Babs & Aggie
The Good, the Bad and the Vegan

Babs & Aggie
The Good, the Bad and the Vegan

HAZEL HITCHINS

Copyright © 2025 Hazel Hitchins

The moral right of the author has been asserted.

Apart from any fair dealing for the purposes of research or private study, or criticism or review, as permitted under the Copyright, Designs and Patents Act 1988, this publication may only be reproduced, stored or transmitted, in any form or by any means, with the prior permission in writing of the publishers, or in the case of reprographic reproduction in accordance with the terms of licences issued by the Copyright Licensing Agency. Enquiries concerning reproduction outside those terms should be sent to the publishers.

This is a work of fiction. Names, characters, businesses, places, events and incidents are either the products of the author's imagination or used in a fictitious manner. Any resemblance to actual persons, living or dead, or actual events is purely coincidental.

Troubador Publishing Ltd
Unit E2 Airfield Business Park,
Harrison Road, Market Harborough,
Leicestershire LE16 7UL
Tel: 0116 279 2299
Email: books@troubador.co.uk
Web: www.troubador.co.uk

ISBN 978 1 83628 143 6

British Library Cataloguing in Publication Data.
A catalogue record for this book is available from the British Library.

Printed and bound by CPI Group (UK) Ltd, Croydon, CR0 4YY
Typeset in 11pt Adobe Caslon Pro by Troubador Publishing Ltd, Leicester, UK

For Mark, William and James for all the tea, tech advice and hugs.

And for my mum, who would have damn-near widdled herself with laughter over this.

Chapter One

I heard House arrive before I saw it – the click and scrape of claws on concrete cut through the double glazing. I groaned. I might have known one of them would show up when the news broke about the cat but did it have to be her? How long was it since I'd last clapped eyes on her? A hundred, a hundred and fifty years? Around the time she had all that nonsense with Rasputin, anyway. And now she was here. And there was me with a sink full of dirty dishes. *Oh well, nothing for it*, I supposed. I dusted the biscuit crumbs off my chest and stepped out onto my doorstep to greet her.

Her house stepped over the box hedging and nestled itself on the lawn. I winced at the sharp crack of my granite sundial under its weight. There'd been a nice heather bed there I was fond of too. The painted wooden door flung open and there she was, arms spread wide, silhouetted against a backdrop of ethereal mist – all sham, of course. I know for a fact she would have had a pot steaming for hours to create the effect. Still, we all have our quirks. I know I do. Or did. It's been a long time since I used my pots for anything but cooking.

She sashayed down House's steps and walked toward me, a bottle of clear brew swinging from her hand.

"Privet, Comrade." She engulfed me in a bear hug that nearly cracked my ribs. I gasped and promptly choked on her heady perfume, the feathers of her coat collar tickling my nose.

"Babs," I managed to splutter. She pushed me away, holding me at arm's length to look me up and down. I tugged my cardy to cover the grease-stained joggers I was wearing but Babs didn't seem to notice. Instead, she frowned at me.

"What is this? You are not happy to see old friend?"

I grimaced. "Of course, I am but, Babs, this is a quiet neighbourhood." I looked beyond her. Mavis Leadberry's curtains were twitching. Babs followed my gaze and tutted.

"Bof!" she said and waved her hand. The shimmering glamour settled and House became a gypsy caravan to anyone who cared to look – remarkable, yes, but inclined to raise significantly fewer eyebrows than a walking house with chicken legs. Babs shook the bottle in my face and pulled two shot glasses from her coat pocket. Her eyes twinkled at me like the sins of angels – the more interesting ones, at least – and she grinned.

"Now, to business!"

I don't drink much as a rule, not anymore. The occasional sherry at Christmas or a medicinal brandy to keep out the chill, but nothing on par with Babs' brew, not for centuries. A lethal haze rose off it as she sloshed it into the glasses. I toyed with refusing but I didn't want to be rude, so I told myself I'd just have the one. Babs had already raised a plucked eyebrow at the electric fire and chintz armchairs. I didn't want her to think I had completely changed since the old days. Ha. As if I could hide it. She'd see the piled-up pots and pans soon enough and it was only a matter of time before she discovered the balled-up pants on the bathroom floor. I'm not usually slovenly, you understand, but things had been difficult lately, ever since Misty... well. I took the glass. The drink hit the back of my throat; my lungs burned and my eyes streamed. I could barely breathe for spluttering. Babs, on the other hand, smacked her lips and casually refilled the glasses.

"Again."

I held up my hand, wheezing my objection, but Babs pressed the glass firmly into it.

"Da, darling. Again."

It wasn't such a shock this time and by the time the third one slipped down, the burning in my throat had become a comforting warmth that spread from my stomach to the tips of my toes. My lips tingled and I found I was holding out my glass before Babs was ready with the bottle. She nodded approval. We sat in the armchairs, the bottle between us. The room looked brighter somehow, shiny around the edges like I was looking at it through a crystal and I swear the scent of woodsmoke billowed from the false flames of the fire. Oh, she's good. It's clear *she* hasn't lost her knack. She stared at me, her face solemn.

"So. You hev problem." It wasn't a question.

I sat for a moment then nodded mutely. I grabbed the bottle off the table and poured myself another shot. My hand shook. Babs waited while I necked the drink. I took a deep breath and opened my mouth to calmly tell her I was fine, but the instant I met her gaze, my eyes burned, my heart clenched and I flung myself into her arms.

"He's dead, Babs. The bastard went and killed him."

Babs' eyes flicked to the empty basket by the fire and I looked away so I didn't have to see her sympathy. Instead, I gulped down yet another shot, fished a tissue from the sleeve of my cardigan and blew my nose. I looked around. The room closed in around me. The walls pulsated in a way that had nothing to do with Babs' glamour. The paisley carpet swirled. My face felt quite clammy now and a ringing in my ears set my teeth on edge. Babs tilted my chin and peered at me with a professional eye.

"Okay, Comrade. Enough Slivovica for you, I think." She led me to the sofa and I let myself be swallowed by it.

"We will talk tomorrow," Babs said. I closed my eyes and heard nothing more.

I woke with a screeching head and a tongue like the floor of a barbershop. From the kitchen came the clunking of pans and the clatter of plates; above it all, Babs' warbling voice casually butchered a folk song. I peeled my face off the cushion, raised my head and sniffed the air. Rich, red aromas wafted through – deep, spicy paprika, fresh, bright tomatoes and peppers and the brown comfort of toasted bread. I'd barely cooked since the cafe closed and my mouth watered. I heaved myself upright and stumbled into the kitchen. The pots and pans gleamed on the draining board – no doubt I'd find the bathroom similarly pristine and my dirty pants now in the washer. It's what we did, after all. There are so few of us left that when one of us puts out the call, we rally to do what we can. And in my anguish, I guess I must have made the call. I shifted uncomfortably, rubbed my clammy hands on my cardy and cleared my throat.

Babs was as she ever was, fresh-faced and dewy-skinned. In fact, the only difference in her appearance from the last time I saw her was that the sleek bob she sported was now silver, the same silver you see reflected in moonlit ponds. I ran my hand through my unruly mop and got my fingers snarled in the knots. For a moment, I hated her – she had drunk at least as much as me last night – but one look at the stew bubbling on the hob and I forgave her. She cracked two eggs into it and set the cover on the pan to steam them. She turned to me then and I quailed under the severity of her glare.

"Agnes, Agnes, Agnes." She shook her head and waved her arm at my pantry shelves. "What is this?" My cheeks burned at the sight of the jars of shop-bought herbs and spices. I hadn't grown my own in years, though this would be the least of my worries when the news broke of precisely how far I'd slipped.

"Well, it's tricky to get hold of the right seeds…" I muttered. She cut me off with a tut.

"Not that. Supermarket is very easy – yes, fine. I mean *this*." She pointed at another jar. "*Instant* coffee, Agnes?" She reached over and patted my hand. "I am sorry, my friend. I did not realise things were so bad." She reached behind me, pulled a mug from the tree and lifted a copper turka pot off the stove. The coffee she poured was tar thick and pungent. She pressed the mug into my hand.

"First, we will eat and drink *real* coffee, then you will tell me of this man who has wronged you and why you do not currently wear his eggs as earrings. *Then* we will talk of the dead cat in your freezer."

Chapter Two

The light inside the chest freezer spewed onto its contents and poor Misty looked even worse in its harsh glare. I'd avoided the freezer since I put him in and now I bit my lip to hold back the tears. Babs drew a breath beside me.

"Ahh." She placed a gentle hand on his head and stroked him. "He's looked better."

I nodded. I couldn't reply; my throat was too tight and my eyes swam. Babs fished a hanky out of her pocket and handed it to me. I turned away and blew my nose loudly. "Sorry," I said to Babs.

Babs shrugged. "Is no problem."

"I know I'm being ridiculous. Other people would say, 'It's just a cat, get over it,' -"

"Other people are khuylos – they hev penis for head," Babs replied. "Nothing is ever 'just' anything and even if it was, we both know Misty was more than 'just' cat." I nodded. There didn't seem much to add. Babs closed the freezer lid softly. "What happened?" she asked, eventually.

I let out a shuddering breath. "He disappeared. He's done it before, for a day or so, but it was different this time because I couldn't sense him." It slipped out before I could catch it. *Damn.* Babs frowned. I carried on quickly, hoping to gloss over my error. "A day went by, then two, then a week. I did all the usual things – put up posters and whatnot," another frown from Babs, "and then one day… I felt him go."

The words were inadequate. I knew it and Babs knew it. She'd have felt him go too, they all would, but not the way I did. The words I couldn't say screamed so loudly in my head I felt certain she must be able to hear them. I felt him die, yes, but more than that, I felt every indignity inflicted on him first. I felt him go like the ripping of a plaster from my soul, leaving me raw and exposed.

I couldn't say those words. Instead, I said, "And then, he dumped him on my doorstep like he was a piece of rubbish." This final insult had been salt rubbed in the wound. The bastard wanted me to know it was no accident. Hot tears spilled down my cheeks and heavy sobs raked in my chest. Babs rooted in her pocket again and this time drew out a paper bag. She plucked out a toffee, unwrapped it from its paper twist and popped it into my mouth before I could protest. The caramel began to dissolve instantly, coating my tongue in a thick paste that slid smoothly down my raw throat. I sucked at it, letting the motion steady me. The hard outer broke apart and a burst of apple and ginger syrup danced across my palate, warming and comforting and uniquely Babs. Her gift has always shown itself through her cooking. Mine shows through healing. Or at least, it did.

I let the toffee work its magic and my sobs subsided to occasional hiccups.

Babs led me back to the kitchen table. She poured us more coffee from the turka pot and paused to look at the pictures of Misty that adorned the walls: photographs, oil paintings signed by long-dead hands and the oldest, a wood carving, blackened with age. She smiled at this.

"He was good friend to you. You knew him almost as long as you know me." We sat quietly for a moment. Then she took my hands and looked me in the eyes.

"I cannot help you resurrect him, my friend. I will not do you that disservice."

I gave her a watery smile and shook my head. "No, that's not what I was thinking. I don't know why I've kept him in there, I just couldn't bring myself to bury him. Stupid, really."

"Not stupid," Babs disagreed. "He was your companion for long time. Is natural you are not ready to say goodbye."

Her kindness made my eyes well again. I pressed Babs' handkerchief into my face. Her perfume lingered in the folds and I let the woody scents of vetiver, thyme and rosemary soothe me.

"I remember the day we made him."

"Da, was same day we built House." There was a dull crack from the front lawn where Babs' house, as if hearing its name, shifted and demolished another part of my rockery. It had never been particularly graceful, even that night by the bonfire.

I smiled weakly at Babs. "A house on chicken legs as a familiar. Only you would think of that!" Babs grinned back at me and doffed an imaginary cap. "To be honest, we all thought you were pissed when you came up with the idea."

Babs nodded. "Da, darling. I was rear end of rodent!"

I turned the phrase over in my mind a few times.

"You mean you were rat-arsed?"

"Da, this is what I said!"

Well, at least she was honest about it. I remembered her staggering into the circle we'd formed. Truth be told, I was worried about her getting too close to the fire, the way the fumes were rising off her. Still, there were enough of us there to deal with it if she got into mischief. There had to be… it's tricky magic, is forging a familiar.

Painful too. You have to carve away a piece of your very essence to put into the creature, but what's the alternative? We're not social creatures, as a rule – as the writer once said, the collective noun for more than one of us should be an argument – but once you've watched those you care for wither and die a couple of times, you realise you need *something* to keep you company, *something* to ground you, otherwise, you end up like poor Morgana, talking to the crows.

I called for a cat – useful, tactile, discreet. Babs reeled and swayed her way into the ceremony and called for "House… no, bird… No, *housebird!*" Moments later, an egg the size of a skull rolled from the fire. It pulsed and grew, larger and larger, until finally, it split to reveal House, wobbling on its chicken legs with its downy shingles still damp. I cradled my kitten and laughed along with the rest.

Another crack from the garden brought me back to the present.

"I thought you were daft at the time," I admitted. Babs chuckled softly.

"Da, I remember, but I think I am heving the last laugh, no? Can you imagine Siberian winter without House?" She shuddered and looked over at the window where House was crushing my rose bush in its attempt to peer in. Her expression softened for a moment and even I had to smile at its pot-bellied bulk. The respite was short-lived. Babs clapped her hands. The steel was back in her eyes and I sat straighter in my chair.

"Now," she said, "tell me of this man."

Chapter Three

I nearly widdled myself when we opened the cafe the next morning. The keys rattled and my nerves jangled and in my haste to unlock the door, I couldn't find the keyhole. I don't know what I was thinking – that we could nip in, reopen, do a day's business and close up again before he noticed?

I've really only myself to blame. What did I expect to happen once Babs knew the truth? Well, the part of it I told her. I had to wait for her to stop laughing about the fact *I* owned a cafe. I don't know what's so funny. I may not be up to Babs' standard but I know my way around a kitchen and my flapjacks are to die for... poor Misty learned that the hard way. Those bloody flapjacks are what brought me onto that bastard's radar in the first place. I'd popped round with a batch while he was out, ostensibly to see if they wanted to sell them – they ran the health food shop opposite the cafe, you see.

In reality, I wanted to get a better look at the girlfriend. Sophie. I'd been watching her from a distance for a while and now the babby was here... well, it can be a difficult time. I didn't tell Babs that bit. I hadn't expected Sophie to love the flapjacks as much as she did. She ordered a batch for the very next day. It was her shop, she said, bought with money her dad left her, and she could stock what she wanted. I caught the flick of her eyes searching the shadows. Her tone was defiant, though. I didn't say anything. The reminder of her dad barbed my conscience and I was temporarily lost for words, though I didn't tell Babs that bit either. I agreed a price with Sophie and went back to the cafe to start work on the order.

Course, it was only a matter of time before His Nibs appeared, the Vegan – or so he claimed. Sophie's vegan, but it *means* something to her. For him, I think it was just another way of controlling the world. He smarmed in, all charm and patchouli oil, Sophie at his elbow, to cancel the order. He did the talking – Sophie wouldn't meet my eye. Blah, blah, such a shame, blah, cost of living, blah, blah, Sophie shouldn't make decisions without him. It pulled me up short, that last bit did.

"Why not?" I frowned. "It's her shop, isn't it?" And then I saw it. I saw *him*. It was blink-and-you-miss-it but I saw the cracks behind his smile.

It didn't take long for things to deteriorate. A complaint that the smell of my cooking was driving away his customers, a scathing review on social media claiming he'd found cat hair in his pasty (I didn't serve pasties), and finally, a nasty report in the local rag that I deliberately doctored all my dishes with pork fat because I hated… well, everyone apparently – vegans, veggies, Muslims, Jews. You'd have to go a long way to find a more rabid bigot than me. There was other stuff too, smashed windows and cancelled orders. I fought back, I really did, but it was exhausting and then when Misty disappeared…

I'd trailed off then and stared at the kitchen table, awaiting Babs' judgement.

"I will meet this Vegan," she declared.

"Oh, really?" I said. "You want me to knock on his door and say, 'Babs, this is the arsehole who killed my cat; Arsehole, this is Babs, my nine-hundred-year-old friend who would like to separate you from your testicles.'?"

"Do not be stupid, that would be awkward. No. You will open cafe and he will come... and I hev twenty-four years before nine-hundredth birthday."

So that was that. Babs had spoken and now, here we were, opening the cafe. She placed her hands on my shoulders and her breath tickled my neck. I forced myself to take a deep breath and steady my hands. The key found the hole and I opened the door. Everything was exactly as I had left it. Even in the pre-dawn gloom, I could make out the pattern of the tablecloths, the gleam of the crockery stacked, waiting... tears pricked my eyes.

A match scratched and hissed behind me and the scent of burning herbs wreathed the air. Babs went from table to table wafting burning sage, and her guttural muttering brought forth golden-hued spectres – people eating, drinking, laughing; the tinkle of china, cutlery ringing in the air. Ghosts of the past... and possibly the future. It's a simple trick to perform but it reminded me of the potential of this place. The cafe already felt warmer.

I watched the flames licking the slender sage branch and let my mind wander, testing if I could grasp a glimpse of what the future may hold. For a brief moment, the sage blazed hot, the pale, healing smoke became a greasy pall and the chatter and hum of customers morphed into terrified shrieks. I gasped and reeled backwards. Babs shook a cloth from her pocket and deftly patted out the fire, then slapped the light switch on the wall. I winced in the harsh buzz of fluorescence. Babs inspected the charred sage in the cloth and pursed her lips, then sniffed and bundled the remains into her handbag.

"So. To work," she said and made for the kitchen. I put a hand on her elbow.

"Hang on a minute. The future. I saw fire…" Babs made an indelicate sound.

"Bof. There is always fire. You look far enough and you see Mother Earth consumed by the sun – now *that* is a fire, Comrade."

I went to object but stopped. "Wait, you've actually *seen* that?"

Babs stared off into the distance and nodded slowly. "It was long winter and they were strange mushrooms." She snapped back to here and now. "But what happens between now and then is for us to write. If there is to be fire, then *we* will light it."

I bit my lip.

Babs' shoulders slumped and she rolled her eyes heavenward. "ENOUGH!" she shouted. She faced me then, her eyes level with mine, our noses almost touching. "*I* remember when they called *you* Black Aggie," she whispered. "Mothers scared their children into submission with your name, grown men bolted their door against your anger and now what? You want to be timid little mouse. I think not." She stepped back and let her words sink in.

The years rolled across my memory, who I was… and what I had become. I shook my head.

"That was a long time ago."

"Not so very long," Babs replied. "You will remember. I will help you remember." She set her jaw and tilted her chin. "We will open. He will come and when he does, you will face him." I swallowed. "I will be here," she continued, "and all will be fine." I nodded – there seemed little else to do. Babs shucked off her coat and breezed past me into the kitchen. "And now I will make Borscht."

Chapter Four

Sure enough, during the afternoon lull, he came. My last customer had just left and I was wiping down the table. I knew it was him by the way the door jangled and my stomach twisted into knots. From the anxious shuffling I could hear, he must have dragged Sophie with him again. I busied myself straightening the salt and pepper whilst his shadow fell over me. Babs started warbling a tune in the kitchen. Finally, I took a deep breath and forced myself to face him.

"Can I help you?" I asked. I kept my tone bright and my expression neutral. God alone knows how – it took all my strength to keep the quiver from my voice. He looked around at the freshly wiped tables and newly-stocked chiller.

"You're open," he said, eventually.

"Yes, well, difficult to feed people if I'm not, love," I said. I peered behind him and sure enough, there was the girl, her baby in her arms. She jigged gently from foot to foot, though whether she was anxious or trying to soothe the child, I couldn't tell. I gave her a smile – a real one.

"Alright, love? Haven't seen you in a while."

She wore her usual pinched, ferret look and for a moment, in the garish light, the side of her face looked pink and raw. I blinked but the next moment it looked fine. I tried to get a better look but he stepped between us.

"I thought we agreed you were shutting up shop for good." His voice was low, intimate almost. He was close, very close. My pulse thudded in my throat. Babs' voice faltered slightly in the kitchen. I swallowed and lifted my chin.

"I don't remember agreeing to that," I said.

He smiled sympathetically. "I've heard the memory can play tricks on you when you're more…" he looked me up and down and I twitched my cardigan shut over my chest, "… advanced in years. We'll have to see what we can do to jog your memory." He reached beyond me to the salt and pepper on the table, forcing me backwards. His breath was hot on my face and I couldn't help but frown. There was a familiar odour to his breath, salty and slightly sweet, like…

"Bacon?" The word was out before I could stop it and his eyes narrowed further.

"Babe!" Sophie was less adept than I was at keeping her voice level. He didn't even spare her a glance. He picked up the pepper pot, bounced it in his hand a couple of times and then casually let it drop to the floor.

"Whoops."

I closed my eyes, anticipating the tinkle of breaking crockery but it was drowned out by another sound. A silken hiss rang through the air, the rhythmic rasp of blade on steel. Babs came from the kitchen carelessly sharpening my favourite knife. She stopped by my shoulder.

"Agnes, darling, you should hev said we hev more visitors."

He had jumped back from me at the sound but now his shoulders dropped as he saw just another old lady. He looked from Babs' close-fitting crimson blouse to my rusty cardy and didn't bother to hide his smirk.

"Friend of yours?" he asked.

I floundered briefly. "This is my… er… sister –"

"—*younger* sister," added Babs. He cocked an eyebrow at her.

"Is that so? Well, maybe you can tell your *older* sister she needs to close."

Babs shrugged.

"Of course, we will close…" I frowned at her and she looked at her watch, "in precisely one hour and we will open again tomorrow for breakfast." She looked at me then and pursed her lips as though weighing up an important decision. "I think I will make… hmmm… da, syrniki. I will make these pancakes and your customers will love them." His Nibs shifted his weight at that and shouldered forward again. He fixed his full attention on Babs, who blinked as though surprised he was still there.

"If you think you're opening tomorrow, you're as senile as this old bag." He waved his hand at me. *Old bag*. I glanced down at my frumpy skirt and cardy and a flush of shame crept up from my neck. And then, something else. A white-hot bead of indignation. I squared my shoulders but Babs shook her head almost imperceptibly and I let them drop again. It was her time to play. She gasped in mock horror.

"Tsk. Such language! That is it, no syrniki for you."

His mouth dropped open. How I managed to keep a straight face, I'll never know. He was scowling now. He spread his hand on the table and leaned in towards us both. Babs smiled back, unconcerned. He pushed his face closer to hers – it's easy to be brave when you don't know any better. His lip curled in an ugly sneer and he dropped his voice again.

"You want to be careful with that smart mouth of yours. Your sister had a run of really bad luck when she last opened. I'd hate for you to be unlucky too." He flicked his eyes to me and smirked again. "I heard you found your cat."

THWUNGGGG.

The knife wobbled between his fingers, its point buried deep in the table before I had time to react. Himself could only stare at it. Sophie stopped her incessant jig and the baby made a faint whimper in the silence. Babs looked from the knife to the man.

"Whoops, I hev butter on my fingers." She whipped in front of me cobra-quick until she was eye-to-eye with the Vegan.

"You are Big Man, da?" She looked him up and down and smiled. "I like big men. They make such pretty clatter when they fall. You should go now. I do not think you should return."

He stepped back and stood a moment, sizing us up. I folded my arms and glowered at him in return, for all the good it did.

The doorbell jangled again and a flock of hi-vis jackets and helmets tumbled noisily into the cafe. The Vegan took one look at the newcomers, turned on his heel and left without a word. His girlfriend gave us an apologetic half-smile and turned too. Babs placed one hand gently on her elbow and softly brushed a strand of hair off her face and frowned. For a moment, I saw it again – Sophie's skin, raw and pink with patches of purple and yellow. It was gone again in a heartbeat but I'd definitely seen it. The promise of a bruise. Babs had seen it too. She looked the girl in the eye.

"You, however, should come back *soon*." The girl swallowed, tears brimming in her eyes before she too fled. Babs sighed, then turned to the gaggle of workmen and flung her arms open in greeting.

"Gentlemen, is your lucky day. I hev Borscht for everyone!" She turned to me and jerked her head at the retreating form of the Vegan. "I thought he would be bigger," she said and marched off to ladle Borscht.

I watched her for a moment then pulled off that bloody cardy and stuffed it in the bin.

Chapter Five

The builders left looking bemused. They were certain they'd wanted bacon butties when they came in but suddenly discovered what they really craved was thick beetroot soup served with soured cream and hefty chunks of freshly baked bread. They wiped their bowls clean just like their mothers had taught them and trotted away with full bellies.

Babs locked the door behind them and turned the sign over to say we were closed. I ferried bowls into the kitchen, wiped down the tables and studiously ignored her whilst she set about brewing more coffee. Finally, though, there was nothing left to clean. Babs made her way to the table where the knife stood, its tip still buried in the wood. She set down the tray she carried and tugged the blade out with a grunt. I joined her at the table and sat down with a sigh. Babs said nothing. She poured two cups of coffee and pushed a slice of yabluchnyk towards me. I stared at the cake. The warm fragrance of cinnamon and sugar mingled with the bitter aroma of the coffee. I inhaled deeply and let the scent weave around me, comforting me. Babs said nothing. I picked up a fork and plucked a piece of baked apple from the depths of the cake. Babs said nothing.

"Alright! You don't have to go on about it!" I shouted.

Babs held up her hands in protest. "I did not say dicky bird!"

"You didn't have to," I grumbled and popped the cake in my mouth. I let it dissolve, savouring the flavour. When I spoke again, I was calmer. "I don't know why I've let him get to me. Heaven knows he's nothing special, though he clearly thinks he's the—"

"Oh, I know this one," Babs interrupted. "The dog's pyjamas, da?"

I chuckled in spite of myself.

"Something like that," I said. "The thing is, I *know* he's just another bully. I KNOW he's no worse than a hundred or more like him that I've dealt with over the years…" I sighed. She was waiting for an answer and I gave her one. "Maybe that's it, Babs. Maybe I'm tired of having to deal with his sort over and over again."

Babs frowned but yet again, said nothing. I bit into another forkful of cake.

"And then there's the girl and her babby."

Babs blew steam off her coffee.

"What about them?" she asked and I hesitated. How much should I tell? How much had she already guessed? In the end, I kept it vague.

"I don't want them getting hurt. You saw what he's like." I didn't mention the promise of bruising we'd both glimpsed.

"Then we make her leave. Is simple, we just…"

"NO!" I spoke louder than intended and Babs froze in the middle of the gesture she was making. "We can't just go interfering in other people's lives."

Babs gave me another look. "Since when?"

I shook her question away.

"If she leaves him, it has to be *her* choice. We can't make it for her. Though Lord knows why she stays with him."

"Maybe you should ask her." Babs nodded at the door where Sophie's anxious face peered in at us. I snicked open the lock and Babs wordlessly brought another coffee cup and piece of cake to the table. Sophie glanced over her shoulder before coming in with her baby. I ushered her to the table and she eased herself into the chair looking miserable. She sat silently, taking breaths, priming herself to speak. I could almost see the jumble of thoughts jostling to get out of her but each time she tried, no words came. Babs nudged the cake and Sophie opened her mouth to protest. Babs cut her off.

"Don't worry, is vegan. And you should keep your energy up for feeding the baby. May I see her?"

I blinked at that. Babs normally avoided babies like the plague – more than the plague, in fact. Sophie held out her child for Babs to take and Babs crossed her arms. Instead, she looked at me. I sighed, reached forward and twitched the baby's blanket from its face. Babs peered at the child, then nodded in satisfaction and sat back in her chair, her inspection apparently complete. Sophie shot me a questioning look but I just shrugged.

"Babs doesn't do babies," I said.

"Nyet, darling, I do not, but tell me, does he know baby is not his?"

The tick between the seconds of the clock stretched for an eternity. I'll say this for Babs, she's good. It took me nearly forty minutes to figure that one out.

Sophie stared at Babs, her jaw slack. Her lips were even more bloodless than usual and for a moment, I was worried she might faint. I moved to take the babby but she pulled the little mite closer. Fair enough. I sat back down. Babs, on the other hand, stood up.

"Cake is not cutting it for you. You need *real* food." She marched into the kitchen leaving Sophie and me to our awkward silence. We listened to the clock's apologetic ticks for a minute or so. I took a leaf from Babs' book and said nothing. Finally, Sophie spoke.

"How did she know?" It was scarcely more than a whisper.

"Perhaps I am witch!" Babs' voice made us both jump. She glided back in holding a steaming bowl of Borscht and another generous slab of bread. "Perhaps I am really Baba Yaga, come to eat your baby." Her eyes sparkled with mischief. Sophie pulled the baby closer to her and I scowled at Babs and placed my hand lightly on the poor girl's wrist.

"You'll have to excuse Babs, Sophie, her sense of humour is an acquired taste," I said. "We only figured it out because your little one is so adorable, we simply can't imagine that fella of yours having any part in her."

Well, that and the fact that in all my years, I'd never seen two blue-eyed parents have a brown-eyed child. She'd better hope nobody sits that man of hers down and explains basic genetics to him. Babs raised an eyebrow. I've got to admit, the response I gave sounded weak, even to me, but Sophie didn't seem to notice. She just stared at her lap and toyed with a loose thread on the baby's blanket. Everything about her was strung so tightly she practically twanged.

Eventually, she lifted her head and looked from Babs to me and back again. "Will you tell him?" she asked. Her voice was sandpaper. Babs shook her head.

"It is neither my circus nor my monkeys," she said. Sophie looked at me, puzzled.

"She means it's none of our business," I translated. "You and your baby are perfectly safe with us."

"Da, darling," agreed Babs. "Now eat." She set the food on the table and, seeing Sophie's expression, added, "Don't worry, is vegan."

That was true, at least. While she normally used good beef or venison for her soup, she hadn't had time to get any yet and obviously anything from my freezer was out of the question. Instead, Babs set to work, turning basic kitchen scraps into a rich, fragrant stock and simmering it with sauteed beetroot, carrot, onion, potato, lemon, dill and a whole host of other herbs and spices from her personal store. I know it set my mouth watering and I don't even like Borscht. Sophie pushed the spoon around.

"Come on, Love," I said. "It'll do you good and you do need to keep your strength up." I nodded at the babby. "She'll be taking a lot out of you."

Sophie swallowed and bit her lip.

"I'm not supposed to," she said finally. "I'm on a diet." You could have heard a mouse fart in the silence that followed. I think poor Sophie must have realised how ridiculous she sounded as her cheeks went the colour of the soup. She cleared her throat. "It's just… well, he said he went off me when I was expecting so he wants me to lose the weight quickly." No need to ask who 'he' was. "I know it sounds bad, but he's just showing he cares…" Sophie finished, somewhat feebly.

Again, Babs and I were silent. For my part, I was trying to arrange the slew of thoughts chasing round my head so that they didn't come out as me simply shouting at her not to be so bloody stupid, whilst also preparing myself to smooth everyone's feathers after whatever Babs said. Her filter isn't as sophisticated as mine – I'm not sure she even has one – so there was no telling what to expect. What I didn't expect was for her to stand and gently remove the baby from Sophie's arms. She passed the child to me, barely sparing it a glance, then took the plate with the bread on it and pushed it closer to Sophie.

"I hev seen more meat on butcher's pencil, darling," she said softly. "Eat." Sophie's resolve evaporated in the fragrant soup steam. She gripped her spoon and ate.

Chapter Six

She stayed for two bowls of Borscht, speaking a little between mouthfuls, spoon-feeding us morsels of her life. Most of it I knew already; raised by her gran, dad dead, mum not on the scene – best to gloss over that for now – loves animals and nature. She bought the shop and the flat above it a couple of years ago when she came into her inheritance. She didn't mention the Vegan and I was happy to keep his name out of her mouth for as long as possible.

"I was sorry to hear about your cat," she said when she'd set her spoon down for the last time.

"Mmmm," I said. I didn't want to talk about Misty with her. I was almost certain she hadn't had anything to do with his death, but I've been wrong about people before. Instead, I let the silence stretch. Sophie opened her mouth a few times as if to say something but obviously thought better of it. It was Babs who spoke next.

"What is her name?" she said, nodding at the infant drowsing in my arms. Sophie let out a breath I doubt she even knew she'd been holding. Her face softened and she looked at her daughter.

"Grace," she said. "It's kind of a family name."

Grace. I jiggled the baby softly and stroked her cheek with my finger. For a moment, I was back in a smoky, thatched cottage long since ground into history, and I was cradling my own baby's head, still slick with caul. She had the same eyes.

"Yes," I said. "She looks like a Grace." Babs cleared her throat and I snapped back to the here and now. Some of what I'd been feeling must have shown on my face though because Sophie was staring at me, her head tilted. I shook her unspoken question away. "I had a Grace of my own once," was all I said. Sophie delicately let the subject drop and it was Babs who broke the silence. She sniffed the air like a gun dog.

"Well, whatever the name, she does not smell so Gracious at the moment." I sniffed the baby's rump and my eyes watered.

"I'll say," I coughed. Sophie jumped up, looking crestfallen.

"I've not got any nappies with me," she said. "I didn't think I'd need them. I was only going to be five minutes." She glanced at the clock then and the Borscht drained from her cheeks. "I've got to go. He'll be..." She bit her lip, clamping down the rest of the sentence so it didn't escape. Instead, she scooped baby Grace into her arms and headed for the door. I opened it for her and she paused before leaving and stared at her toes.

"I'm sorry about how he was today," she muttered, "it's just after he read that newspaper report..." Sophie trailed off. She scuffed the tile with her toe. Ah yes... Bacongate. All his handiwork, I had no doubt. "I've told him it's a nonsense," she said, "but he's convinced you'll try and trick people." I waited and, to her credit, she didn't add the word 'again' to the end of that sentence. She, at least, believed me. Still, it took a lot of effort to swallow the bile in my voice and when I spoke, my voice still wasn't steady.

"And that's all there is to it, you think?" Her head whipped up and she looked me in the eye.

"Of course," she said, a little too quickly if you ask me, "what else could there be?" She jiggled the baby again as she'd done when she was here with *him* earlier. "Look, I know he's not everyone's cup of tea, but I'm sure once he realises that article was just a mistake, we'll all be able to get along nicely." From the lilt in her voice, she wasn't even convincing herself. "It's just he's so passionate about veganism," she finished lamely. She looked from me to Babs and back again, wide-eyed and earnest. I could have shaken her. Finally, her shoulders slumped and she sloped out. I bolted the door behind her with a sigh.

"There's none so blind as those that will not see," I muttered, half to myself.

"Da," said Babs, "and if he is vegan, I will eat hat."

"You smelled the bacon on his breath?" I asked. Babs shook her head.

"Nyet. Egg yolk on his collar." I'd missed that. Made a change from lipstick, I suppose.

We walked home through the arcade and I showed her the other shops. It was a small but beautiful setting, all cast iron arches and glass roofing. We all made a bit of an effort with our exteriors – window boxes, miniature trees in pots, that sort of thing. I'd planted lavender and rosemary and had a couple of lemon trees. I could give all kinds of mystic and arcane reasons for my choices, but in truth, I just like the smell and they're hard to kill... much like me, I suppose. The owner of the pagan tat shop had planted a money tree, and much good may it do her. All in all, though, there were worse places to be. There'd been some grumblings about one of the big supermarkets taking it over and knocking it down but they couldn't convince anyone to sell up. There were five of us in total. Sophie's health food shop was already shuttered up for the day, as was the tat shop next to it – *The Wiccan Way – Emporium of Magick*, to give it its proper name; utter rot whatever you call it. Two doors down, Margot sat at a Formica table in her ice cream parlour. She had a calculator in her hand and a frown on her face, never a good combination. I waved, but I don't think she saw me. Then there was Burt in the greengrocers. Barrel-chested and open-faced, he grinned happily when he saw us and set down the crates of produce he'd been heaving indoors.

"Aggie! I saw you were open again. Don't let the bastards grind you down, eh?"

I smiled back at him – he was easy to smile at, Burt. His eyes drifted past me to Babs, who was staring at Burt from beneath her eyelashes. She smiled at him coquettishly.

"Another Big Man! But this one I like. Tsk, Agnes, you should have told me you had such a handsome neighbour." I gaped at her. The last time I'd seen behaviour like that was when next door's cat came into heat and made a fool of herself in front of Misty. Now, Burt looked just as embarrassed as Misty had. His ears turned pink and he cleared his throat.

"I see the Prodder paid you a visit," he said. I frowned at him.

"The Prodder?" He waved his hand in the direction of the health food shop.

"Young Sophie's fella. Waste of skin and air if ever I met one. Always in here, prodding my goods -" Babs opened her mouth and I stepped on her toe quickly to shut her up. She glowered at me briefly but closed her mouth. Burt didn't seem to notice. "And the questions he asks – 'Is this fair trade?', 'What's the carbon footprint of that?', 'Do I think it's ethical to sell asparagus out of season?' I told him, if I only sold it in season, you'd blink and miss it." He shook his head. "Nah, can't take to that one. He's been on at poor Margot too, you know."

I tilted my head. "Oh?"

"Aye, telling her she's pandering to bovine rape by making ice cream. She was in a right state about it." He ran his fingers through his thick, curly hair. "I was all for having a word with him, but she begged me not to."

It seems I wasn't the only one on the Vegan's radar. That was interesting. I waited to see if Burt would say any more – they say women gossip but if you really want the juicy stuff, you should stick around middle-aged men. They'd put washer-women to shame. It seems we'd had the best of it though. Instead, Burt checked we were okay following the afternoon's adventures.

"I'd have popped in," he said, "but them builders showed up and you seemed quite busy..." He looked at his crates, most of which were still full. "Wish I could say the same." He sighed. Babs stepped forward then.

"Well, perhaps we can be of assistance..." She placed

her hand on his arm and let it rest there. "Tell me, Mr Greengrocer, how big are your plums?" By rights, there should have been a seductive silence, but I was choking on my laughter. Poor Burt didn't know where to put his face. Babs rolled her eyes at me and turned back to her prey – I mean, Burt.

"You must ignore Agnes," she practically purred at him. "She has the filthy mind. I will be making slivovyi pirog and I will need many plums… and beetroot for Borscht," she said.

"You and that bloody Borscht," I muttered. She whipped around to look at me.

"Da? What of it? Borscht is life!" She turned back to Burt then and led him inside to discuss her needs – those that were suitable for a PG audience, anyway. I shrugged and left them to it.

I stood by his door and stared at Sophie's shop. When the Vegan was first stirring up trouble for me, he'd been cunning about it – clearly, Sophie was innocent in the matter and I hadn't mentioned it to anyone as I'd had no proof. It got to the point that sometimes, I even doubted it was him. My gut said it was, but my gut had been wrong before. Now, though, he was bolder. My gut was right. And with his jibes at Burt and poor Margot, perhaps his initial attack on me hadn't been personal… for him, anyway, though I wasn't sure if that was a good thing or a bad thing. I rubbed my chin. What was his game?

The window in the flat above the shop glowed yellow. If only I knew what was going on behind those walls. I glanced behind me. Babs was still deep in conversation with Burt. I took a deep breath, drew myself up and relaxed my mind. I felt it unfurling, weaving up, out of my head. I focused on the slash of yellow from the window and felt my mind reaching for it, moving up, past the shutters of the shop... Sophie's shop... Sophie's shop, bought with money from her dead father... My mind crashed back inside my skull and I gasped. It was like being dunked in icy water and I should know, that's happened to me more than once. I pinched the bridge of my nose and took some deep breaths to steady my shaking hands. I should have known it wouldn't work. My stomach was like lead. After all these years to wind up like this... Babs' tinkling laughter sounded by the door. I swallowed hard and blinked away the tears and she smiled brightly at me, seemingly oblivious to my turmoil. At least that was a blessing.

I should have known better. We came to my front door. I rifled in my bag for my keys and Babs placed an affectionate hand on House, who quivered excitedly in response. And then, as casually as if she was asking what was for dinner, Babs said, "So, Agnes, when were you going to tell me you can no longer do magic?"

Chapter Seven

I was going to throw up. I had that same clammy feeling, the same ringing in my ears and sudden lurch in my stomach I'd had the other night, only this time without the alcohol. I caught a glimpse of myself in the window; I'd seen marble busts with more colour. In fact, I knew exactly how I looked. I looked just like Sophie did when Babs confronted her about Grace. I must have a word with Babs about how she drops these bombshells, it's really not good for the nervous system. I stood there, feeling my world drop into my knees. Babs reached past me and snicked the key in the lock. She guided me through the door, into the living room and sat me in the armchair. Then she placed her hands firmly on my shoulders and shoved my head down between my legs.

Something pinged in my back and it didn't half hurt. I batted her away and flung myself upright. "What the bloody hell do you think you're doing?" I yelled. Babs stepped back and cocked her head.

"I am being caring and considerate friend. This is not obvious?"

"Who taught you the definition of caring and

considerate? Nurse Ratched?" I rubbed my throbbing back. Babs rolled her eyes.

"Oh, stop being baby," she said, then she smirked, "besides, it snapped you out of it, didn't it?" I froze, a dozen or so unspoken retorts dying on my lips. Bugger, she was right. I'd been spiralling into… something and she'd nipped it in the bud before it could take hold. It probably wasn't the best way to manage the situation but it had worked. She raised an eyebrow at me, following my train of thought. My hand twitched and for a second it took all I had not to slap the smirk off her face. The moment passed though, and I slumped back in my chair. My back twinged again. I'd have to get some camphor oil on that later.

"How did you know?" I asked. Babs shrugged.

"The Vegan still lives," she said, still smirking, then she caught my expression and sighed. "I saw you outside Burt's." Ah. I wasn't as discreet as I thought then. "I did not need Sherlock Holmes to put pieces together," she continued, counting off reasons on her fingers. "You couldn't sense where Misty was; you *know* that man is responsible for your misery but you are looking for *proof* because you no longer trust your instincts; you hev sat by and allowed these things to happen to you when in the past, there would be scorched earth leading to the Vegan's door and yes, I say again, that the Vegan still lives is proof enough something is up."

She stared at me then and waited for me to speak. I couldn't. I couldn't think how to begin. I closed my eyes and tried to marshal my thoughts. Truth was, she'd cut close to the quick. I'd felt a flare of anger in my bones when she said I'd let things happen to me but it was quickly doused as I realised she was right. The old me – or the younger me, if you prefer; the me of a thousand, a hundred, even twenty years ago wouldn't have been cowed by the Vegan's campaign of hate. She'd have dragged him out into the light for all to see. Now, I was left cowering, forced to confess I was impotent, about as much use as the proverbial glass hammer. I rubbed my forehead.

"What happened?" Babs asked quietly. "Was it back-firing spell?" I blinked.

"A what? That's not even a thing!" I said.

"Da, it is! I hev seen it."

"You never have! Who?" Babs pulled a face and waved her hand airily.

"Just someone… you do not know her. It was very tragic, very messy but she was not good to begin with – you, I think, are much stronger and so you will make full recovery." I stared at her for a minute. I knew what she was doing, trying to goad me, prod me into a state of anger, or at least irritability; that was practically meat and drink to the old me. I dare say it might have worked at one time, but I was too long in the tooth for such tricks now. I shook my head.

"It wasn't a back-firing spell. It was…" I sighed. "I made a mistake." I let the sentence fall, giving it the gravitas it deserved. Babs sat, her head tilted forward, looking puzzled.

"And?"

"And what?" I said.

"You made mistake? This is it? *This* is why your magic is…" she snapped her fingers, looking for the right phrase, "…on the fritz?"

"It was a big mistake. I bound someone -"

"- Da, you always were good with binding spells."

"I bound someone... and they died." Babs nodded along slowly, trying to make sense of my words.

"So, you did wrong spell? You *meant* to bind someone but killed them instead?" She shrugged. "I mean, is a little careless..."

"NO!" My voice was louder I expected. Misty would have jumped if he'd been here. My fingers itched to feel his fur between them now. Instead, I let out a long breath and tried to explain to Babs. "I bound someone, a man, to stop him from hurting someone else..."

"Da, you bound Sophie's father to stop him hurting Sophie's mother." I know my mouth dropped open because Babs rolled her eyes at me, "Again, Sherlock Holmes is not required. Why else would *you* open cafe *here*?" I gaped at her. What else had she figured out? "So, then what?" Babs asked.

"Well, if you must know, she killed him. She told me he was violent. I bound him so he could never lift a hand to her again and then she killed him." Babs frowned.

"Right there in front of you?"

"No. I found out afterwards she'd done him in..."

"How? Why?" The questions were fired bullet quick and I flicked them away impatiently.

"I don't know!" The truth was, I hadn't looked any further into it. I didn't want to know all the gory details.

"You. Don't. Know." Babs looked at me like I had two heads. "You don't know and you have punished yourself for... how long? Twenty years?"

I gritted my teeth.

"A man died, Babs."

She shrugged. "Men die all the time. It is what they do."

"And you'd be saying that if *you* were in this situation, would you?"

"I would not be in this situation," she replied.

"Because I suppose *you* never make mistakes." I'd meant it sarcastically but her reply was a slap in the face.

"Nyet. Never."

She'd done it. Despite my best efforts, that bead of anger grew hot in my chest again and any number of retorts crawled up my throat, ready to fly at her. How dare she say that? I could list any number of her mistakes – Rasputin, for one! I sucked in a deep breath, ready to let rip but Babs raised her hand to silence me before I could utter a word.

"Nyet, I hev never made mistake," she repeated. She held her hand in front of her and waggled it like a see-saw. "I hev had things not end as I anticipated. I hev had consequences I did not expect."

"*Cough* Rasputin. *Cough*" She ignored my jibe and continued.

"But if I was in the same situation with the same information, I would take the same action, so nyet, I do not make mistakes… I do, however, learn lessons." She paused to let that sink in and I swallowed down some of my anger. "Tell me," she said, "if you went back to your 'mistake', knowing only what you knew then, would you do the same thing?"

I hesitated. Would I? I remembered the woman – of course, I did. She was so earnest, so… believable. And him… I'm ashamed to say it but he seemed the sort. There was something intrinsically unlikeable about him. He had a shrewd, ferret look; Sophie wears the same expression and it sets my teeth on edge. *She* – Sophie's mum – had me believing it was a look of calculation and shrewdness, that he was watching her every move and finding her wanting. I realised too late that it's a look born from spending all your time walking on eggshells. She spun a good story; I'll give her that. And in my heart, I knew, if I went back to that moment, I'd believe her all over again.

I dragged myself out of the black hole of my memory and met Babs' steady gaze. I nodded. Yes, I would do exactly the same thing. Babs nodded along with me.

"Good. So, we are agreed, it was not mistake. It was lesson." I half laughed under my breath.

"How lovely it must be to see the world in black and white like that."

"Da, I sleep very well."

"Well, good for you, but it's not that simple for me," I said.

"Da, darling. It is that simple. If is not, you hev been learning wrong lesson. You helped someone you believed was in need. You were deceived. Is the lesson you learnt to never help anyone else because *one* person lied?" She got up, strolled to the window and stared at the world beyond the pane. "There are people here who need help, Agnes. I can feel it. You would too, but you are so scared of the past, you will not allow yourself to feel the future."

Her point made, she patted my hand and wandered into the kitchen. I sat with my head bowed. She returned, moments later, with a couple of Slivovica glasses. She handed one to me and I took it wordlessly. We sat for a minute.

"I've been such a coward," I whispered. Babs shook her head.

"Nyet, you hev been scared – but now, I think it is time to not be scared… or to be scared but not let it stop you." I said nothing so Babs spoke again. "I could make the Vegan disappear," she clicked her fingers, "but I do not think that would solve your problem. Instead, I will stay with you while *you* deal with him, magic or no, da?"

I swallowed and nodded.

"Da," I whispered. "I mean, yes." Babs nodded with satisfaction and my lips twitched into a faint smile. My chest felt lighter than it had in years. I might not know what I was going to do, but at least I'd have Babs in my corner while I did it. She leaned forward then and took my free hand in hers.

"My friend, it is also time to remove Misty from the freezer." My smile froze and my throat tightened. I wasn't ready. I opened my mouth to say as much to Babs but she squeezed my hand to silence me. "Nyet, I know you are not yet ready. This is why you should move him into House – we hev cold cupboard that could give ice cream in the Sahara… is just, should anyone stir up trouble for your cafe, a dead cat in the freezer would not look good. We must be squeaking clean." She wasn't wrong. I gave a final nod of agreement and I downed my drink. Babs smiled at me as I spluttered and raised her glass in salute before knocking hers back.

"Good," she said, smacking her lips appreciatively, "because we have tweaked your Vegan's nose today and I think it will not be long before he bites back."

Chapter Eight

Babs was right, we didn't have to wait long for the Vegan to react. We found Burt waiting for us at the cafe the next morning. Beyond him, the remains of my shop window grinned like broken teeth. The culprit, a common house brick, sat on the nearest table, next to the scar Babs' knife had left the day before. My stomach dropped into my boots. *Here we go again,* I thought. And I'd started the day feeling so much lighter, too.

Burt shuffled his feet. "Sorry, Aggie love. I was in the back, getting your order ready." He nodded at the box of veg overflowing next to him. "I heard the smash but by the time I'd got out, they were already halfway down the arcade, so I thought it best to wait here, make sure nothing else happened." He hesitated and glanced down. "Truth is, I'd never have caught up with them," he admitted, "not with my legs."

I gave him a watery smile.

"We're none of us as young as we used to be," I said. I stared at the damaged pane, mentally working through the next steps. I'd need to get the glaziers in – assuming they were even available today. No point going through the insurance, they'd need a police report and that would slow things down even more. As it was, I'd need to make it safe, clear up, and secure it, which would all take time. I'd have to shut for today, at least. Probably tomorrow, too. The bastard had closed me again… I closed my eyes. What wouldn't I give to just turn around, go home and crawl back into bed? I bet I could find an old movie on one of the channels, perhaps a Western with John Wayne. Instead, I was stuck here, thinking about glaziers. My head throbbed behind my eyes and I closed them even tighter to hold back the tears that threatened to form. I felt Babs' hand on my elbow. She gave me a gentle squeeze.

"Agnes? Agnes, open your eyes." I turned to look at her, opened my mouth to take a deep breath and she promptly popped a toffee in. I slurped and spluttered my way around it until all that remained was the thick aftertaste that coated my tongue. "Better?" said Babs.

"No!" I said. "You can't solve every problem with sweets, you know." Babs' eyes glittered with mischief.

"Want to bet?" She winked at me and then clapped her hands. "Now, to important business. Burt?" Burt snapped to attention; I half expected him to reel off a salute.

"Yes, Babs? What can I do?" Babs smiled sweetly at him.

"You can tell me why it is you think your legs are not good." She pursed her lips speculatively, examined his legs and then looked at him from under her eyelashes. "You hev magnificent legs, darling. You hev my word on the matter." Burt blushed and shifted his gaze from her and I puffed out my cheeks and blew in exasperation.

"Da, darling? Is problem?" Babs asked me.

"Oh no!" I replied, waving my hand. "You carry on. Don't let my personal tragedy get in the way of you flirting!" Babs glanced behind me at the remnants of the window and wrinkled her nose.

"This? This is not tragedy. This is barely inconvenience and already is dealt with." I frowned at that.

"Eh?" I said. Babs nodded her head in the direction of the building site across the way, where the gaggle of hi-vis jackets were flocking in our direction. The foreman reached us first and doffed his hard hat. He squinted at the damage and tutted.

"Aw, no way, Hen. What wee jobbie's done that tae ye? We were on our way over for some brekkie, we did nae expect tae see this." I shook my head, unable to answer. He beckoned his team closer. "Have youse lot seen the state of this?" There was much disgusted sighing and shaking of heads. "Well, I'm no standin' for it," said the foreman. He rubbed his chin, then looked at his team. "Alright, lads, here's what we're going tae do. Tony, I want you with a sweeping brush, clearing up. Jason, ye tae get Sammy from the glazier's down. Tell him tae bring the pane from that order he messed up yesterday and we'll say no more aboot it. Dave, I want you on the phone tae Simon. He owes me a favour and I'm wanting shutters fitted so there'll be no more bricks, right?" Dave muttered something to the foreman who promptly rounded on him. "I dinnae care if he tae wed today, tell him I want him here in an hour or he'll have no need fae a honeymoon." The foreman turned to me then and spoke gently. "Sorry about that, Hen, but you've no tae worry about anything. We'll take care of this." I nodded mutely, still trying to catch up with all the instructions he'd fired out. Babs shouldered her way forward.

"Excuse my sister. This has been big shock and you hev been so kind. And whilst you work, I will make you all Borscht." The foreman tilted his head.

"Is that yon pink soup we had yesterday? Aye, that was proper nice. That'd be grand, Hen." And with that, he strode away.

"I *like* him." Babs chuckled, then she nudged me. "And *you* should never underestimate the power of Borscht – it is never just soup."

"Clearly," I replied, watching the yellow jackets swarm over my shop front. "I'd never have expected a bowl of boiled beetroot could have such an effect." I noticed Burt frowning at us then.

"You never said you were her sister," he said to Babs.

"*Younger* sister," corrected Babs. I rolled my eyes.

"—different mother."

"—different father," we said, at the same time. Burt looked puzzled. I didn't blame him.

"Is very complicated family tree," said Babs. "Perhaps I can explain it to you over hot drink?" She nodded toward the cafe – *my* cafe. Burt looked from Babs to his shop, clearly sorely tempted, then he looked back, crestfallen and sighed.

"Thanks, but I really should be getting back – hey, you won't believe this but I had a load of new orders come through last night." He rubbed his hands together. "Looks like business is finally looking up. You must be my lucky charm, Babs." Then he smiled at us, nodded to the workmen – one of whom had carried our order from Burt inside – and scarpered back to the safety of his own shop. Babs watched his retreating form.

"I will be his 'lucky charm' alright," she muttered. I slapped her on the arm.

"Behave, will you? And get inside. We've work to do."

She raised one impeccable eyebrow. "Really? Then lead on." She motioned me into the cafe and followed behind me.

I'd had several thoughts fizzing round my brain while Babs had been ogling Burt's plums, and they all came back to the Vegan… or, more to the point, who he'd been harassing. He'd started with me. When it seemed I was out of the picture, he'd moved on to poor Margot at the ice-cream parlour, as well as taking a few side-swipes at Burt – nothing too serious, he wasn't that brave… yet. He'd stuck to the ones he thought were the easy targets: the old woman and the widow. The problem was, one of them was starting to fight back, so he'd struck again, hard and fast. I knew it had to be him; it was too much of a coincidence to be anyone else.

Babs set to work in the kitchen, the rhythmic sound of her chopping accompanying the less-than-rhythmic warble of her singing voice. I stared out through the window and looked across the arcade. Hmmm, there was something more going on here, I could almost feel it in my gut. I hadn't listened to my gut for a long time, but perhaps it was time I started again.

I was interrupted in my reverie by Margot, her anxious face appearing as if summoned. I motioned her past the bustle of builders and in through the door. She heaved a sigh when she reached my side.

"Oh, Aggie, I can't believe this has all started up again. I had to come and check on you. You must be devastated." I shrugged. It wasn't great, but somehow, it didn't feel so bad this time. Margot nodded toward the workmen. "Still, at least you've got them fixing it quickly enough. How'd you manage that? I can't get a plumber to answer the phone without three weeks' notice."

"That would be thanks to me," called Babs. Modesty was not a word she was familiar with. She came from the kitchen, drying her hands on a tea towel and I introduced her to Margot. "You own ice cream parlour, da?"

Margot toyed with the wedding ring she still wore.

"Yeah… well, for now," she said. I frowned at that and looked at Margot – properly looked and for the first time, I saw the coarse strands of grey that streaked her dark hair. There were new lines etched around her eyes and the corners of her mouth and she stood with her shoulders hunched as though trying to hide in the centre of the room. She looked up at me. Her eyes shone with barely suppressed tears. I recalled the furrow of her brow yesterday evening when I'd seen her scowling at her calculator. A dark maggot of guilt started to worry away in my stomach. How long had she been struggling? How many other people around here had been crying out for my help and I hadn't heard them? I took Margot's arm and gently guided her to a table away from the hubbub outside.

"Come on, Love. You've time for a cuppa before you open up." One of the workmen poked his head through the empty window frame.

"Did someone say cuppa? We're all gasping." Babs shooed him away with her tea towel.

"Da, I will make coffee now. You work." The workman pulled a face.

"Any chance you could make it tea? Four sugars?" he said, then returned to work. Babs froze in her tracks, her smile twisting into a grimace.

"Tea." She practically heaved on the word. She shook her head and headed back to her domain behind the counter to start the drinks. Margot sniffed and dabbed at her eyes, seemingly grateful for the distraction.

"Does Babs not like tea?" she asked.

"About as much as she likes babies," I chortled. Then, seeing Margot's puzzled expression, I explained, "Babs only drinks tea when there's no alternative available."

"Like coffee?" said Margot.

"Like sewer water," muttered Babs, darkly. Margot smiled and her shoulders relaxed somewhat. The guilt maggot wriggled a little deeper and I thought back to Babs' words the night before. I'd been punishing myself for twenty years… but I'd been punishing others, too. How much good could I have done if I'd taken my head from out of my own arse for long enough to look around? What of Margot's husband? What comfort could I have offered there? Not a cure, certainly, but I could have eased those final months. Instead, I hid myself away, too scared to put a foot wrong to put a foot right. Well, not anymore. Things were going to change, starting here and now. I straightened my shoulders and set my jaw. From the corner of my eye, I saw Babs looking at me. I met her eye and she gave me a single, solemn nod.

Chapter Nine

Margot cradled the cup in her hands and blew across the rim to cool her drink. She was onto her third cup and had demolished a hefty slice of Babs' yabluchnyk. She hadn't needed coaxing like Sophie. She wanted to talk and I wondered how long she'd kept it all bottled up inside her. How many nights had she paced the floor of the flat above her shop – her home ever since Derek had passed – with all these thoughts brimming inside her, desperate to burst out?

Her financial difficulties were easy to track. She and Derek had bought the shop when he was in his prime. They rented out the flat above whilst they lived in a modest terrace nearby, where they planned for a future that wouldn't happen. I remember Derek as he was: tall and handsome, with arms built for churning ice cream. They laughed a lot. Then he became ill. Margot's transition from wife to widow was swift, which some people chose to say was a blessing. It should be against the law to utter the words, "at least he didn't suffer long," at a funeral.

She struggled. Of course, she did. Time and loan repayments wait for no man. She sold the house and moved into the flat. That bought her a bit of breathing space but without Derek, it was hard to regain the momentum the business used to have; running the parlour, making the ice cream, managing the stock… it was a lot on her own and she couldn't afford to pay anyone else. And now the Vegan had started on at her.

"*Bovine rape!*" Margot blew air through her teeth. "It's not like I don't have vegan alternatives either – I've spent ages perfecting recipes to shut him up, but he won't give over and it's driven more than a few customers away. I mean, no one wants to think about that when they're eating their ice cream, do they?" She sighed heavily, blew her nose and I patted her arm sympathetically. It wouldn't be long until the wolf found its way to her door again. I bit my lip thoughtfully, then swirled the dregs of my own tea gently around the cup.

There's nothing mystical about tea leaves. I know there's a lot of guff about them but really, they're just something to look at while the mind does the real work. I stared at the smattering of leaves in my own cup now, trying to get a feel for how valid Margot's fears were. I let my eyes unfocus and felt my jaw slacken. My breath slowed and my mind drifted out of my body. I willed it forward, a week, a month, a year into Margot's future. There was fog, too much fog; I couldn't see anything. I flicked my head, like a cow trying to shoo a fly, but still, the fog didn't lift. Then I felt the familiar warmth of Babs' hand taking my own. She squeezed it gently and the mist parted, rolling back like storm clouds. I saw Margot's shop, but it wasn't her behind the counter; the melamine tables and bright orange chairs were gone and in their place was... I squinted but couldn't see clearly through the shop window. My shoulders dropped. It looked like she was right to be anxious.

"Aggie?" Margot's voice dragged me back through the fog, back into the here and now of my own shop but Babs still held my hand. She gripped it tightly now and I looked as though staring through a kaleidoscope. She gave a subtle move of her head and let her eyes take in the rest of the cafe. With the future echoes still swirling around us, I caught a glimpse of it – a snapshot of potential. An ice cream stand in the corner of the cafe, Margot behind it, smiling, her face young again and beside her a man... Burt!

I gasped and snatched my hand away from Babs. The cafe snapped back into sharp focus and I fought down a wave of motion sickness. Margot leaned towards me, her face a picture of concern.

"Are you alright, Aggie, Love? Is the shock of the morning getting to you?"

"Sell the shop," I said, without any preamble. Margot blinked and sat back, folding her arms.

"Well, it's not that easy."

"Yes, it is," I said. "Sell it, all of it, the flat too. Set up a stall in here," I pointed to where I'd seen her stand in the vision, "over there. You can move into the flat upstairs, too. Heaven knows I've been letting it go to waste. Nothing up there but cobwebs and old crockery – it could do with someone living in it." Margot pursed her lips and stared at the currently vacant corner. Babs reached forward and, seemingly innocently, patted Margot's hand.

"It is good idea," she said. "You should definitely

consider it." Margot's mouth had formed into a little o of wonder and I knew she could see it all as we had – well, not all; I assumed Babs had left Burt out of the equation. Margot would believe it was all in her imagination, of course, but it might be the little nudge that got her moving. Margot's brow furrowed then.

"What about Himself?" she said, nodding in the direction of Sophie's shop.

"The Vegan, you mean?" I said. "Well, obviously, I can't guarantee he'll stop bothering you, but I will say he's less likely to be 'brave' when there are two of us to contend with."

"Three," corrected Babs, "and one of them knows how to butcher a carcass in two minutes flat!" She grinned wickedly. Margot and I glanced at each other for a moment before the sniggering began. It wasn't a great joke, I'll grant you, but it was what we needed to break the ice. The sniggers became snorts that scoured the insides of our noses before morphing into full-blown belly laughs that saw the builders looking around warily in the way men do when they hear women laughing. It made us laugh all the more. Finally, we settled down. Margot's laughs dissipated into little hiccups, Babs dabbed her eyes and I rubbed my aching ribs.

"It's been a long time since I laughed like that," Margot admitted.

"You should do it more often, darling," said Babs. "It is taking years off you." Margot blushed prettily. It was easy to see how she'd appeal to someone like Burt. I told her a little of some of the problems I'd been having – not too many; I didn't want to overwhelm her, but enough so she'd know we had a common enemy. She listened quietly.

"To be honest, it's a bit of a relief to know I'm not the only one that fella of Sophie's has been having a pop at," she said, then she clamped her hand over her mouth. "Oh, that's awful, isn't it, saying I'm glad he's caused you trouble. I'm not, obviously…" she stammered. I waved away her concerns.

"Don't worry. A trouble shared and all that. Burt's had a couple of issues too. In fact, it seems like all of us in the arcade have had some bother with him… well, almost all of us." I let my sentence hang in the air and glared over at the Magick shop. The others followed my gaze.

"Ugh," said Margot. "*Her*. Face like a dog licking a pissy thistle, that one." Babs glanced sharply at her, frowning, but Margot was still talking. "I wouldn't be surprised if she and the Vegan were knocking boots, the way she simpers and fawns over him." That was interesting. Margot glanced at the clock then. "Look at the time, I must get on. Thanks for the tea and sympathy, Aggie – and you, Babs." Babs nodded; she was still staring at Margot looking perplexed.

"No problem, Love. Have a think about my suggestion, yes?" Margot swallowed.

"I will," she said, then navigated the clan of builders who were peering, meerkat-like, through the window, wondering if there was any chance of a little taste of something…

I grabbed a plate, stacked it with flapjacks and passed it out to them, while Babs cleared the table.

"That was interesting," I said. "Looks like I'm not the only one with suspicions about that little madam in the magic shop" – just because it's spelt with a K, doesn't mean I have to pronounce it.

"Hmm," said Babs, still frowning. "What is pissy thistle dog..." She paused and I chuckled. I sometimes forget English isn't her first language.

"Face like a dog licking a pissy thistle?"

"Da. Is this woman unattractive?"

"No, not as such..." I rubbed my chin trying to think how to describe it. Eventually, I conceded defeat. "You know what? You'll understand when you see her," I looked across at the shop again, "and I think we'll want a chat with Little Miss MagicK before she's very much older." At that moment, the bell on the door jangled and a host of customers thronged through the door... Miss Magick would have to wait.

Chapter Ten

It was late afternoon before business slowed, which I should have been grateful for but I was itching to get finished. I was wiping the tables down before the last customer had drained their cup, which Babs clucked her tongue about. I took her point and sent the customer on his way with a complimentary flapjack by way of an apology. Babs had started her prep for the next day, but once I'd turned the door sign to closed, she wiped her hands, took off her pinny and followed me outside.

The workmen had done a fantastic job. The window had been replaced and polished until it shone and I was the proud owner of a set of shutters that would stop brick-throwing vegans in their tracks. I'd watched each of the men as they went about their business and had made a note of who seemed to suffer from what: the foreman would be getting a jar of my special camphor rub for his neck tomorrow, Big Dave would have a blend of hibiscus and nettle tea for the gout he didn't know about yet, and Babs had already presented young Simon with a packet of spices to make his wedding night go with a bang. The poor lad had turned so red, he was practically a fire hazard, but

I noticed he tucked them carefully in his breast pocket, nonetheless. I rubbed my hands together. It felt good to be doing proper work again.

Out in the arcade, Burt's shop buzzed with activity. Burt caught sight of us as he bagged up some grapes and motioned to queueing hordes with an exasperated smile that wasn't fooling anyone. He was like a pig in muck. Babs blew him a kiss and I looked at her curiously.

"That's the busiest I've seen Burt in... well, ever," I said.

"Hmm?" She gave me a look of wide-eyed innocence that was a trifle overdone.

"What did you do, Babs?"

"I did nothing... merely placed some reviews in some strategic places on internet... I *may* hev added merest hint of glamour to make sure they were seen, but clearly, Burt really *does* hev greatest plums in the area." She smiled archly but I was agog.

"Wait, *you're* on the internet?"

Babs looked heavenwards. "Da, darling. *Everybody* is on internet."

"I'm not!"

"This is because you think it is still twentieth century."

"It is..." I paused and did some calculations in my head. "Oh..." I thought for a minute. "And is that why we've been so busy?" Babs gave me her best duchess look, the one she pulls out when she wants someone to know their place.

"Nyet. *We* hev been busy because *my* food is glorious. Now, let us see the thistle-licking canine." I fought a losing battle against a grin and led her to the magic shop.

The shop was as pretentious as they come, right down to the Hamsa symbol – an eye in the palm of a hand to protect against evil – etched on the window. As with the money tree, much good may it do her. A jangle of windchimes announced our entrance and the woman behind the counter looked up with a salesman's smile that stopped short of her eyes.

"Blessed B…" The rest of the greeting trailed off along with the smile.

There she was, the owner of the Emporium of MagicK in all her glory. As I said before, she wasn't unattractive; she filled her clothes nicely and had a pretty enough face, it was just that sour look she always wore (sales smile, excepting), like she'd trodden in something and sniffed it. It gave her the look of, well, a dog licking a pissy thistle.

"Pissy dog face!" Babs' eyes danced with glee as she finally understood the comment and I was scarcely able to suppress my own mirth. Pissy Dog Face's expression hardened into one that could turn mere mortals to stone. I dare say it would have worked too, had we actually been mere mortals, but I cut my teeth on slate-faced harridans who probably *could* turn men to stone and she wasn't anywhere near their league. I batted my way past the swags of dreamcatchers and returned her look with a beatific smile, guaranteed to get right up her nose. It worked. I saw her jaw tighten as her teeth clenched.

"Can I help you?" she asked, barely moving her lips. Yes, that was a point, why was I here? I could hardly ask her outright what was going on with the Vegan. "Er, can you not touch that, please?" she added. "It's very expensive." I looked around and realised Babs had wandered off and was inspecting a polished sphere that had a pinkish glow to it – pink amethyst if I'm any judge. Babs bounced it gently in her hand a few times for the pleasure of seeing her wince, then set it back on the counter. The woman turned back to me then.

"*Was* there something?" I was better prepared now. I'd seen her security cameras and a wicked little plan was brewing in my brain.

"Yes, actually, Love," I said. "I don't know if you noticed, but I had my window done in again this morning."

The girl sniffed. "Is that what all the fuss and noise has been about?"

"Ohh, has it disturbed you? I'm ever so sorry. All that bother must have knocked your chakras way off kilter." Pissy Dog Face pursed her lips, clearly trying to decide whether she preferred to accept my comment at face value or live in a world where I was mocking her. She pitched for the former.

"Well, just make sure it doesn't happen again… and that's expensive too," she said, the latter directed at Babs, who was now holding a carved fertility idol in an inappropriate manner. Babs raised an eyebrow and set it down.

"You want we should visit all criminals in the area and ask can they pretty please not throw more bricks because it upsets lady in magic shop?" she said. She took a step closer to the counter and her voice was deceptively neutral. Pissy Dog Face was braver than I thought; she didn't even flinch but then, she didn't know Babs like I did. I placed a soothing hand on my friend's shoulder.

"Come on now, Babs. You know these misfortunes

aren't just our own. This young lady here has a business to run, just like us, and it's perfectly natural that she should want as little disruption to that as possible..." The woman behind the counter gave a nod and a sniff of satisfaction – she didn't know me very well either. I nodded along reassuringly before continuing, "...and *that's* why she's going to give us access to the footage her security cameras will have taken, isn't that right, Love?" I turned to her, still nodding agreeably and she found herself nodding back before her brain had a chance to catch up.

"My what?"

"Cameras. You've one there, another there and, oh look, one by the door that will capture anything going on outside. I bet it got a decent look at my phantom brick thrower."

The girl shifted her weight awkwardly and toyed with a strand of her hair. "Oh, those..." she said. "They... er, they don't work. They're just for show, to put people off, that kind of thing."

"Is funny," said Babs, peering past the girl to the office behind her, "because *that* would suggest they are working in tiptop condition." She pointed one long finger in the direction of the office and the monitor just visible inside it – a monitor, moreover, showing multiple images of the shop and surroundings, including a freeze-frame of Babs, face pinched in an accusatory scowl, finger outstretched. I leaned back on my heels and crossed my arms.

"Lucky for us they've chosen today, of all days, to start working again, eh? So, shall we take them with us now, or shall we just tell the police to collect them later?" I asked. The girl blushed and looked down.

"I'll download them for you later," she muttered. I turned to Babs so she could translate that for me, but her attention had wandered again. She drifted over to the wiccan section which was festooned with pewter and silver jewellery – tree of life amulets, triple moon goddess earrings, green man brooches. Babs clapped her hands and her face split into a joyous grin.

"Agnes, look! Is dress-up section for baby witches!"

Well, that broke the spell, if you'll pardon the pun. Pissy Dog Face did some pointing of her own and ordered us off her premises.

Babs raised both eyebrows at me. "Rude!" she huffed.

"I don't think she likes us very much," I said.

"Not like us!" she said incredulously. "You, I can understand, but me? I'm adorable." I didn't bother to respond. I was already tugging her elbow, guiding her next door.

"Come on, next stop."

Sophie looked up from her seat behind the counter. Her smile was genuine… or at least it was until *he* joined her from the back room. The dark clouds rolled across her face then; it hurt to watch. He stood in front of the counter and crossed his arms.

"What do you two want?" he said.

"For the record, he *definitely* doesn't like us," whispered Babs. I elbowed her into silence.

"I came to speak to Sophie about the vandalism to my cafe this morning," I said. I managed to keep the tremor from my voice, though my stomach writhed. He looked me up and down but I wasn't going to be cowed this time.

"She doesn't know anything about that," he said. I stared at him, not blinking.

"Oh, I'm certain *she* doesn't, but it's her I wanted to speak to, not you, Love." The muscles shifted under the skin of his jaw.

"I'm not your 'love'," he said. I saw Sophie shift uncomfortably behind him. I let a saccharine smile crystalise on my face before I replied to him.

"I know you're not, *Love*, but given the other names I could use, I think we'd better stick with love, don't you, Love?" I ignored Babs' snickering behind me and kept my eyes fixed on the Vegan. His jaw was working overtime, clenching and unclenching. I'm surprised he didn't crack a tooth. It must have been hard for him. After all, this wasn't how these meetings usually went. He shifted his shoulders and nodded at the workmen who were just clearing up.

"Got it sorted, I see," he said, sourly.

"Oh yes." I gave a cheery wave to the workmen. "You'd be surprised how many *decent* people object to unpleasant things happening to old—" Babs coughed significantly, "—old-*er* women," I said. "They've even given me some shutters too, to make sure there'll be no more bricks." The Vegan's nostrils flared.

"I wonder how much their bosses will appreciate them bunking off a day's work like this," he said. Babs spoke up then.

"Oh, I think they will not mind too much," she said, "not when the local press declare them heroes for today's work... remarkable, the power of the press, is it not?" Oh, that was slick, but it was time to draw this meeting to a close. I shifted myself so I could see Sophie behind His Nibs. "Anyway, I just came to say you don't need to worry,

Love. Magic shop next door got it all on CCTV. Police should be able to find the bugger with that, so there's no need for you to fret."

I heard Babs' little intake of breath and just about managed not to smirk. To his credit, the Vegan hardly even blinked, but I noticed he looked a bit paler and his voice when he ordered us out was not entirely steady. We left without a fuss though.

Once outside, Babs gave a happy sigh.

"That was fun," she said. "What's next?"

What was next was a waiting game. I hurried Babs back to the cafe and pulled down the blinds so we could watch. Sure enough, no sooner had we settled ourselves when we saw him come scurrying out of the health food shop like the weasel he was. He paused and looked around furtively before sidling into the magic tat shop. He'd make a rotten spy.

I sat back in my chair. I know I looked smug because Babs told me so.

"So, what is it you are hoping to achieve?" she asked. I cracked my fingers.

"Oh, I don't know," I said, "put the cat amongst the pigeons a bit, maybe. Get him worried – worried people make mistakes. *Then* we'll know what he's up to, because there's more going on here than him simply trying to make my life miserable and I want to know what it is."

Babs chewed her lip thoughtfully. "You know what would be easier would be if you..." She weaved her hands in a little motion I assume meant 'scrying'. "You did well with Margot this morning, after all." I looked away and concentrated on teasing a bit of nothing out from under my thumbnail.

"We both know that was down to you," I said, finally.

"Nevertheless," she said. I waited, but she said nothing more. Instead, she stood and patted my shoulder on her way into the kitchen. "Today has been good day," she called over her shoulder and I smiled. She was right, it had been. And who knew what tomorrow would bring?

Chapter Eleven

To the surprise of absolutely no one, the morning brought the arrival of Pissy Dog Face. She deigned to drop by while Babs was enjoying her morning flirt with Burt. She'd convinced him to join us for coffee before the morning rush and honestly, the sight of her fluttering her eyelashes at the poor man over a slice of apple cake was almost enough to make me lose my cornflakes. Throw in Little Miss Magick's sour face to curdle my milk and that was breakfast ruined for me.

Anyway, young Miss came to tell us that, tragically, there'd been a glitch in the system and the CCTV from yesterday morning had been wiped. I nodded my head with the look of someone who had no idea what she was being told but didn't want to admit she was clueless – not much of a stretch if I'm honest. It confirmed our suspicions that there was something going on in that quarter and the conversation would have ended there had Burt not been with us.

"That's terrible. What service are you using?" he demanded. The girl was taken aback and stammered some kind of answer. "You want to get on to them. They'll have a backup server for sure. It may even be linked to your original system. How often does the scheduled backup run? Does it do a differential or full copy over? Is it in the same data centre? What's the latency? Could it have ended up on the dead letter queue? Is it over WAN or LAN? I can bob over and take a look for you if you want?"

I almost felt sorry for her. Her eyes had glazed over at the word *server* and would likely not go back to normal for several hours. My own were probably fairly glass-like at this point too. Babs' eyes were also glazed – but with admiration for Burt. They had never been normal to begin with, though. Either way, Little Miss Magick snapped out of it quickly enough and drew herself up to her full height.

"No, thank you. I'm quite capable of taking care of the matter myself. The content is gone, that's all there is to it." Babs smirked at me. I had to hand it to the girl, she wasn't shy about doubling down on the manure she was peddling. Burt looked taken aback for a moment then shrugged.

"Suit yourself," he said and turned back to his coffee. I shook my head, feigned disappointment and thanked her for her trouble. She tossed her head and didn't even look embarrassed. I offered her a flapjack. "It's the least I can do." That gave her pause.

"Don't worry," I said, "it's vegan."

"Da, we hear you like all things Vegan," added Babs. The girl finally had the decency to blush before turning on her heel and stalking back to her own territory.

"I like her," Babs declared as we watched her through the window. "She is cowbag, but does not pretend to be otherwise."

"Yep, she's got some brass neck, I'll give her that," I said.

"Well, if she's 'lost' that security footage, it'll be no accident," said Burt. "Glitch in the system, my eye." Babs rubbed his arm, presumably because she couldn't reach anywhere else.

"Da, darling. She is lying, we know this."

"Then why…?" She pressed a finger to his lips to silence him. I cast my eyes around for a sick bucket.

"Don't you worry. It was test to see where her loyalties sit. Now we are on to her game and playing one of our own."

Burt held her gaze for a moment then shook his head.

"I will never understand women," he said. He brushed cake crumbs off his top then and got down from the stool. "Must be off. Thanks for the coffee and cake, ladies."

"Any time," purred Babs. "Perhaps I will pop over later for some beetroot." I didn't know anyone could make the word *beetroot* sound salacious until that moment. Burt's ears turned pink and he scarpered back to the relative safety of his shop. I rounded on Babs the instant he was out of sight.

"What are you playing at?" I demanded. I followed her through to the kitchen and she looked up from the batter she had picked up.

"I am making syrniki, is not obvious?"

"With Burt, I mean." I put my hands on my hips. "You be careful there. He's a good 'un – technobabble aside – and I don't want to see him hurt."

Babs looked at me, pityingly. "Oh, Agnes. He is already hurting; can you not see? Can you not hear?"

I swallowed whatever response I could have made and stopped to listen.

"Lovely apples and pears. Get your strawberries," Burt's voice boomed out across the arcades, as loud and jolly as ever but there… I strained my ears and heard it: a slight discordant tone weighing down his words. I could see him now, the buttons of his white greengrocer's coat straining at the chest, his habitual open smile in place. How had I not noticed the grey cloud that hung across his shoulders? The guilt worm wriggled again. *You know why*, it said. I took a deep breath and let my mind unwind. Burt was completely surrounded by rolling mist now. Babs took my hand as she had done with Margot and the mist dissipated.

I saw Burt in the front room of his house, just across the street, almost directly opposite mine. I saw the chair in the corner where his mother used to sit. I watched him take his single plate and cup through to the kitchen and carefully wash and put them away. I saw him sit and flick through channel after channel on his television, before sighing and switching it off. Now he picked up his phone and scrolled through the numbers. He paused over one of them, his thick fingers hovering over the green call button before that too was turned off and set aside.

I snatched my hand away from Babs and Burt was back as he ever was, cheerfully cajoling the natives to purchase a punnet or two. But I'd seen the cloud now. I'd heard the lead in his voice. It wasn't so very long ago I'd have picked up on it without Babs guiding the way. I had seriously let things slide. I remembered Burt when I first arrived. He'd not long lost his mother. He'd cared for her until the end, I'd heard, so hadn't had much time for personal relationships. That was a good couple of years ago now and it hadn't occurred to me that he might still be single. It hadn't crossed my mind that he might be lonely.

"Why didn't he say something?" I muttered, half to myself.

"You know why," said Babs, unconsciously echoing my guilt worm, and I nodded. I'd seen enough men drink themselves to death because liquor is easy but saying *I need help* is hard. It's not something they're taught, men, is it? Everyone assumes they'll just get on with it, whatever *it* is, and not need anyone to talk to... or to simply be around. Only women and weirdos talk about their feelings and asking for help is right out the window. No wonder so many of them lost their way. I balled up my fist and slammed it onto the countertop.

Babs calmly picked up the syrniki bowl and started beating the batter again. She knew my anger was not directed at her but at life, the world... but mostly myself. Finally, she cleared her throat.

"Is no good beating yourself up about things you hev missed." My jaw clenched and I stared off into the distance. She was right though; the past was done. I couldn't change it. But I could make a difference to the future and I could make sure he didn't get hurt.

"So," I said, "Burt..." I winced at the forced casual tone in my voice and Babs threw her head back and laughed.

"You are *bad* at this."

"Still..." I said, determined to carry my point.

"Still..." she said. Then she went quiet and finally

shrugged. "He is not mine. His heart belongs elsewhere, though he does not admit it yet, even to himself." An image flashed across my mind. Burt and Margot, standing close together, laughing – the image I'd seen in my vision yesterday. I felt a pang for my friend. Babs saw what I saw; of course, she knew.

"Then why?"

She put the bowl down. "Because, as it stands, he will never hev courage to approach her; not romantically, anyway. He needs confidence to make the next move. I can provide that." I swallowed a small lump of pity.

"And what about your needs?" I asked. Babs' answering laugh was throaty and earthy.

"*My* needs are much more basic, darling."

"Doesn't it bother you, though?" I asked. Babs looked thoughtful for a moment then picked up her bowl again.

"The only thing that bothers me is that I still haven't cooked these syrniki," she said and walked back to the kitchen.

And that was that. There was nothing more to be said on the matter, nothing anyone cared to listen to, in any case. I sighed, dusted my hands off on my pinny and made the decision to put them out of my mind. Burt was a grown man, after all, and heaven knows Babs had been around long enough to take care of herself. The bell jingled. The first customers came and I smiled in greeting. It would be nice to have a busy but unremarkable day for a change.

Chapter Twelve

I was wrong, of course, though not about the busyness – the bell never stopped chiming; it seems the local populace has developed quite a taste for beetroot soup and apple cake. I was wrong about it being unremarkable.

The reporter arrived that afternoon, a full day earlier than we expected. I'll say this for the Vegan, he doesn't let the grass grow under his feet. It had been barely twenty-four hours since Babs had subtly planted the idea in his head and now, here he was. I recognised the greasy oik the instant I saw him – it was the same hack he'd set on me last time. My stomach seized up at the sight of his smarmy face and I was sorely tempted to show him the back of my ladle. I don't mind the press as a rule. Most of them are hard-working and dedicated to their job but this one was the lowest of all gutter dwellers. Oh, I don't mind that he was obnoxious and aggressive with his questions – I dare say I've rubbed one or two people up the wrong way myself, over the years; it's par for the course when you're trying to eke the truth out of them. No, what I objected to with *this* one was that he was lazy. Not just for running with the story in the first place when five minutes of research would have shown it for the sham it was, but also in his reporting. It was sloppy andlacklustre. Even the headline looked like it had been dialled in: *Local Caff in Bacon Gaffe*. Personally, I'd have gone with *Arcade Eatery's Pig Mistake*, but not everybody has my finesse. The rest of the article wasn't much better – full of boring tautologies and cliches. If you're going to be bad, at least be good at it.

Still, at least I was better prepared for him this time – I rolled my shoulders back and told my stomach to behave itself. He swaggered up to the counter and eased his buttocks onto one of the stools there. I pretended not to notice him and carried on carving up the honey cake Babs had baked, but I could feel my lip curling involuntarily. Finally, I looked up, locked eyes with him and raised an eyebrow. He spoke first.

"I see you're open again."

"No thanks to you." I'm surprised the words made it out between my clenched teeth. "Shouldn't you be off ruining someone else's business with your lies? I hear the magic shop across the way only sells *white* rabbits to pull out of hats – that's got to be racist, hasn't it? Maybe you should write one of your nasty little articles about her."

He smirked then, not one of the wicked ones Babs and I do, but a proper oily one.

"Nah, I think I'd do better to revisit your story—"

"Good, because you had some terrible spelling errors last time." His nose twitched at that. Ha.

"I mean, I wonder how many of these good people here -" he threw his arm wide to incorporate the humming cafe "- know about your sordid past?" Ha, none of them, unless they'd researched ancient folklore, and even then, that only covers a fraction of it. But the journalist was still talking, so I gave myself a shake and tried to focus. "Tell me, was that stunt with the window yesterday a deliberate ploy to garner public sympathy? It worked well with those poor builders, didn't it? No doubt they'll be docked a day's pay but what does that matter as long as everyone comes flocking to your door?"

Really? So that was what the Vegan was putting about, was it? I had to give him credit; after all, if I denied it, there'd be no CCTV evidence to the contrary. The journalist tilted his head then as if another thought had occurred to him.

"Your cat died recently, didn't it? That sort of thing gets bags of sympathy…" He left the sentence hanging and I tightened my fingers around the knife handle. Babs wafted through then, serving tray balanced on one hand, and deftly removed it from my grip with her free hand.

"Agnes, darling, what is the golden rule?" she said. I looked down sullenly.

"Don't kill the customers," I muttered, then brightened, "but he's not a customer!" I said, eyeing the knife.

"Yes, I wouldn't eat here if you paid me," the journalist said, but his words didn't reach his eyes. In fact, he was no longer looking at me at all. His attention had drifted to the tray Babs held, heaped with delicacies. She set it down on the countertop before him.

"Are you certain? Surely you will need energy to write all your clever words?" Tiny beads of sweat were now forming on the journalist's top lip. Tendrils of steam coiled off freshly baked pyrizhky; you could almost see it forming fingers and beckoning him closer. He swallowed, clearly struggling with his watering mouth. Babs took a fork. She used the side to cut into the pasty-like dish and the flaky pastry, golden and buttery soft, gave way to reveal a filling of minced beef in a dark, rich gravy. I swear I heard the journalist moan. As it was, he stared, his lips parted in an expression of utmost longing. Babs pressed the fork into his unresisting hand.

"Well," he said, "maybe just a little bite…"

I'd expected him to fall into his food like a pig to trough. Instead, he was like a pilgrim at prayer. Each forkful was savoured, his face awash with blissful reverence. The buzz and hum of the other customers had disappeared, the clink of their cutlery now mere white noise to him. I'm not even certain he was aware that Babs and I were still there. There was just him and the food. Babs gave me a knowing look. Of course, she'd have done her homework. Whilst he demolished the pyrizhky, she slid a golabki onto his plate – a cabbage leaf Babs had stuffed with sauteed porcini and chestnut mushrooms, their earthiness a perfect foil for the nuttiness of the red lentils and rice she'd added. The stuffed parcel was then cooked in a thick stew of tomato and paprika and the journalist didn't even bother to hide his salivating chops this time.

"Don't worry, is vegan," Babs said, somewhat redundantly given he'd already proven himself a carnivore. Borscht followed next, naturally, served with soured cream and thick slabs of good, brown bread, still warm from the oven with soft yellow butter pooling to oil on them. The journalist was silent now, save for the gentle smacking of his lips or the occasional moan of ecstasy. Then came the dessert. Babs placed the tray in front of him and the open look of desire on his face was positively wanton. First came the syrniki Babs had been preparing earlier, slightly sweet drop-scone-like pancakes, served with sharp red berries, then a slice of the honey cake I'd been carving earlier – Medaus Tortas – layers of sweet pastry interspersed with angel-light frosting. Then there was simtalapis – hundred leaves cake, poppyseeds and raisins folded into sheets of pastry and sugar, served with yet more cream, and to finish, Varskes Surelis, my personal favourite.

If I didn't know better, I'd assume Babs' plan was to feed him to death. The journalist's cheeks were flushed now but he still happily lifted the dessert to his lips. The chocolate cracked as he bit into it, revealing the stark white curd cheese within. Another bite and he would discover the golden nugget at the heart – caramel or maybe hazelnut or poppyseed, maybe a thick, sharp fruit syrup. I never found out which as he'd devoured it within moments. He sat back then and folded his hands across his stomach.

"That was…" he looked up and his eyes were shining. "I haven't tasted food like that in a long time."

"Da, since your mother passed away," said Babs, not unkindly. The journalist's jaw dropped.

"How did you –" Babs cut him off with a shrug.

"It stands to reason. You are young… ish man. You hev not tasted the like for long time – probably since you were boy so most likely your mother cooked and she is now not able to. Is simple deduction."

What rot! You could practically see the waves of mummy issues rolling off him by this point. He shook his head.

"I was twelve." That was all he said. It was enough. I

saw him, a pink-faced boy at a scrubbed pine table, delving his spoon into a bowl of hearty vegetable soup. A woman sat next to him. Her smile painted the room – I could imagine the same smile on the journalist's lips should he deign to try it. She ruffled the boy's hair and the look he gave her was warm and liquid.

The scene changed with a screech of tyres. The woman was gone, the bowl was empty and the colour in the room drained to grey. I gasped at the strength of the vision and blinked sudden tears from my own eyes. Babs barely had her fingertip touching my hand this time but that meant nothing. Sometimes, a person's pain is so intertwined with who they are, it's etched into every line on their face; every movement they make betrays them. You can see the story of it practically bursting to get out of them, if you only stop and listen… no, I'm not going to berate myself for not seeing it when he was last here. It was a brief encounter when he had his agenda and I was already on the ropes – we were neither of us in the mood for stories, be it telling them or listening to them. But now… I cleared my throat.

"She was a good cook, then, your mum?"

He smiled his mother's smile.

"The best," he said, then hesitated before adding, "or so I thought, until today." He smiled, somewhat ruefully. "Perhaps I should have let you feed me last time I was in." Babs gave a snort of derision and I shot her a sour look before turning back to the journalist.

"What my sister—"

"—*younger* sister—"

"—is trying to say is that I'm not responsible for the food you've eaten today." He frowned and looked at Babs.

"Oh, are you saying her food isn't good?"

"Nyet, darling. I would never say that." She patted my hand reassuringly. "Your food is very adequate," she said, then shrugged, "but mine is better."

I could feel my cheeks burning.

"And you're going to let her get away with saying that, are you?" The journalist was talking to me now. His eyes glittered with malicious glee and my fingers itched for the ladle again. Instead, I swallowed my pride and met him with a steady gaze.

"Can't argue with the truth," I said. "You of all people should know that. Her food is better than mine."

"Except for flapjacks," said Babs. "Her flapjacks are to die for. Try one." She pushed a plate full of them towards him. You wouldn't think he had room for anything else, given what he'd already put away, but he bit into one with as much relish as he had done the other courses. It was just one of my simple oat and fruit ones but the look on his face as he chewed was that of a child on Christmas morning. His eyes widened suddenly – every trace of bitterness replaced with delight and I knew he'd just had a zing of cranberry shoot across his palate.

"Guaranteed one hundred percent pork free," I said. I couldn't resist it and I'm not ashamed to say I was gratified by the heat that came off his cheeks.

"Why are you here?" His question came out of the blue and I think it took him by surprise as well. He toyed with a flapjack crumb before pinching it between his thumb and forefinger and popping it in his mouth. "What I mean is, with food like this you could be anywhere. You could have a Michelin-star restaurant in London, or a boutique patisserie – you could charge what you like and instead, you're here." He waved his arm at the world outside my window. One of our customers came to the counter to pay her bill. She'd been in every day for the past few days, dragging her wheeled shopping bag and asthmatic pug behind her. I let Babs deal with her, one ear on their easy chatter. I looked the journalist squarely in the face.

"I dare say you're right, my lad. Babs could make the greatest chefs in the world tremble with a simple bowlful of Borscht. And my flapjacks are decent enough, I grant you. I could package them in pretty boxes and charge five, even ten pounds a pop and there would certainly be those that would buy them."

Babs continued to talk with the customer. She placed a couple of complementary Varskes Surelis into a paper bag for her, along with the turmeric and ginger powder I'd prepared for her arthritis. The old woman gave a squawk of delight and fished around in her purse. Babs waved her money away. The bell jangled cheerfully as she left the shop and I brought my attention back to the journalist.

"But what about Mrs Simpson?" I asked.

The journalist frowned. "Who?"

"The lady that just left. Lives on her own, with just the dog for company and he's not much longer left in him, if I'm any judge. Where would she go if we left? Or the builders who were good enough to fix my window? Or the mother who brings her toddler in for a change of scene because if she has to watch one more episode of a cartoon pig, she will completely lose her marbles?" He squinted at me and I could tell he hadn't got it yet. "These are normal, everyday people," I explained. "They are nothing special and they are everything special. Shouldn't *they* have access to reasonably priced, good food? Just because something is good, doesn't mean it should be exclusive. This food, this cafe," I spread my arms wide to mimic his earlier gesture, "this *arcade* is a safe space for people to shop and eat and relax, regardless of their bank balance." I fell silent to let that sink in. Babs joined us again and the journalist toyed with another crumb. He shifted uncomfortably in his seat and cleared his throat.

"So, my previous article…"

"Was completely wrong, yes."

"And you're really not against anyone?"

"No."

He cleared his throat again. "Only, I heard you hated…" he blushed again "… well, everyone, but I heard you particularly hated vegans."

Babs placed her hand to her chest and her jaw dropped – she'd barely scrape by as an actress.

"Hate vegans? Nyet! Do we hate vegans, Agnes?" I shook my head and smiled softly.

"No. We've nothing against vegans," I said. "It's arseholes we don't like."

He stared at his feet for a minute after that, as well he might. Finally, he stood up.

"Well, I think that's it. It's probably time to go." I refused his offer of payment and he slid off the stool like a barely tethered balloon. He was a different person from when he'd walked in, that was for sure, but was it enough? Could one good meal make that much difference? Or should I give it a helping hand? I bit my lip, hating myself a little for what I was about to do, but sometimes, you have to rip the plaster off to start the healing process.

"Tell me," I said, "would she be proud?" He stopped short and gaped at me. "Your mother, I mean," I continued. "Would she be proud of what you're doing now? Scavenging for slander? Muck-raking?" The balloon deflated. He looked like I'd slapped him. Tears welled in his eyes but I swallowed back my guilt and drove home my point. "And it's not just the content. I've read some of your other work. You've talent, lad, that's for sure but it's so… bland. It's like you know you're writing utter tripe so you're deliberately trying to make it boring… and it's working – you could hand it out in operating theatres and they wouldn't need the anaesthetic."

He tugged at his collar, his neck now as red as his face. I didn't give him time to speak. "Now, imagine if you put that talent to good use writing about something you actually cared about, something like…" I puffed out my cheeks and stared at the ceiling for a moment, as if considering options, "food, for example. You certainly know your food. Imagine how far you could go writing about that. Something to think about, eh?"

Babs pressed a couple of her chocolates into his hand and I caught a fleeting glimpse of the glamour she flung at him – here the hot, sour soup eaten standing by a stall in a bustling, exotic market, there a bite of velvet octopus, slow cooked in red wine and served at a beachside taverna where white-shirted waiters greeted him like an old friend and the taste of salt lingered in the air; a life full of sensuous colour and fragrance and flavour, just waiting for him to commit it to paper and deliver it to the salivating world so they could live vicariously through his words. He could do it, too, if only he was brave enough. His eyes were wide and his mouth was an O of wonder. I let Babs' vision sink in then patted his hand, kindly.

"I'm glad we've had this chat. I look forward to reading your next article." I turned my back on him then so I didn't hear him leave. I carted his tray of dirty dishes back to the kitchen. It shook in my hands so much the crockery clattered. Had I said enough? Had I said too much? Only time would tell.

Chapter Thirteen

We closed for the day not long after he'd left. I washed up and wiped down the tables, Babs devised her menu for the next day and then we locked up to walk home. I paused while Babs rolled down the shutters, and I looked over at Sophie's shop. I could just about see her, restocking the shelves. It was the first whiff I'd had of her since I'd popped in the day before. I caught her eye and raised my hand in a half-wave and she looked away, quickly. Himself came out from behind the counter and strode over to the door. He stepped out into the arcade and leaned against the shop window, arms folded, watching us with a smug expression on his face. I nudged Babs who made a great show of rattling the new shutters then turned and blew him a kiss. I chuckled when I saw his jaw clench. He turned abruptly and went back into the shop. He barked something at Sophie and stalked off into the back. She stared after him, hurt plastered over her face and my good humour evaporated.

We'd have walked home in silence if Babs hadn't kept humming tunelessly beneath her breath. I wanted to think about everything that had happened – Pissy Dog Face,

Burt, the Journalist, Sophie… There was so much swirling round my head but every time I came close to unpicking it, Babs' grating hum would intrude. It wouldn't be so bad if it was a melody hummed off-key, or badly rendered scales, anything other than the rusty-chainsaw trill that cut through my thoughts. By the time we reached my front gate, I was clenching my teeth so hard my jaw ached.

"Must you do that?" I snapped at her.

Babs looked surprised. "Da, darling. It helps you not to think." I blinked at her then sagged. Sometimes it seemed she knew me better than I knew myself. I was a champion at overthinking these days. I sighed and pushed the gate open and peered into the garden. House was there in an instant and Babs rubbed her face against its feathered shingles.

"There you are, my Mielasis. What have you been up to today?" she crooned. House ducked low, looking almost shy for a moment, then adjusted its bulk to hold out one of its chicken legs. There, clutched between its claws was a bunch of flowers which it presented to Babs. Roses – my roses, to be precise, picked from the rose bush I'd cultivated for years and which was now being crushed by House's rump. Babs gave a delighted squeal.

"Oh, my darling one, they are beautiful!" She held the roses up to her face and inhaled deeply. House waggled from side to side, as if wagging its tail and a green cloud of envy swirled briefly in my stomach. I looked away quickly and blinked back sudden, hot tears when I realised I'd been unconsciously looking for Misty when I opened the gate. He'd always been there when I came home, particularly when he sensed I'd had a trying day. Granted, he wasn't much cop at giving flowers – a dead rodent or two was more his thing – but he would weave around my ankles and later, he would creep up onto my lap and knead my worries into submission. I thought of him now, resting in the cold store inside House's belly and blinked again. I risked a quick glance at Babs' joyous face as she stroked her familiar and the green cloud coiled inside me again. It wasn't fair! Why should I be so alone when they still had each other?

I felt a gentle nudge on my hip as House tried to get my attention. It wobbled precariously for a moment while it changed legs and then held out its other foot to reveal a second bunch, slightly more wilted than the first, but still pretty. House held this second bunch out to me and the swirl of envy was quenched by scarlet shame. It wasn't their fault Misty was gone. Why shouldn't they have each other? I patted House gently.

"Thank you," I said hoarsely and stepped inside to allow House and Babs to have some time together.

By the time she came in, I had arranged my flowers in a jam jar and had coffee brewing for Babs and a pot of tea steeping for me. She practically glowed when she breezed in and I felt another brief pang of envy. She paused briefly to add her flowers to mine, then squeezed my shoulder as she walked past me to get the mugs.

"You handled the journalist well today," she said. I grunted in response and Babs raised an eyebrow at me. "You do not believe so?"

"I don't know, Babs. What if I went too far? You saw him. I didn't notice it last time, but he clearly hasn't ever come to terms with his loss." That was putting it mildly. The journalist was little more than a twelve-year-old boy who missed his mum and I'd poured an ocean of salt into that gaping wound today. Babs' hum rent the air again and I waved my hand at her.

"Knock it off, will you?" I said.

"Depends. Will you also be knocking it off? This self-flagellation is becoming wearisome. I am all for causing suffering, darling, but not to ourselves." I rolled my eyes and huffed at her.

"Well, excuse me for having a conscience. I was a healer, you know, and the cornerstone of healing is 'first, do no harm'."

"Wrong," said Babs. "You *weren't* healer; you *are* healer. Great healer. Almost as good as I am at cooking." I gawped a bit at that. She *must* be in a good mood. She poured the drinks, wrinkling her nose at the tea and sat down opposite me. I fiddled with the frayed cuff of my blouse for a moment, then reluctantly met her gaze. "Tell me," she said, "in all your years of healing, how many broken bones have you set?"

I shrugged. "Thousands."

"Da, and how many tonics and tinctures have you given out?"

I shook my head. "I don't know. Millions, probably."

"Exactly. And I'm guessing they didn't all taste of sunshine and rainbows, nyet?" She wasn't wrong; I'd had patients declare they'd sooner die than take their treatment… of course, they soon changed their minds when faced with the reality of their sentiment, but still… I saw where Babs was going.

"I know. The break hurts to set and the medicine isn't always sweet but it's necessary to get better."

Babs smiled like a nursery teacher whose pupil has finally learnt to use the toilet instead of sitting in their wet knickers.

"Exactly," she said. "And is same no matter what the injury – body hurt, mind hurt, soul hurt… fixing it will not taste nice, it will make the hurt worse for a while, but it is so much better than staying injured." She sat back in her chair and folded her arms across her chest, looking insufferably smug.

"Alright," I conceded, "you've made your point. You don't have to lay it on so thick, though. Talk about using a sledgehammer to crack a nut!"

"In your case, nut is particularly dense," she retorted and I chuckled.

"Aye, I suppose I am, at that. My head's not been right for a number of years now."

"Since 'mistake'?" She did the little air quotes thing with her fingers.

"Yes," I replied. She picked up her coffee mug and took a sip.

"Tell me of it," she said. I sighed. I placed my elbows on the table, rested my chin on my hands and stared out of the patio doors into the overgrown back garden. The lawn was long overdue a mowing and the bindweed had got a stranglehold on my bay tree. I'd have to sort that soon. Babs didn't rush me and finally, I sat back and looked at her.

"I ran a different shop back then – 'alternative medicine' they'd call it now. It didn't make a fortune but…"

Babs nodded. I didn't have to explain. Once you realise you're likely to be around longer than most, you make sure you've always got funds to support yourself. The savvier ones of our number have invested wisely over the centuries – after all, rolling in muck is only fun if you know you've got somewhere to get clean afterwards. This particular shop hadn't been my first apothecary, and it did a steady trade. After turning away from traditional remedies, people were beginning to wonder if there wasn't something in it after all, and there I was, with my herbs and my jars of ointment. And they actually worked, not like Pissy Dog Face and her crystal enemas or whatever it is she offers.

I could still see that shop clearly in my mind, the shelves of blue glass jars, the wooden boxes which housed my sachets of dried herbs. The scent of lemon, thyme and eucalyptus hung in the air, partly because it was an uplifting smell that cleared the stuffiest of noses and minds, but mostly because I liked those fragrances. I even used lemon oil on the old pine counter. There was a small kitchenette at the back, where I put my mortar and pestle to good use, and a bell by the door to announce visitors. It chimed the day she first came in. It was an ill wind that blew her over my threshold, that's for sure.

Dead leaves skittered around the hem of her old-fashioned wool coat – I suppose it'd be called vintage now – it was two sizes too big and she looked like a kid playing dress up. With hindsight, that was probably part of the plan. I knew who she was, of course, though she wasn't aware. I'd seen her around with the baby, Sophie. I came through from the kitchen when the bell tinkled, wiping my hands on a tea towel. She rested the baby on her hip, looked around furtively and asked if I had any arnica. Two days later, she was back. This time, the bruises were on her arms and neck. I'd seen this pattern countless times before, so I sat her down and gave her a cup of tea while she turned on the waterworks.

He wasn't a bad man, she told me, he just had a temper. Oh yes, I was well aware of what a man with a temper could do and there was always a reason – she answered back, she made him look bad, she laughed. I shook my head, dabbed her wounds and tutted over the fragile male ego that saw men afraid women would laugh at them and women afraid men would kill them. God, I was so stupid. She must have been laughing her socks off at me. Even now, my blood boils when I think of it. You'd think after all these centuries, I'd know when I was being strung along but she was so charming, so vulnerable… and honestly? I wanted to believe her. It fit the pattern I'd seen so often.

She was in most days after that, always with a new tale of woe to tell that set me grinding my teeth. It didn't occur to me she was paying similar visits to various shops around the place, establishing her victim credentials with anyone she saw as a soft touch. Well, she'd have struggled to find a softer touch than me. I could easily have got to the truth had I taken the trouble and done a little scrying, but I didn't have any reason to doubt her and the day she showed me the bruise on Sophie's cheek was the day I snapped.

She wouldn't have known what I could do, of course. No doubt she was just showing me to build up her alibi, but the second she was gone I focussed my mind, pooled my energy and cast a binding spell so strong it left me laid up in a dark room with a cold cloth over my eyes for three days. But it was worth it, I told myself. He wouldn't be able to raise his hand in aggression ever again. I needn't have bothered. He was dead before the week was out.

I heard it from the florist over the road. "Self-defence," she said. Well, I knew that was a load of codswallop straightaway. He couldn't have attacked her, I'd seen to that, whether she knew it or not. And then his mam came from the north and set the record straight. She'd been terrified for years of something like this happening. She'd watched him change from a happy, outgoing young man to someone so cowed, he would scarce move without *her* say so.

He'd finally plucked up the courage to leave when she fell with Sophie. After that, his mam said, the last of the fight went out of him. There was no way he'd leave a baby in her care and the way she was putting it out that he hit her, there was no way he'd get the child if he left. He never showed his bruises or cried on the shoulders of strangers. Who'd have believed him anyway? I remembered the times I'd seen them together, how I'd thought it was like watching a game of cat and mouse. I'd been right… only I'd been so caught up in her stories, I'd forgotten to check which one was the cat.

I couldn't face the florist after that, or any of the others. I couldn't bear to hear the whispered tittle-tattle. None of them knew my role in it, obviously, but my head pulsed with guilt and shame. I shut up the shop and avoided the news. Even so, it wasn't long before I heard she'd been arrested and Sophie was taken back up north with her gran. I sold the shop and followed them there. The least I could do was keep an eye on her. I owed him that, at least.

I sat back in my chair and Babs wordlessly passed me a box of tissues.

"So that was that," I said and shook my head. "She led me a merry dance, I'll give her that. I should have checked her story before acting. I always have before but this time…" I fell silent, not wanting to say any more.

"You put your trust in wrong person," said Babs. "You know who you should have trusted?" Despite my tears, an impish glimmer bubbled inside.

"You?" I asked innocently. Babs reached over and cuffed me round the earhole. "Alright, alright!" I giggled. "I should have put my trust in myself. I should have stuck to my own rules and checked things for myself. I should…"

"Da, you should. But at end of day, you acted as you did to protect an innocent." I nodded and dabbed my eyes one last time. "Do you believe Sophie is dancing you merrily?" she asked. I did her the credit of considering her question before shaking my head.

"No," I said. I balled up the tissue and straightened my cardy. "Something stinks in that shop and it's not Sophie or the baby. And he's up to something else, too… I just wish I knew what."

Chapter Fourteen

I poured water into a shallow bowl and sat at the table. Babs lit a tallow candle and discreetly left the kitchen. Her presence would only muddy the waters. It was her idea I try scrying again and she was right; if I could get a sense of the Vegan's plans, if I could just reassure myself of his true nature, I'd know what to do, how to act. Everything would be simpler. We both knew she could do it herself in a heartbeat – she could stare into a dark mirror or look at the tea leaves or the shape of some dropped twigs… knowing Babs, she could probably glean a glimpse of the future from chicken giblets or beetroot stalks. The point is, she *could* do it and report back and we could deal with him and that would be that. But what about the next bully, or the one after that, or the one after that? There was always another Vegan out there. That's why I had to deal with this one.

I took a deep breath, placed both palms on the table and let my mind drift. The reflection of the flame flickered and danced on the water. I kept my focus on it and let it fill my mind until there was nothing beyond its glowing aura. My breathing slowed until everything hung in a frozen moment. It was working; any moment, I would see images skitter across the water, breaking the flame, moving in a frenetic jumble at first then steadying, forming a story in the ripples and eddies. I must have done it a million times. *But not lately.*

The treacherous thought sneaked in before I could stop it and my mind ran into a cold wall of concrete and the kitchen flashed back into stark relief.

Bugger.

I blinked, rolled my shoulders and tried again… and again… and again but it was no good. Everything dragged my attention from the bowl of water – the greasy pall of smoke from the candle tugged at my nostrils, the insect hum of the fridge buzzed in my ears, even the chair I sat on thrust hard edges into my backside. I glanced at the guttering candle, sighed and snuffed it out between my thumb and finger. The flame would keep its secrets tonight.

I rose heavily and went in search of Babs. She was seated on top of House, who had graciously flattened its roof to accommodate her. An extra chair was set out and a heavy metal pot steamed on top of a camping stove. House shifted its weight and held out one of its massive, clawed legs to lift me onto the roof. Babs greeted me with a questioning tilt of her head and I shook my head in response.

"Ah," she said and busied herself with the stove. I plonked myself into the spare chair and sat with my head in my hands. It had been a long day. My sojourn into the past had taken a lot out of me. I'd hoped that talking about it might unlock the magic again, but clearly it was going to take something more. My head throbbed and I pinched the bridge of my nose. Eventually, Babs nudged my elbow and passed me a tin mug brimming with her special blend of herbal tea. The vapours made my nose stream. I'd have known it was alcoholic even if I hadn't heard the telltale squeak and glug of her medicinal bottle being opened and poured. I didn't care. I sipped the tea, looked up at the clear night sky and counted the constellations. Cassiopeia blurred into a milky smear and I surreptitiously dabbed my eyes on my cuff. Babs cleared her throat and waited. I tried to organise my thoughts so I could explain but I needn't have bothered. The second I opened my mouth, the words tumbled out in an ungainly heap.

"What if I've lost it for good, Babs? What if I can't do magic ever again?" I stared at my hands. Fat teardrops splashed onto the liver spots. "What if the Vegan is right and I am just a stupid old woman?" I whispered. Babs waved her hand and made an indelicate sound to show me what she thought of that. I waited for her to expand but she simply stared up at the stars. A greasy little thought slithered into my brain – what if *she* was embarrassed by my impotence? Was she ashamed of me? Was that why she wouldn't look at me? My cheeks flamed and my throat felt like I'd swallowed marbles. I had to get away. I stood up with forced casualness and straightened my top when finally, she spoke.

"Do you remember summer of 1771?"

I frowned. "1771?"

"Da. There was great plague in my country." Something stirred in the depths of my memory and I nodded. Babs still stared at the stars. "It was almost too much for me to handle..." She glanced at me and flashed a quick grin. "Almost! I put out the call and you were first to answer."

I nodded again as the memory took hold.

"You were with the blacksmith's wife when I arrived. She was having a bad time of it as I recall."

"Da. Life in the midst of death is always a precious thing but this was not going well. She had been labouring for three days and we were both exhausted. I was at the wit's end, certain I was going to lose one or both."

"I remember," I said, and I did. I remembered the stink of sweat and shit and blood. I remembered the matted straw and the girl's whimpers and the bruises on her body in places she had no business being bruised. Babs was looking at me now, following the path of my thoughts.

"Da," she said. "She was in bad way but then you were there and you were so calm and kind. You brewed nettle tea and soothed and talked us both through what to do. We turned the babe and her daughter was born." I smiled but Babs' face darkened. "Then the husband arrived, full of piss and bluster, reeking of the alehouse." She wrinkled her nose. "He took one look at the baby and screamed he wanted son. Pfft." She shook her head. "I tried to reason but he was heving none of it. He seized the poker and raised it in air to bring it down on his wife, and you..." she pointed at me, "quick as lightning, you catch the poker as it comes down, wrench it from his grasp and hit him hard across leg – thwack."

She smiled wickedly, "I still hear crack of his kneecap." She fell silent for a moment. The smirk on her face showed she was clearly relishing the memory. I have to admit, my own lips were twitching. She picked up the story again.

"He screams like stuck pig and you tower over him, poker tip pressing right into end of his bulbous nose and you say—"

"—you raise your hand to a woman again and I'll have your arse as a wheelbarrow stand." I finished the memory and Babs howled with laughter. I chuckled a bit myself. "Broke four bones in my bloody hand that day," I said, ruefully.

"Da, darling, but he never raised *his* hand to her again *and* he walked with limp for the rest of his life…" she shrugged, "…which was only five months before plague took him, but still…" She resumed her scrutiny of the stars then said quietly, "You were my hero that day. That day and every day since, magic or no."

I sat back down. My throat tightened again and Babs made a great show of ferreting an old pipe out of her cloth bag to give me time to pull myself together. Entire decades have gone by where I've remained stoically dry-eyed, but lately, I must have cried a river… or a decent-sized puddle, at least. I dabbed my eyes, blew my nose and cleared my throat.

"Strong tea," I muttered. I didn't trust myself to say much else. My head felt like it hadn't stopped swirling in a month.

Babs didn't answer but set to work with her reamer and scraper, clearing out the pipe bowl. I'd almost forgotten about the pipe. I hadn't seen it in years. She'd carved it herself out of a briarwood burl; I could still see the notch marks of her pocketknife. Of course, back then, it was pale golden in colour. Now, it had darkened with age and use until it was almost black. She turned the tools gently in her hands, stripping back the layers of tar and ash. She grunted. "Even when fire is gone, there is still work to do."

I nodded and watched her set the tools aside and pull out a polishing cloth. She rubbed the outside of the pipe bowl until it almost glowed. Only then did she reach back into her bag and pull out a plug of something I assumed was tobacco, but knowing Babs, I couldn't swear to it. She carefully unwrapped the wax paper and, taking her trusty pocketknife, sliced a thin shard off the plug, folding the flakes and pressing them down into her pipe bowl before carefully folding the plug back into the paper, tying it with string and returning it to her bag. The ritual complete, she took a few test draws on the stem, then held a taper to the stove and used it to light the pipe. She sat back in her chair and puffed gently, her eyes half-closed.

I sat back too and let out a slow breath. I hadn't realised how much my heartrate had slowed while watching her and how much steadier my breathing had become. Babs glanced over at me and winked. She was a sly one, alright. She passed the pipe over to me and a rich, almost chocolatey aroma wreathed around me, undercut with deep burgundy scents of cherry. I wrinkled my nose and sniffed again. Could I detect a more herbal backnote? I couldn't be certain, even with my experience, but decided not to think too deeply into it. I took a few draws, then handed it back to Babs.

We sat in companionable silence for a while, her puffing away, me sipping my tea.

"Who was your first?" she said suddenly. I sprayed my tea across House's roof and the poor thing shuddered briefly in protest. Babs bent and stroked its shingles. "Sorry, darling," she murmured, shooting me a reproachful look.

I patted the roof myself. "Yes, sorry House," I said, then turned back to Babs. "You can't expect me to answer that. I mean, it's been centuries. I can't even remember the name of the village I was in, let alone *his* name…"

Babs waved her hand irritably. "Nyet, not *that* first! Of course, is too long ago. So many centuries…"

"*Alright!*"

"I mean the first to use the 'W' word."

"Ah, that first," I said and the lead weight of the memory dropped into my head. You forget many things in this life, but never the first time someone tries to have you killed. The 'W' word was always an effective weapon. It tapped into all those dark little insecurities, those nasty little secrets you're too ashamed to show to the sun and gave them someone to blame for them all. It gave them a name: Witch.

A woman could be a witch for being wiser than a man, or daring to speak her mind, or for not having children, or for having too many, or the wrong kind… she could be a witch because she'd had more sex than was deemed acceptable, or for refusing to have sex, or for looking different, sounding different, being different… Occasionally, she could be named a witch because she actually was one. Like me. I let the memory unwind and answered Babs' question.

"The thane of the second village I lived in. He had an eye for the girls, the younger the better. The village was lousy with his bastards." I stared off into the past. "I must have been barely twenty. Young enough to know everything, anyway." I chuckled, ruefully. "I came from the birthing room of another of his conquests. She was scarcely more than a child herself and it hadn't gone well. I was seething with righteousness. I lured him into the stables, got his attention with a set of gelding clamps and warned him if he didn't keep it in his breeches, I'd see it hung from a horseshoe."

Babs passed me her pipe and I took another draw. "I don't know what I thought would happen – that he'd miraculously see the error of his ways and crumble beneath my steely gaze, maybe? He didn't, obviously. Instead, he sought to silence me by crying witch. He shouted for his men and declared I'd attempted to unman him with sorcery." I handed the pipe back to Babs.

"What happened?" she asked.

"Well, in all the furore, he spooked his horse and it kicked him in his unmentionables." I spread my hands wide. "Can't say I didn't warn him! Anyway, it became infected and he died. He wasn't well-liked and there'd been enough witnesses that practically everyone believed it was nothing more than a nasty accident."

"*Practically* everyone? Who did not believe?"

"His wife."

"Oh? And what did she say?"

"I believe it was, 'Thank you.'" Babs' laugh startled a nearby fox out from between the rubbish bins and I tried to shush her while stifling my own mirth. Finally, we calmed down. We sat for a while and then I asked, "What about you?"

She shrugged. "Much the same. Big man did not like

being told he should not behave badly, so he threw me in prison while he built my pyre."

My mouth dropped open. "No! How did you escape?" Babs' lips wobbled and her eyes sparkled with barely-suppressed glee.

"Jail was House in disguise. The instant door slammed behind me, House stood up and ran off, trampling big man underfoot on the way!"

This time, it was my laugh that set the windowpanes rattling and distant dogs howling. Babs joined in and by the time we stopped, I thought I'd strained a rib. I caught my breath and dabbed my eyes again. Then I sighed.

"All these big, bad men and I've let a little vegan get to me!" I tugged at my collar and straightened up. "Not anymore. Tomorrow, one way or another, I'm going to figure out his game and then…"

"You will hev his arse as wheelbarrow stand?" asked Babs.

"Precisely," I replied.

Chapter Fifteen

Of course, it was all well and good *saying* I was going to figure out his game but quite another putting it into practice. The morning rush came and went and by the time we'd seen the last of the breakfast customers out of the door, I still had no clue what I was going to do about it *and* I had a tea hangover to boot.

Still, at least I wasn't the only one suffering – oh, I don't mean Babs; she was as irritatingly chipper as ever. Across the way from the cafe, the Vegan looked like a dog chewing a wasp. I could see him scrolling urgently on his phone, clearly expecting to see something that simply wasn't there. It became apparent what that something was when he ventured out and returned with a copy of the local paper. He was waiting to see what his pet journalist had said about us.

I could have saved him a wasted journey. There was nothing about us in there, or online, according to Babs. Clearly, something had hit home yesterday, and our literary friend had chosen to sheathe his claws. I just hoped he was alright.

The Vegan threw the paper down in disgust, earning

him a sharp reprimand from Burt, who happened to be refilling the crates outside his shop. His Nibs made a gesture in return. I didn't hear the rest of the exchange but I saw the set of Burt's shoulders. I wasn't the only one to note it, either.

"Oh, he is so masterful," Babs simpered. We peered out over the top of the *Open* sign. Enough of a crowd had gathered around the duo now to leave the Vegan with no option but to clear up after himself and he snatched up the scattered pages and stuffed them in the bin. His face was a picture – the kind Oscar Wilde would have hidden in an attic – and I permitted myself a few moments of well-earned gloating. I was glad I did, or I'd have missed what happened next. He twitched, mid-paper-stuff and pulled his phone out of jeans so tight, they were practically indecent. He'd been a satisfying puce colour up until that moment, but one look at whatever was on his screen sent him the colour of rancid taramasalata. I nudged Babs and we watched him check over each shoulder, then furtively answer the call.

"That's the face of someone taking a telling," I said and I wasn't wrong. The last time I'd seen such a miserable expression had been on the face of a small boy who'd been frogmarched to my door to apologise for accidentally breaking my window with his football.

Babs sniffed. "Perhaps Pissy Thistle girl is cross with him," she said. I shook my head.

"No, look, she's over there." I nodded over to the magic shop where she stood, watching the Vegan's every move with undisguised longing. I tutted. "Who wears crushed velvet at 10:30 in the morning?"

"I would," said Babs.

"Yes, but you would wear it because you're a brazen hussy, not because you want to look gothic and mysterious," I said. Babs grinned, then chewed her lip.

"Perhaps is Sophie on the phone, then?"

I frowned.

"Unlikely. He looks worried and I don't think Sophie would make him feel that way – oh, he's looking over, quick, duck!" We sequestered ourselves behind the curtains and watched him finish his call. I haven't lip-read for a while but you don't lose the knack.

"I'll phone her, have a naan," I interpreted confidently. Babs tutted.

"*Aroma, half an hour*," she corrected. That made more sense. There was a cafe the other side of town called Aroma. He gave another surreptitious glance over his shoulder, pocketed his phone and strode out of the arcade. I reached for my coat.

"Come on," I said. Babs looked at me quizzically and I huffed impatiently. "Look, he's upset about something and I'd bet good money it has something to do with that phone call. I say we follow him and find out what's going on."

"But what about—"

"Oh, hang the cafe! We'll just close for the day, it's not like we don't deserve it. Come on!" Babs didn't move and I shifted from foot to foot and pointed at the Vegan's retreating back. "He's getting away!" Babs pursed her lips.

"I was about to say, what about disguise? We do not want him to be seeing us, nyet?" Actually, she had a point. If he saw us, that would definitely put the kibosh on things. I dropped my coat and hurried towards the stockroom.

"Where are you going?" called Babs.

"Lost and found," I said. "There's bound to be something in there we can use as camouflage…" The silence that followed was stonier than Medusa's mirror. I didn't have to look at Babs to know she'd rolled her eyes heavenward. I turned to face her.

"Did you lose sense as well as magic?" she asked through gritted teeth. I frowned at her, confused and she waved her hand irritably. The air around Babs shimmered as the glamour settled on her. Her sleek, silver bob stretched into a brunette plait that hung by her waist, and her hips and chest widened – clearly she'd drawn inspiration from Little Miss Magick. The nurse's uniform was a bit much though. With the low-cut top and red lipstick, she was reminiscent of a character in a 1960s smutty comedy film – and no nurse worth her salt would be seen in stilettos. Still, Babs seemed happy with the overall effect.

I glanced at myself in the reflection of the chiller cabinet to see what she'd done to me and I gasped. She'd easily added twenty-five years onto my perceived age, if not more. Oh, she'd altered the shape of my face and the shape of my body, but mostly, she'd added wrinkles and a few more liver spots.

"Why am I an old woman?" I demanded.

"Because you hev not died yet," she replied. Smart arse.

"You know what I mean," I said. She looked surprised and placed a hand to her now-ample chest.

"Well, no one would believe *me* to be old woman!"

"I don't see why either of us has to be an old woman!" I protested.

"The Vegan will not think to look past wrinkles," she replied, then pointed at herself, "… or cleavage."

"Well, no one's going to buy you as my carer in that get up," I grumbled, nodding at her outfit. She sighed, shrugged and waved her hand again. The lipstick vanished and the uniform and shoes morphed into a modest blue dress and sensible pumps.

"Better?" she asked.

"Barely," I muttered, but we were wasting time, so I left it at that. It still smarted though and as we shut up the shop, a wicked thought occurred to me.

"Quick, take the glamour off me," I whispered. Babs looked puzzled but waved her hand and I watched the wrinkles on my own hand smooth out a little. "Right, I'll meet you in the alley behind the arcade," I said and popped across the way to Burt's.

He was busy serving when I went in, so I called over the customer's head.

"Burt, you still got your mum's wheelchair in the back?" He frowned but nodded. "Mind if I borrow it?" I called. He shrugged his agreement so I nipped out back and grabbed it before setting off to meet Babs. If she wanted to play silly buggers, I was more than happy to oblige.

Her jaw tightened when she saw the chair.

"What is this?"

"Well, we'll never catch up with him if I have to walk – no one would believe someone as old as me could walk fast, so I'll just have to depend on my trusty carer to push me." Her eyes narrowed and I knew she was thinking of all the places she'd love to push me. I grinned widely and sat in the chair, wiggling a bit to make myself comfortable.

"Come on then," I said. "Glamour me up." She scowled but there was nothing else for it, so she waved her hand. I'm fairly certain she added a wart or two to the glamour this time, but I could live with that. "Through the park is the quickest way across town," I told her. It was also the route that included a steep hill, but that was no hardship for me. "Better get a pace on, or we'll miss him."

Babs muttered something I chose to interpret as, *"Why, yes, of course, my dear friend, I will move with alacrity."*

Two minutes later, we were on the incline and she could hardly say anything. Her hot breath warmed the back of my neck. "Bet you're glad you changed those shoes," I said. She muttered again and I felt the wart on my nose grow. I cackled. It was important to stay in character, after all. Anyway, it was only a short walk and within a few minutes we were on the high street. We turned the corner by the lingerie shop and nearly walked smack bang into the man himself.

"Quickly, in here," hissed Babs, and she wheeled me into the shop next door. She parked me next to the window and I damn near pulled a muscle, craning my neck to see what Himself was up to. He stood staring at the scantily clad dummies in the window for a few moments before venturing into the store.

"Hmpf, pervert," I muttered.

"Who is?" said Babs and I realised her voice was some distance away from me. I looked around the shop for the first time and saw shelf after shelf of spices, elegantly labelled jars of cooking sauces, delicately shaped pasta in paper packages with the instructions all in Italian. Babs was standing at the counter, where a flushed woman fed her samples of cheese and olives. Trust Babs to find a delicatessen to hide in.

"Oi!" I said, "We're on a job, or had you forgotten?" Another thought occurred to me. "Hold on, we're in disguise. Why did we need to hide? He wouldn't have recognised us!"

Babs looked genuinely confused. "Hide? Who is hiding?" She pointed at the various tins and jars amassed on the counter. "I am simply needing more spices."

I scowled at her. "This is important," I said through gritted teeth.

"Da, darling, so is paprika. We know where he is and we know where he is going. You hev nice sit in chair and I will chat to this lady." She turned her back on me and returned to her conversation, which seemed to revolve around the extortionate rent the shopkeeper was paying and the best thing to do with kale (throw it in the bin, if you want my opinion). I did as I was told and sat by the door, grinding my molars.

It wasn't long before the Vegan slunk back out of the lingerie shop. In his hand he clutched a pink paper bag.

"Babs!" I called over my shoulder. "It's showtime." She gathered up her purchases and wheeled me out of the shop.

We were practically on his heels when he entered the cafe. He didn't hold the door for us, which earned him a few tuts and disapproving looks from the cafe's patrons, especially when Babs made a great show of struggling in backwards, banging into tables and chairs. I think she was doing it more to irritate me than anything else, but I wouldn't grumble at anything that set people against the

Vegan, so I grinned good-naturedly while she manoeuvred me and apologised to the customers.

"Aw, sorry, luv, I'm dead clumsy, me," she said, as she nearly sent a plate flying. "Me mam always said the only safe place for me to work was the pillow factory."

It was strange. I could hear her usual voice and accent in my mind, but now it was overlaid with a broad Liverpudlian lilt, and the locals were lapping it up, jumping up to move seats and tables. Nobody does a glamour like Babs. As luck would have it, we managed to get a table right next to him – well, I say *luck*. In reality, Babs batted her eyelashes at a few of the gents in there and they promptly rearranged the room around her. They'd have stayed slurping their tea if it had been me.

The Vegan glared at us once the hubbub had died down and we were seated. Babs smiled at him.

"Alright, luv? Good 'ere, innit?" He said nothing but his eyes flicked to her chest. He glanced at me and I grinned gummily back at him. He wrinkled his nose and turned away from us. Looks like Babs was right about the disguise. She smirked and leaned over to me.

"You order. I'll be back in moment. Am going to powder nose," she said and promptly disappeared. I frowned briefly but if you've got to go, you've got to go. I busied myself watching the Vegan, peering at him over the top of my menu. The waitress took his order and then came to take ours. He brazenly ogled her backside and I fought to stop my lips from curling. He really was loathsome.

The doorbell announced a new arrival. The man in the doorway had slicked, silver hair, creases in his suit trousers sharp enough to shave with, and I could practically see up his nose from the reflection in his shoes. He stood blocking the doorway for a moment, partly to scan the cafe to see who was there but mostly, I suspect, to give everyone a chance to admire him. I blinked as a jolt of recognition shot through me.

He locked eyes with the Vegan and made his way over to his table. He took the silk handkerchief from his pocket and placed it on the seat before deigning to sit himself. I was so distracted by this pantomime, that I nearly missed the other person who slipped in after him and secreted herself in a quiet corner of the cafe, well out of the Vegan's sight – Sophie.

Chapter Sixteen

Well, well, well, you could have knocked me down with a feather. It seemed the Vegan hadn't been as subtle as he'd thought, though if she was expecting to catch him with another woman, she was in for a surprise. It made things tricky though. If he saw her here, I couldn't help but think she'd be letting herself in for a world of pain. Babs nudged me out of my reverie.

"What did I miss?"

I nodded over at the Vegan and the silver fox.

"I recognise him," I told her. "He's the fella from the developers who tried to convince me to sell up a while back." Babs raised one eyebrow.

"Hmm," she said.

"That's not all," I replied and sat back in my chair so she could see Sophie, looking smaller than ever without the baby strapped to her. Babs' other eyebrow shot up.

"That is setting spanner amongst pigeons." I couldn't have put it better myself. "She suspects his affair?" Babs asked me. I shrugged.

"We only know he's got Little Miss Magick wrapped around his little finger," I said. "We don't know that he's *actually* playing away."

"I am begging to differ," said Babs and nodded to the bag on her lap. It was the Vegan's lingerie bag.

"You nicked his shopping?" I said, impressed.

"Borrowed," she corrected. "I was curious as to what he bought."

"Ha! Nosy, you mean," I said and leaned forward. "Go on, then, let's have a look."

She pulled out a flimsy creation in burnt orange.

"This is definitely not Sophie's size," she declared and I had to agree. Sophie could have worn one of the lace cups as a hat. I peered into the tissue-papered depths and saw matching knickers – well, I assumed they were knickers. Dental floss doesn't come in that colour.

"Be good to know if this really is for Pissy Dog Face or if he's stringing someone else along too." I pulled a face at the underwear. "I don't think much of his taste. That fabric'd chafe."

"I do not think they are to be worn for comfort," replied Babs, "… or for very long." She twanged the thong. "I think colour is meant to make you think of heat, like chilli, or paprika or cayenne pepper…" She trailed off and our eyes locked as the same devilish thought occurred to us both.

"We couldn't…" I whispered.

"We shouldn't…" Babs whispered.

"On the other hand…" I said.

"We'd know if they were for her or someone else," finished Babs. I grinned at her and, quick as a flash, her hand darted into the bag of goodies she'd got from the deli and pulled out a jar of burnt orange-coloured powder. She broke the seal and I placed a hand on her wrist to stall her.

"We're certain these aren't for Sophie?" We both stole a glance at the waif-like creature in the corner then looked again at the generously proportioned fabric in the bag. "Fair enough," I conceded and Babs sprinkled the powder into the bag. It blended so well with the material that I couldn't even see it. We put our heads together and snickered like naughty schoolgirls. I pulled myself together and dabbed my eyes.

"Still," I said, "it looks like Soph's not going to catch him in the act she thought she was." I frowned at the men. The waitress was at their table now. She placed an egg and bacon roll in front of the Vegan and Babs and I shared a look. Ha! Vegan, my eye.

"I'd love to hear what they're talking about," I said. Babs grinned at me and took out her phone and a pair of – well, she said they were headphones but they looked more like hearing aids to my mind. Ah well, at least I was keeping in character. I popped one of them in my ear and Babs did the same. I could hear the faint murmur of their voices but there was too much background noise. Babs waved her hand irritably. I felt a subtle wave of power ripple outwards from her and the background noise faded.

"... just need a bit longer." The Vegan's tone was petulant. "We agreed this was going to take time."

"You've had well over a year already. I've already lost one prospective buyer because it was taking too long. I want to see a return on my investment." The silver fox was tetchy and the Vegan's shoulders squared off as he leaned forward.

"You will. The ice cream place can't keep going much

longer and the sad cow that owns it will be practically begging you to take it off her hands. Then the old bird at the cafe…"

"I'll give him *old bird*," I harrumphed. Babs nudged me into silence. The silver fox was talking.

"…heard she'd been giving you some trouble?"

The Vegan tutted in response and sat back, his arms crossed in front of him.

"Nothing I can't handle. She's got some psycho pal helping her out but I'll have her back where I want her soon enough and once she's gone, the fat old grocer will follow."

Babs snorted at the word *psycho* but then shook her head.

"*Tsk*, he should not be speaking of Burt so." I opened my mouth to speak but she shushed me into silence and we carried on listening. The fox was speaking again.

"…don't want a repetition of that business with the cat. What if the press had got wind of it? They'd have had a field day – a supposed vegan murdering family pets…"

"Relax. No one knows…"

I didn't hear what he said next. I gripped the edge of the table. My ears were ringing and I had black dots swirling in front of my eyes. *Misty*. Babs grasped my hand and squeezed hard, hard enough that my knuckles whitened and my vision cleared. I gasped with pain and wriggled my hand free. The look she gave me was full of sympathy but her message was clear – not here, not now. My breath quivered in my chest but I nodded and drew myself up. Luckily, our food arrived at that moment.

Babs took one look at the order and hissed. "Tea?" Then she prodded the food on the plate. "And what is this?"

"Toast," I said. "Wholemeal… well, brown, at least. It's good for you."

Babs picked up a slice between her thumb and forefinger and stared at it like it was some strange insect. It wilted under her stare. She used one corner to nudge the plastic pot of jam that came with it off her plate.

"This is not food," she declared. To be fair, the cartoon picture of a strawberry on the jam lid was probably the closest it had come to actual fruit, but still, she didn't need to be so judgemental. And she wouldn't even look at the teapot.

"Well, what did you expect?" I said. "I couldn't have you getting distracted. Give you a whiff of something tasty you'd have been off to the kitchen and rifling through their pantry to see what brand of beans they used, or some such nonsense."

Babs folded her arms across her ample bosom and scowled at me but I saw the glimmer in her eye. Her bad temper was just another ruse to distract me from Misty. I smiled gratefully and the hard line of her mouth wobbled a little.

"At least now we know," I said.

She nodded. "Da…" She looked back at the offending square in her fingers. "Though we could have known *and* had good breakfast."

I waved away her comment irritably and tapped my earpiece. "Shush, I'm still listening."

Babs dropped the toast and pushed the plate away

from her in disgust but she stopped grumbling. I tuned back into the Vegan's voice.

"If you don't like my methods, hire someone else." His tone had the usual cockiness to it and by now he barely even looked at his companion. Instead, he was tucking into his sandwich. Bright yellow drips of egg yolk plopped onto his plate. The silver fox stared at him, his nose wrinkled in distaste. Finally, he sighed and sat back.

"Just be careful. And if any of this gets out, we've never met."

The Vegan shrugged as if this was of little importance to him. "Like old times then, eh, Dad?" he said and carried on eating. Babs and I shared a look. *Dad!* She mouthed to me. Her eyes were saucers and I'm sure mine were the same. The silver fox scowled at his son and adjusted his tie.

"And what of the other two shops?" he asked, no doubt keen to change the subject. "What of your little… ahem, harem?" Another shrug as if this was of even less importance.

"They'll do as they're told," said the Vegan, "one way or another." His words were barely comprehensible through his mouthful of bacon and egg. "God, this is good. You've no idea how sick of tofu I am." The silver fox clearly didn't care. He pushed back his chair and stood up. The Vegan cleared his throat significantly and nodded at the bill the waitress had left on the table. A look of abhorrence shuddered across the older man's face but he pulled out his wallet, threw down a twenty and turned to go.

He wasn't the only one leaving. From the corner of my eye, I saw Sophie shift herself and head for the door. I swivelled in my chair and tried to catch her eye but she didn't look. Why would she? As far as she was concerned, I was a stranger. Her face was pink and blotchy and the haste with which she was gathering her belongings told me she wasn't paying attention to anything else going on around her. My insides ran cold. If the Vegan so much as tilted his head to see his colleague out, he'd see her and all hell would break loose, I was sure of it.

I tugged Babs' sleeve and motioned towards Sophie. Babs looked from the girl to the Vegan and nodded once, then she shoved the lingerie bag into my lap and thrust her chair back with such a jolt that the table juddered. The teacups toppled with a clatter and all eyes turned to us. Babs' broad Scouse accent cleaved the air.

"Awww, no way, Doris! Not again. Which poor sod's shopping have you got now? Give that to me." I took my cue from her and clutched the bag close to my body.

"No! Shan't!" I shouted. Babs made a lunge for it, catching the table with her hip and sloshing steaming tea over the Vegan's coat. He leapt up to avoid getting any more on him and noticed the bag.

"Oi! Give that back!" If I wasn't prepared to hand it over to Babs, I certainly wasn't handing it over to him. I stuck my hand in the bag and rummaged around, finally pulling out the thong, which I promptly twirled around one finger above my head.

"Wheeee!" I cried. Babs fussed around me, looking like she was trying to retrieve the knickers but in reality, blocking Sophie from the Vegan. For her part, Sophie was frowning at us. She shook her head like she was trying to see through fog but then shrugged and sidled closer to the door. Babs kept up her work with the Vegan, chattering away at him, getting underfoot, keeping his attention on us.

"Aw, I'm dead sorry, luv. She can't help herself when she sees a fancy bag like that – I think it reminds her of her younger days as a burlesque dancer." I froze for a moment and narrowed my eyes at her. Burlesque dancer! I'd get her for that later, but for now, I'd use it to my advantage. I leaned forward and shimmied my shoulders towards the Vegan.

"Would you like me to dance for you, sexy?" I breathed huskily. The Vegan turned green. In fact, the entire room seemed frozen in a horrified moment and the only sound was the tinkle of the doorbell as someone left. Sophie was clear.

The door slammed shut and broke the spell. The room breathed again. The Vegan reached forward, red-faced and panting now. He plucked the pants from my hand and seized the bag.

"They're mine," he snarled.

"Not my colour anyway," I sniffed.

Babs filled the cafe with apologies and left enough money on the table to cover breakages. We made our way out of the cafe with the Vegan declaring I should be locked up and it was only when we were round the corner and well out of sight that we creased up and laughed.

Chapter Seventeen

I hadn't laughed that much in a long time. My ribs and jaw ached. I was pretty sure I needed a change of underwear. My cheeks were wet and it took a while for me to realise they weren't tears of laughter. You can only push away emotion for so long and the tears I'd fought back in the cafe now surged forth. Poor Misty. I'd wanted proof and now I'd had it straight from the horse's mouth but it didn't make anything better. Misty was still gone.

I thought of those desperate days when he was missing. I wandered the arcade for hours, calling and whistling then standing stock still, willing my heart to stop thudding so loudly so I could hear if he meowed. I knew he was somewhere nearby but couldn't pinpoint him, not like I used to be able to. All I could sense was his fear and confusion and then… nothing. And now I knew he hadn't been killed in the passion of hatred but because the Vegan wanted me broken so they could swoop in on my property. My cat – the best part of me – was murdered because a rich man wanted to be richer.

Babs tapped my shaking shoulders and handed me a

tissue. I could tell by the wrinkles on her hand that she'd let the glamour fade. She pushed the wheelchair slowly through the park while I let my tears fall. A fine mist of rain fuzzed my hair. The first bite of autumn snapped at the air and the trees wept their own tears of gold and russet. Finally, I dried my eyes and blew my nose.

"Better?" asked Babs.

"Yes." And I was a bit. "So… burlesque dancer?" I said and Babs snorted.

"It worked, didn't it? Sophie was able to leave."

"I hope she's okay. I wonder what she was expecting to find. She can't have heard what they were talking about from where she was. It was tricky enough for us."

"Da, I am still not fully understanding," said Babs.

"Well, the grey-haired bloke came round a couple of years back, wanting to buy the arcade. There's money to be had in property at the moment. I imagine he has plans to convert the arcade into luxury apartments."

"Hmm," said Babs. "I hev seen the prices of similar properties. They would fetch the pretty penny, I think."

"A fair few pretty pennies, I'll wager," I agreed. "Anyway, it came to nothing because we all – Burt, Margot, Soph and me – we said we weren't selling. I'm assuming Miss Magick did too. He tried again and again and got quite stroppy when we refused. You know that type, can't stand being told no. Eventually, he stopped and we all assumed that was an end to it. Life went on."

"But it was only beginning."

"So it seems. Himself – the Vegan – pitched up in Soph's life a few weeks after it all died down. I didn't think anything of it. Seemed nice enough at first and Sophie seemed to like him; why would we think anything amiss? Besides, we were all busy with our own lives. Burt was still grieving for his old mum, Margot's husband had fallen ill and I…"

"Hed head stuffed up backside?" finished Babs.

"Oi," I protested, but the shameful heat crawling up my cheeks acknowledged the truth of it. "Yes," I said quietly, "I was busy wallowing in self-pity."

Babs squeezed my shoulder. "Never mind, you are done with that now, da?"

"Da – yes," I agreed, then I tutted. "Damn, I wish we could have got some proof." Babs jerked the wheelchair to a stop.

"You are *still* doubting Vegan is up to no good?" she said incredulously. I half-turned in the chair.

"What? No, I mean, I'd still like to know what else he's got planned but no, he's a bad 'un alright. I mean proof for when we tell Burt and Margot."

"Ah, yes, they should know what he is up to," agreed Babs, grunting slightly as she started pushing the chair again.

"Yes, and somehow, I don't think telling them we magically altered our appearance so we could follow him is going to be the best opening for a rational conversation."

"We could say we slipped recording device into his jacket," she suggested.

"That's not much more believable," I said. "Besides we don't have a recording, do we?" Babs' answering silence was weighted. "Do we?" I repeated.

"I don't know, perhaps *someone*, some wise and beautiful person hed bright idea to press record button on phone and captured entire conversation, maybe this thing happened."

I swivelled around to look at her.

"You never did?!" I exclaimed. Babs grinned devilishly. She stopped the wheelchair again, pulled out her phone and pressed play. The Vegan's voice rang out: *"The ice cream place can't keep going much longer..."* She pressed stop, looking as smug as anything and pocketed her phone again before starting up the chair again with another grunt. I sat back.

"Well, that makes it easier," I said.

"Mmm," agreed Babs, panting a little with exertion.

"You know, you're quite clever sometimes, aren't you?" I said.

"Only sometimes?" she replied, catching her breath. "I think you will find I am clever at all times."

"As you say," I said, mildly, then paused for a moment. We were at the other end of the park now. "Only... the thing is..." I said as the wrought iron of the arcade came into view.

"Da?"

"You know you lifted the glamour off us so we look like ourselves now?"

"Da?"

"Why did you push me all the way back to our cafe when I could have walked?"

The crunch of the wheels on the ground stopped and was replaced by the sound of Babs' teeth grinding together. I stood up and patted her cheek.

"Thanks for the lift," I said. "I'll pop this back to Burt now, shall I?" And I skipped off with the chair, leaving her to mutter words I didn't want to know the meaning of. Ha! That'll teach her – burlesque dancer, indeed!

She caught up with me and we rounded the corner into the arcade together. The foreman was pacing the pavement in front of the cafe and let out an explosive breath when he saw us.

"There youse are! Are youse alright?" I peered behind him to check on the cafe but everything seemed to be in order. I gave him a bemused smile.

"Of course, we are. We just had a personal matter to attend to." He gave the slightly hunted look most men give when women say the words 'personal matter' and the poor man let out another breath, slower this time. He ran his fingers through his hair.

"It's just…" He looked away, his cheeks reddening slightly. "… that is, me an' some of the boys dropped by to check everything was ok with the shutters, ye ken? An' when we saw you were shut an' no one knew where youse were… an' then yon grocer blokey said youse were after borrowin' a wheelchair… an' then the wee lassie from the health food shop comes back greetin' an' whatnot…" he trailed off, looking sheepish while I quietly translated his Caledonian brogue for Babs. She patted his cheek.

"Ah, you were worried for us," she said and his cheeks burned brighter still.

"Aye, right enough," he said, "but what with youse havin' that bother with the window…"

Babs beamed at him. "You call your boys," she said. "I will hev special syrniki pancakes ready for you all in moments." I passed her the keys and she started to open the cafe. I touched the foreman's elbow.

"You said Sophie was crying?"

"Aye, she was," he replied. "She was picking up her wain—"

"—baby," I interpreted for Babs.

"—aye, well she'd left her with the lady at the ice cream shop and was collecting her and I could tell she'd been greetin'-"

"—crying."

"—an' what with youse being AWOL, I put two and two together and got…"

"Six?" I said. He went red again and I felt a swell of affection. "I'm touched by your concern," I said. He coughed and scuffed the floor with this boot.

"Aye, well…" He looked around, fishing for another topic of conversation. "That fella of hers is a jobby and a half, right enough," he said.

"Jobby?" said Babs.

"I'll explain later," I said to her, then turned to the foreman. "You're not wrong. He's worse than the smelliest jobby you couldn't flush."

"Ahh, 'jobby', I am understanding," said Babs.

"And have you seen him? The jobby?" I asked.

"Aye, he got back aboot ten minutes before youse. He was surprised to see the shop shut up and I heard him causing a ruckus inside, shouting for her. I coulda told him he was wasting his breath; she was nae there."

Babs grinned at him. "You could hev told him… but you chose not to."

He grinned back. "Ah'm not one tae go sticking my nose in someone else's business," he said.

I bit my lip and tried to sound unconcerned. "I don't suppose you've any idea where she went?"

The foreman shook his head. "Sorry, Hen, she just grabbed the wain and scarpered." He hesitated. "Is something the matter?"

Babs breezed forward. "Nyet, darling. Nothing at all. Go, get your boys and I will cook." He wandered off, casting worried looks over his shoulder at us as he went.

I squinted up at the roof of the arcade. The fine mist from before was getting the hang of it now and the first heavy drop of rain splattered against the glass. I bit my lip. Babs nudged me.

"She is big girl, she will be okay."

"I hope you're right."

"When am I not?" she said indignantly, then held up her hand before I could reply. "Okay, I may not always be right, but I am never wrong. Sophie will be fine." I gave her a watery smile and she squeezed my arm. "Go to Burt and Margot. Tell them to come when the shops close. We will tell them what we have learned."

I nodded and Babs went into the cafe. I gave one last look at the gloomy sky through the glass ceiling before I set off and tried not to think of Sophie out in the weather.

Chapter Eighteen

The afternoon passed more quickly than I expected. We opened so we could feed our pet builders but didn't expect many other people to brave the wind and rain. Far from keeping people away, though, the bad weather drove them into the arcade and we were busier than ever. Just as well, really, as it kept me from fretting too much about Sophie and the baby. That said, I still found myself peering across the way at the Health Food shop every couple of minutes, hoping to see some sign of life. Babs tutted at me whenever she caught me looking but I noticed her craning her neck and pursing her lips at the dark windows of the shop as if she could will Sophie there by the sheer force of her frown. Part of me was surprised it didn't work.

Four o'clock rolled around eventually. The last customer left and we set about clearing up and preparing for the next day. At five, there was a tentative tap at the door. Burt and Margot arrived at the same time and faffed around in the doorway, stuck in a loop of "after you, no, after you." I rolled my eyes, grabbed Margot's arm and dragged her in. Burt trailed in after her.

"What's going on, Aggie?" he asked. "You looked ever

so worried when you came in earlier." Margot nodded her agreement. Babs was busy frying something in the kitchen so I sat them down at the nearest table and called her through. She joined us and took out her phone.

"What's this about?" asked Burt again, but I waved him into silence and Babs pressed play.

"The ice cream place can't keep going much longer…" the Vegan's voice rang out of her phone.

"Here, that's -" began Burt but Margot shushed him and sat in silence for the rest of the recording. When it was done, they both sat back and I filled them in on some of what had happened at the other cafe. Burt was hard-eyed and red-faced. Margot was grey. Her shoulders were slumped and her hands were shaking. I reached over and patted her hand. I had known this would be hard for her to hear, but she looked like she was going to faint. Babs looked at her for a moment, then she let her eyes linger on Burt.

"Honey balls!" she declared.

I gritted my teeth and glared at her. "Knock it off, will you, Babs? Can't you see now's not the time to be flirting? You're embarrassing poor Burt."

Babs' mouth opened in an O of outrage. She looked at the other two, one hand clutched to her chest in a mockery of indignation.

"You must forgive my friend. She is heving mind like miners' railway – one track and dirty." She stood up and sashayed to the kitchen, returning moments later with a plate sporting a golden pyramid of deep-fried batter balls, drenched in sweet syrup. "*I* was referring to my freshly made honey balls." She placed the plate on the table and fetched us each a fork. I didn't bother protesting; my mouth had started watering the second I got a whiff of the fried batter. I swirled one of the balls in the syrup and popped the whole thing in my mouth. The batter was light and fluffy. The syrup sparked across my palette, first soft and comforting with notes of cinnamon, then sharp and refreshing with the lemon she'd zested into it. Warmth spread out from my cheeks and down into my stomach. Babs smiled at me, knowingly.

"Is good, da?" I nodded. She looked at the others and wafted her hands at the food. "Come. Eat," she said. "Don't worry."

"I suppose these are vegan too?" I asked, a little sourly, if I'm honest. Babs wrinkled her nose.

"Nyet, darling," she replied. "I think we hev had our fill of all things vegan for one day." Margot snorted a little at that and picked up her fork. Burt followed suit and before long, the plate was empty and I was fighting the urge to lick the last of the syrup off it. The sugar had certainly hit the spot though and there was some colour in Margot's cheeks again.

Burt shook his head. "When I get my hands on that long streak of nothing…" he blustered.

"You'll what?" I countered. "Hit him? Get yourself arrested? Play right into his hands? Assuming he doesn't beat you, of course – he's younger than you."

Burt looked down, his face redder still, then he raised his head again.

"We'll go to the police then. You've got the evidence there. He even admits to killing your poor cat, Aggie, they'll have to do something."

Babs and I looked at each other warily. We both tried to steer clear of official channels. They tend to ask awkward questions like your name and date of birth.

"We can't *actually* prove it's him," I said. "He'll deny it was him and it'll be our word against his."

But Burt wasn't prepared to let it lie. "Well, what about the owners of the cafe? The waitress? Surely they'll remember you being there at the same time as him."

I hesitated. "Erm… we were in disguise," I said.

"Really?" said Burt. He raised his eyebrows, obviously trying to imagine what kind of disguise would stop the Vegan from recognising us.

"Was very good disguise," Babs assured him.

"Look, Burt, trust us on this, going to the police is not the answer right now."

Burt shrugged. "Well, what do we do then?"

"Wait him out," replied Babs. "You know what game he is playing now -"

"Yeah, he's playing Silly Buggers," I muttered, darkly.

"Da," Babs continued. "So simply refuse to roll dice and carry on with your life. Show he will not bully you out of business."

"It's not that easy," said Burt.

"It *is* that easy," Babs insisted. She tilted her head and looked him squarely in the eye. "Aggie and I will not be budged, and he has not the yayechka, the iron eggs, to face you without first securing victory elsewhere…"

Margot slammed her hand down on the table and we all jumped.

"But that's the problem, isn't it? He *is* going to 'secure a victory'." She closed her eyes and pressed her lips tightly together while she struggled against her tears. Burt looked at us, his face creased with bewilderment. Finally, Margot opened her eyes and sighed heavily. She looked at Burt. "He was right in what he said," she confessed. "I can't last much longer." She smiled weakly at us. "Even with your kind offer to set up shop in here, I'll still have to sell my place to cover my debts and I can't afford to be choosy about the buyer. I'm sorry," she said and then turned to Burt, her eyes full. "I'm sorry," she repeated. Burt hesitantly reached for her slender hand with his massive paw.

"Margot, love, I had no idea. You should have said something."

Margot shrugged. "You had problems of your own to deal with."

Babs cleared her throat and Burt pulled his hand back, looking a little sheepish.

"How much are you needing to sell shop?" she asked.

Margot took a notebook and pen out of her handbag and did some quick calculations. "This much," she said, showing Babs a figure.

Babs looked at the amount and shook her head. "Nyet, this is too low," she said. "I will pay this and £10,000 more."

Margot let out a bark of laughter and Burt looked at Babs reproachfully.

"Babs, this isn't the time for jokes," he said.

"Who is joking? I am serious as grave." She looked solemnly at Margot. "I will buy your shop and you will open ice cream stand in here."

"But what will you do with it?" asked Margot. "Open another cafe?"

"Nyet, darling, I hev no interest in running business.

Besides, two cafes in one small place will not work – you know this. You hev suffered because of competition." The meaning behind Babs' words sank in and I groaned. Margot was already established when I opened the cafe. I only bought the place to keep an eye on Sophie. It never occurred to me I might be taking business from them. I felt sick to the stomach. It must have shown on my face because Margot reached over and patted my hand.

"Don't you fret, Aggie. Derek and I never saw it that way. He always said there was plenty of room for everyone…" She hesitated. "… but I think Babs is right. Two similar places in such a small space has probably crowded the market."

"Da, this is what I am saying. So, I will buy and rent to suitable business, you will move in here with no debt and Vegan can whistle for his money. Agreed?"

Margot and Burt gawped around the table for a moment, which is the reaction most people have when faced with one of Babs' propositions. Margot swallowed. A hint of a hopeful smile began to tug at her lips.

"Well… if you're sure you can afford it?" she said. Oh, Babs could afford it alright. As I said before, our sort are not short of a bob or two – you never know when you might need to leave a place quickly and start again somewhere new. And, of course, Babs never had to worry about getting a roof over her head… she was right when she said she'd had the last laugh when House was forged.

"I hev sufficient funds," was all Babs said.

"Then, yes! Thank you, yes!" Margot sat back in her chair. Already the lines on her face seemed smoother and her whole body seemed lighter.

"Good, then I will contact solicitor tomorrow but for now…" She spat into her palm and held her hand out to Margot. Margot's eyes widened slightly but she too spat into her own palm and grasped Babs' outstretched hand, laughing helplessly. I clapped and cheered and after a moment, Burt joined in.

"It is agreed," said Babs. "And now we celebrate." The two ladies pulled apart and Babs scooted off into the kitchen. Margot surreptitiously wiped her hand on her skirt. Babs returned with the slivovica bottle and four shot glasses, which I can only assume she carries with her at all times in case of emergencies, since I know I don't stock either the booze or the glasses. She sloshed a generous amount of spirit into each glass and we raised them into the air.

"The future…" said Babs.

"The future," we all intoned.

"And may the Vegan develop a nasty rash in his nethers," added Margot, then she clamped her hand over her mouth as if to stop anything else escaping. Babs lifted one eyebrow and looked at me. I shrugged, biting back a smile.

"May he develop a nasty rash on his nethers," we intoned, although Burt was a bit quiet. I suppose there are some things a man won't wish on another man, no matter how much he dislikes him. I thought of the lingerie bag and the spicy knickers and this time I did grin. Maybe Margot would get her wish. We clinked glasses and, taking their lead from Babs and me, the other two downed their drinks. The charitable thing to do would have been to warn them, but it was getting late and I was running out of charity so instead I watched them cough and splutter as I had done that first time. Babs refilled the glasses.

Burt frowned. "So, is it really that simple?" he asked, still clearing his throat.

Babs patted his cheek. "Da, darling. Most things are. People just make them complicated."

"But what about Sophie and Madam from the magic shop? What if one of them sells?"

Babs' face clouded over. My own mood darkened too.

"That is different kettle of shrimp," said Babs.

I spoke up then. "We've not talked to Sophie yet but I suspect she'll be making some difficult choices in the next few days. We'll all support her whatever she decides."

Burt and Margot nodded.

"So long as she makes correct decision," muttered Babs, so quietly only I could hear.

"What of the other one?" asked Margot. "He's got his hooks into her too. You know they're…" she blushed and gave a sidelong glance at Burt before making an indelicate gesture with her hand.

Babs grinned wickedly. "I would not worry too much about her. She is self-serving cowbag. I do not think she will give up her business easily, no matter if she is…" she mimicked Margot's gesture, "or not. And Burt…" She turned her gaze to the poor man who was lifting his glass for another drink, no doubt to escape the awkward conversation. He met Babs' stare and froze, the proverbial rabbit in the headlights, his glass resting on his lips. "…for the record, I would never call you Honey Balls…" said Babs. Burt sighed with relief and knocked back his drink. "…in public," finished Babs, and Margot and I leapt up to pat Burt's back until the coughing subsided.

Later, Babs and I walked home under the shelter of

an umbrella. The streetlamps bled amber puddles on the glossy pavement and Babs hummed quietly to herself, mercifully more in tune this time.

"Poor Burt," I said. "You'll be the death of him, you know."

"I would like to try." Her tone made my ears burn.

"Did you see Margot's face, though?" I said.

"Da," said Babs, smugly, "she was as green as lady in Tretchikoff painting."

I chuckled. "She didn't look happy. Perhaps she is beginning to realise she's missing out on something good." Babs nodded but said nothing. "So, it's all part of your plan then? You all get something. Burt gets confidence, Margot gets self-awareness and you get la…" But I didn't get to finish my sentence because we arrived home and someone was waiting for us… Sophie.

Chapter Nineteen

She sat huddled on House's steps. The baby was in a sling across Sophie's front, with Sophie's jacket zipped up to protect them both from the elements. House had furtively extended its roof to shelter them and a surge of warmth for it bloomed in my chest. I patted House gratefully as I approached Sophie. She had her head down and didn't notice me until I crouched beside her. Her face was streaked with mascara.

"Sophie?"

"I've left him," she said.

Wordlessly, I handed my house keys to Babs and she opened the door while I helped Sophie to her feet, took her elbow and guided her indoors and out of the rain. I unzipped her coat and eased it gently off her. Baby Grace was sleeping soundly and didn't stir as I steered her mother to the kitchen table and sat her down.

Babs already had the kettle on. She popped back outside to House for a moment and returned with a tin of her homemade baklava. Her hand hovered over my tea caddy and she looked at me, one eyebrow raised in question. I gently cupped Sophie's chin, tilted her head upwards and peered into her eyes. I pursed my lips and considered the situation.

"Hmmm, chamomile, I think," I said to Babs, "with a spoonful of honey – er, maple syrup," I corrected myself, remembering Sophie actually was vegan, unlike her boyfriend… or should I say, ex-boyfriend. I let go of her chin and sat back. "Do you want to talk about it?"

Sophie sniffed. "No… Yes… I don't know," she said.

"Well, I think we've covered all the options there," I said, kindly. I reached behind me and grabbed the box of tissues – it'd had a lot of use lately. I placed it in front of Sophie and she took one and blew her nose noisily.

"You'll think I'm daft," she said.

"Perhaps," said Babs, from her place by the kettle, "but we think many people daft. I see no reason why you should be different." She finished making the drinks and brought them over to us. She took Sophie's hand and spoke gently. "Because he was cheating?" she asked.

I gasped. "Babs!"

"What? He was!"

"I know, but you're not supposed to just come out and say it!" I protested. Sophie giggled and hiccupped, fresh tears spilling down her cheeks.

"It's alright!" she said through the sobs. "I knew. Everybody knew… that's not even why I left him." She started laughing again and I exchanged a worried look with Babs. "You'll think I'm so stupid when I tell you."

Babs looked at her seriously and then clicked her fingers and turned to me. "It is because of egg and bacon sandwich."

That shut Sophie up and no mistake. Her jaw dropped

open and she narrowed her eyes at Babs. "How could you possibly know that?" she said. Babs and I froze.

"Lucky guess," Babs declared, brazening it out. "You knew he was cheating, so it took different betrayal to make you leave."

Sophie sagged, seemingly satisfied with the response. Her eyes welled again.

"It must seem stupid to you but…" she drew a juddering breath, "I didn't really like him to begin with. I mean, he was alright – but a bit too full of himself. He said he'd recently converted to veganism but was struggling and it just went from there. He shared recipes he'd tried and had me in pleats describing all the things that went wrong. He talked about his reasons for going vegan and he was so passionate about it and the way he spoke to me… like I was clever, like I was important…" She trailed off and looked so forlorn I got a lump in my own throat. "He was just so… charming," Sophie said, finally.

Oh, yes, I remembered him. At first, he was just another face in the crowd. Then he pitched up at Sophie's practically every day, sliming in with his oily hair and his creaking jacket, which he probably told her was vegan leather. I didn't like him from the get-go. Something about him didn't sit well with me, perhaps my powers hadn't completely deserted me, but I couldn't scry or use divination anymore and I wasn't close enough to Sophie to warn her off. What would I have said? *"Hi, I'm your shop neighbour who's been following your family for a while and I've a feeling your new fella's a bit of a git. I'd give him the push, if I was you… oh, and by the way, I may have had a hand in your dad's death."*? No, I can't imagine that going down too well. I just waited for Sophie to see it herself and it was a bloody long wait, I can tell you. She toyed with her mug now, turning it by the handle, first one way then the other, keeping her fingers busy while her mind roved the past. She looked up.

"When he finally asked me out, I just said yes. And he was lovely, at first," she said, sadly. "The perfect boyfriend. It was like he had a file on me and knew just what to say to make me love him."

I ground my teeth together to stop myself from swearing. I deliberately didn't make eye-contact with Babs but from the corner of my eye I saw her knuckles whiten on the handle of her coffee mug. That filthy, scheming bastard. It had been bad enough for the rest of us but hearing how he ingratiated himself with Sophie made me sick to the stomach. Sophie seemed calmer now. She took a sip of her tea, taking care to lean to one side so she didn't drip any on Grace. We let her sit for a moment then Babs broke the silence.

"I am taking it honeymoon was soon over?" she prompted.

Sophie sighed. "You could say that. It started to go pear-shaped when he moved in with me. He started to get involved with the business, which I thought was nice, at first – you know, it was sweet that he cared. He quit his job to join me full time and kept making decisions without me, changing stock and suppliers, bringing in products I knew wouldn't sell, but every time I tried to talk to him, he became defensive and said I didn't trust him. He told me he was doing everything for us, to make a better life. He was so adamant we could make it big, perhaps even become a chain..." She went quiet, then whispered, "I never wanted to be a chain. I just wanted my little shop and my little flat. That's all." She took another sip of tea. Babs pushed the baklava towards her. Sophie hesitated.

"Don't worry," said Babs, "is ve- is plant-based," she corrected. Sophie took one and bit into it gingerly. It was good to see the colour flood back into her cheeks. She finished the pastry, then dabbed the crumbs with her finger before continuing with her story.

"It got worse once I fell pregnant. I couldn't make a move without him questioning it, telling me I should be taking it easy, demanding to know why I didn't trust him to take care of us. He kept pressuring me to let him take the burden of the shop off me officially and add his name to the deeds."

I sat up bolt upright. "You didn't?"

She shook her head. "No, I promised my gran I wouldn't. She never did take to him."

No, she wouldn't have. She was a shrewd one; I remembered her well. Sophie's voice cracked. "I've not spoken to her for ages because of it – he'd get arsey whenever I contacted her, so I... I... I stopped." She dissolved into tears again, great heaving sobs that shook her tiny frame and made the baby whimper. "And now I've lost the one person who truly cared for me," she wailed. I scooched around the table and wrapped my arms around her.

"Come on, now, love," I said, smoothing her hair. "Don't get yourself all worked up. You've not lost anyone." I tilted her chin again and smiled at her. "Listen, if I know anything about Jean Letbury, it's that she adores you and will be over the moon to hear from you."

Sophie stiffened in my arms.

"How do you know my gran's name?"

Shit.

I couldn't speak. I just sat there, opening and closing my mouth like a fish in a bowl. Sophie shouldered her way out of my embrace. "Seriously," she said, "how do you know my gran's name?"

"You must have mentioned it..." I began.

"No!" Sophie snapped. "I didn't. What's more, my gran remarried when I was little. She hasn't been Jean *Letbury* for more than twenty years. There's no way I would have called her that!" She backed away from me until she'd positioned the chair between us. She cradled Grace's head and jigged about, seemingly to soothe her but it was the same nervous action she made around the Vegan and my stomach sank to see her use it around me. She looked me up and down as though seeing me for the first time.

"Who are you?" she said.

Babs stepped forward, her hands raised to placate. "Sophie, darling..." but Sophie was having none of it. Her head whipped round to confront Babs.

"And you... you knew about the egg and bacon sandwich. That was way too specific. And you knew about Grace's dad—"

"—well, to be fair, that wasn't exactly hard..."

Sophie's mouth hung open and she stared first at Babs, then at me.

"It *was* you in the cafe, wasn't it? I thought I was going mad because it didn't look like you but I *knew* it was – it was like – like I could see you both just under the surface of the other women." The baby began fussing loudly now and Sophie's jigging became more desperate.

"Soph—" I began.

"—and another thing," she shouted. "Why does that caravan have chicken legs?" She pointed through to the lounge where House was peering in the window. House must have seen her accusatory finger because it ducked low and tried to skulk away to hide behind the lavender, which did nothing to disguise the wooden bulk and only served to highlight that it did, indeed, have chicken legs. I groaned inwardly. There was no way we could style this one out. Sophie's mouth was closed now. She stopped moving and soothed Grace, who was crying properly now. The colour had gone from her face again. She didn't look scared or surprised, she just looked tired and so, so small. And when she spoke, her voice was smaller still.

"I just want to know what's going on," she said.

"It's complicated," I said.

"Is not complicated," said Babs. "We are what you call witches, although we do not use that word. We hev lived for many, many years."

"Well, when you put it like that, it's simple," I muttered.

"You always over-complicate matters," she said to me, then turned to Sophie. "You are correct, we were at other cafe today. We followed your boyfriend and yes, I disguised us." Sophie stared into the middle distance and nodded slowly, as though taking everything in.

"And the caravan?" she asked.

"House is my familiar, my constant companion throughout the centuries," Babs explained, "just as Misty was Agnes'," she added, significantly. Sophie flicked a quick, almost guilty glance in my direction.

"Why does it have legs?" she asked.

"Because jet packs were not available back then," came the reply. The image of House with jets instead of legs lurched into my mind and my imagination baulked at it.

"And nobody else has commented on it?" Sophie's voice was incredulous. "I can't imagine there are many sheds on legs." She practically spat the words. Babs folded her arms across her chest, lifted her chin and eyed Sophie coolly.

"House is *not* shed. House is my heartbeat, my darling one, who provides me with home and warmth and care. This is the way with familiars and if we lose them, we lose part of our selves." Another guilty look from Sophie before Babs continued with her explanation. "People do not notice legs. People see merely a caravan. I hev made this so. I hev disguised House as I disguised us in cafe."

"You cast a spell?"

Babs wrinkled her nose, weighing up the choice of words. "I suppose *you* would say so, da."

"Then how can I see House? Why could I see through your spell at the cafe?"

Babs drew herself up taller still. She answered Sophie but her gaze was fixed squarely on me. "Because blood of 'witches' courses through your veins."

Chapter Twenty

Babs' revelation hung in the air. I held my breath and watched her words work their way into Sophie's brain. Sophie swung around to confront me.

"What does she mean?" she asked. Her voice was low and dangerous. I sighed heavily.

"It means that you, your mother, your grandmother, *her* grandmother, you're all descended from a single 'witch'… me." Sophie stood, statue-still but I could almost hear her mind whirring behind her eyes and I dreaded the next question.

"And it's a coincidence, is it, you living here? Opening the cafe right opposite me? Pure chance, was it?" I swallowed. I could see the slippery slope down which this train of thought would tumble, but she deserved an answer. I met her stare and answered clearly.

"No, I've been watching you – your family – for centuries. I opened the cafe so I could keep an eye on you." Her lip curled. Her skin had a green tinge to it and for a moment, I thought she was going to vomit.

"You've been stalking me," she whispered.

"I've been trying to protect you – all of you," I replied. She jerked her head up then.

"And what about my mum, did you watch her, too? She killed my dad, but you'll already know that from your snooping – did he not deserve your 'protection' from her?" I suppose something of the truth must have shown on my face because her face went paler still. "Did you... did you help her?" she asked. I couldn't answer. My throat had seized up.

Sophie leaned against the wall. "No," she said. "This can't be happening." Her skin was clammy and I followed the rise and fall of her chest as she tried to control her breathing.

"Sophie? Sophie, are you okay?"

Sophie's answering giggle scared me. It was high-pitched and bordering on hysteria.

"He was right," she said. "He said you were mad and he was right. You're bloody delusional, the pair of you."

Babs tutted in frustration and I glared at her. "What?" she said. "She would deny what she has seen with own eyes! She denies what the very blood in her body tells her is truth!"

Sophie's head snapped up at that.

"Truth? What would you know about truth?" she spat. "Either of you?" She whirled around to face me. "It doesn't matter if what you say now is true or if you're as deranged as people say – I liked you. I *trusted* you," she said. "I thought you actually cared for me, and all this time you were lying to me. You're just like the rest of them. You're just like *him*."

My whole body ran cold at her words. I could scarcely bring myself to look at her and when I did, I wished I hadn't. Her eyes shone with years of bottled hurt and I'd just added to the measure. She shook her head.

"I can't handle this," she said. She grabbed her coat and slammed the door on her way out.

The door shuddered in its frame when she left. Through the rain-worsted window, I watched Sophie walk, Lowry-like through the deluge until she disappeared around the corner. Out of habit, I reached down to bury my fingers in Misty's thick fur to calm myself. My fingers found nothing but air and fresh tears pricked my eyes.

The echo of the door faded away and the weight of silence shifted uncomfortably in the room. I took a deep breath and turned to face Babs. She returned my stare, one eyebrow cocked, saying nothing in the way that only she could. Frustration bubbled anew in my stomach. My head was throbbing and my hands were shaking with pent-up anger. The last thing I needed was Babs looking all smug and judgy, like her farts don't stink. I'd had enough.

"What?" I snapped at her. Babs simply raised her other eyebrow but still said nothing. "Fine," I said. "Yes, Sophie and I are related. She's my great-great-whatever granddaughter and maybe I didn't tell you but so what? It's not like you tell me everything and you know why I didn't tell you? Because it's family, that's why and that's something you can't possibly understand."

I was panting now. The words spewed out in such a torrent I barely had chance to draw breath. Still, Babs didn't speak. I slumped into one of the chairs and rested my head in one hand. I waved vaguely in the direction of the door with the other. "Look, just… whatever you're going to do – go or… just do it. I don't care anymore." My pulse swished in my ears. I buried my face in both hands and choked back the sobs that raked at my throat.

I heard Babs shift in her seat. She cleared her throat and finally spoke.

"I hed child once."

My head shot up so quickly I jarred my neck. My anger ebbed away as my curiosity peaked.

"You?" I said. "When?"

Babs shrugged and shook her head.

"Long time past," she said. She picked up the ceramic saltshaker from the table and turned it over in her hands. "Her father drifted like dandelion in breeze before I knew she was growing. Every day for a month, I made raspberry leaf tea and watched it grow cold. I told myself tomorrow I would drink it. But then, one tomorrow I felt her move and I knew tomorrow would never come." I nodded, remembering the bubbles and fizzes of my own child, so long ago. Babs was staring at the saltshaker in her hands now, her mind centuries away.

"She was so beautiful," she said, softly. "Most babies are ugly, you know?" I nodded again. I'd lied in enough delivery rooms when proud parents had declared their fist-faced offspring was the next Adonis. "But not her. She had little kink in her hair so it stuck out here." Babs flicked her hands by her ears to demonstrate. A gentle smile played on her lips. "And she hed the brightest eyes. I would lay her down in the long grass and the blue butterflies would rest on her cheeks to admire them and she would gurgle and chuckle and smile…" She trailed off. This time, I waited in silence. I scarcely dared to breathe. She looked directly at me then, her clear gaze caught me off guard.

"She was beautiful… but she was not strong. One day,

she did not wake and I thought the sun had turned to ash and the earth had devoured itself. I carried her to the forest and howled at the empty sky until my throat was raw and the bears hid in the mountains."

My throat, still tight from my confrontation with Sophie, grew tighter still and my eyes were hot with unshed tears. I swallowed painfully. Babs continued.

"I do not know how long I cradled her – longer than was healthy, I suppose. Some of the villagers stumbled across me, still holding her. I suppose I must have scared them," she laughed mirthlessly. "They called me Baba Yaga, the child eater, and shouted and threw stones." A hot surge of fury unfurled in the pit of my stomach and I drew a seething breath. Babs reached over and took my hand to calm me. "I didn't care. I wanted to die."

That's not the point, I wanted to scream but Babs squeezed my hand to silence me.

"House saved me. He scooped me up and locked me safe in his belly then ran, far from the rocks and the jeers. He carried me to the place where the butterflies swarmed and there we buried her. We roamed then. I do not know where or for how long. House rattled pots and pans to remind me to eat and bundled me in blankets when it was time to sleep. In time, I remembered these things myself. I remembered to bathe in the mountain stream and to see beauty in the sunrise and the crunch of pine needles beneath my feet." She shrugged. "I was still Baba Yaga, child eater, in the hearts and minds of villagers everywhere. Mothers scared their children with tales of me—" her smile twisted somewhat "—yet they still came to me for their potions and herbs."

"And for borscht," I croaked, desperate to break the tension. Babs gave a soft laugh.

"Oh, yes, always for borscht." She looked at me again, her eyes shining. "But Agnes, had my little girl lived, had she had girls of her own, there is nothing I would not have done to ensure their safety." She cupped my face with her hand. "So, you see, I do understand. It is family and we do whatever we must."

We sat like that for an age. The tears I had fought so hard to keep back flowed freely. How long had she carried this alone? How many times had I stung her with my ignorance? I flinched now at the memory of each unwitting barb – *Babs doesn't do children. Babies are wasted on Babs.*

"I should have told you about Sophie," I said. Pitiful words that clawed their way shame-faced from my throat. Then I shook my head. "I should have told *Sophie* about Sophie," I corrected myself. Babs dropped her hand and gave her usual shrug.

"We all hev secrets," she said. "Now we each hev one less."

Chapter Twenty-One

We sat in silence for a while. There seemed to be no more to say. Now the day's battering tide of emotions had ebbed, I was drained. Babs refreshed our drinks and I picked at a piece of baklava, my head drooping. I'd fallen into a gentle torpor when Babs' question came at me from out of nowhere.

"Who was Grace's father – your Grace, I mean? Do you remember?" There was no rancour in her voice, no judgement, merely the acceptance that over time, memory fades, faces merge and lovers become interchangeable. But that wasn't the case here. The centuries rolled back to show me his face as clearly as if he was standing there now. An earthy chuckle bubbled up from my chest.

"Alfred," I said.

Babs' brow furrowed. "The butler?" she said.

"The Great, you dimwit," I replied, swatting her arm.

"Ah," she said, then the penny dropped and her eyes widened. "Ahhh!"

"Mm-hmm," I nodded and my lips twitched into a smirk. "He was great, too." Babs leaned forward, rested her chin on her hands and waited for me to elaborate.

"I was young," I said, "just coming into my power, and I woke one night from a vision telling me to go to the Somerset levels." I took a sip of tea. "I nearly didn't go," I confessed. "Have you been?" Babs shook her head and I grimaced. "Cold, damp and miserable – and that was just me. The weather was worse. Back then, you couldn't take a step without winding up ankle-deep in swamp water and don't talk to me about the smell – murky and fetid and so thick you could practically chew it. You couldn't escape it. I didn't really know why I was there. The vision was vague. All I knew was I was supposed to be there and so, there I was."

"And then?" said Babs.

"There he was," I said, simply. "He'd been separated from his camp – I forget why, probably hunting or looking for firewood, no mean feat in itself. Anyway, he stumbled across my little shack and the instant I saw him…" I let the sentence hang and pulled at the collar of my blouse. I suddenly felt very warm, in spite of the cold weather. I cleared my throat. "He wasn't handsome, as such," I explained. "He was leaner than you'd expect, months in the swamps had done him no good at all, but he had a mop of unruly brown hair that made my fingers itch and there was an intensity about him, a fire in his eyes that was catching – I felt hotter than I had done in weeks and from the glint in his eyes, I knew the feeling was mutual."

I popped a piece of baklava into my mouth and chewed slowly, savouring the contrast between the sharp sweet syrup and the earthy crunch of nuts. I frowned. "Have you tried another recipe?" I asked.

Babs blinked. "What?"

"This baklava. It tastes different from your last batch."

"Da, I used pistachio instead of walnut." I heard the impatience in her voice while she waited for me to get back to the story. I know it was wrong of me, but I selected another slice and took my time chewing again. Babs watched every movement of my mouth as though she was willing me to chew faster.

"Mmm," I said. "I like it. And is that a hint of rose water I detect?" I reached for another bit and Babs' hand slammed down on top of mine.

"Enough baklava. Tell me of your Great Alfred." I laughed wickedly and ran my fingers through my hair.

"What can I say? We didn't waste any time. We stayed in my shack for three days and three nights until the air hummed and the straw in my pallet bed was well and truly flattened. On the third day, he lay back and told me he planned to stay with me forever. That wiped the smile off my face, I can tell you."

Babs tutted. "Men! They always hev to ruin the moment."

"I know! I looked him square in the eye and said, 'You bloody won't, you've a country to lead!'" I shook my head ruefully. "He was not impressed with that. He leapt from the pallet like he'd sat on a hedgehog and paced the floor, scuffing up the rushes with his feet, muttering how a mere woman couldn't understand. The heathen invaders were everywhere, he said, a punishment from God, like locusts sent to ravage the land. 'So, what do you plan to do about it?' I said." I lowered my voice to mimic the ancient king's. "'What would you have me do, woman?' he said. 'Be captured and killed? Or worse, allow them to turn me into some puppet king like my brother-in-law?' He spat on my floor at that."

"Rude!" said Babs.

"I thought so," I said. "'I'd have you be the king I know you are,' I told him, 'one that does not desert his people... or his God.' I knew I'd hit home with that one. Very devout, was Alfred, extramarital dalliances aside. I grabbed his hand and gave him a peek of what the future could be – various snippets I'd glimpsed during our time with each other sewn together to show a brighter future."

Babs hissed. "Reckless, Agnes," she said. "At that time? He could have cried sorcery and hed you killed!"

I wrinkled my nose and shook my head. "Nah, I dressed it up in his faith. Said I was an angelic messenger from the saints."

Babs' laugh was explosive and a little insulting.

"You? Angelic?" she hooted.

"Well, *he* believed me, that was the main thing," I said. "Anyway, then we heard his men approaching and he panicked a bit about being caught *in flagrante* and word getting back to his missus. Oh, don't look like that," I said, catching her frown. "It was a different time and back then, playing away from home was practically part of the job description for kings." I paused. "But, it would still have hurt, I suppose, to hear your kingly husband had been slumming it with some marsh wench."

"You are no mere wench!" exclaimed Babs and I shrugged.

"That's what it would have looked like. Anyway, his wife was a good sort and didn't deserve to hear his men's gossip, so I cast a glamour to make me look like a crone and as they approached, I chased him from the hut, berating him for burning my buns."

Babs was laughing so hard, she had tears streaming down her face. "*That's* where that story comes from!" she cried.

I chuckled too. "Yeah, poor bugger. I had no idea that would be what people remembered about him. Anyway, then his tame scholar, Asser – colossal prick, he was – raised his hand to strike me. Alfred caught his hand to stop him, which was just as well or his biography would have been a lot shorter. Asser stood there, screaming how I should be on my knees before my king—"

Babs snorted. "Talk about closing stable door after horse has bolted," she sniggered.

"Give over," I said, swatting her again. "Anyway, Alfred called for calm. Said he'd had a 'religious experience'. Well, I suppose he had, after a fashion. He gave a rousing speech, there and then, about how they would overcome their foes and lead the country to its glorious destiny, or some such nonsense. I wasn't really listening. I was too busy thinking that his bum looked good in those leather stockings." I sighed.

"Anyway, the rest is history. He did what he had to and became a great ruler and I did what I had to and became a mother. I did hear he returned to the swamp after the fighting was done, to 'pay tribute to his angelic messenger', but I was long gone. I had Grace growing in me by then and it would have been awkward. He'd have felt obliged to take her into his care and I wasn't having that." I took a final sip of tea and pulled a face. It had gone cold.

"All I wanted was for her to grow in peace and she

did." I smiled sadly. "I kept her with me until she was wed, then I moved away for her safety – not too far, but far enough. I returned twice, once to deliver her baby and once to bury her."

My memory searched for Grace's face within its depths and I saw her for a moment before the fog of the centuries swallowed her again. I pressed my lips together and closed my eyes to recover myself. You would think, after all this time, it wouldn't hurt anymore, but my heart still ached to see her smile. I opened my eyes again and brusquely dusted flakes of pastry off my chest.

"I've been watching her descendants ever since," I said, "all through the ages right down to Sophie and her Grace. Kind of like a guardian angel, all without them knowing… until now, that is."

I puffed out my cheeks, but Babs was frowning. "So… Sophie is heir to throne?" she asked.

I blinked. "I hadn't really thought of it like that, but yes, I suppose she is."

"Will you tell her?"

"Probably not. People tend to get a bit funny about that sort of thing. Besides, I'm not likely to get the opportunity now, am I? I can't tell her anything if she won't speak to me." I thought of Sophie storming out into the cold. I felt heavy all of a sudden and slumped in my chair. "Blimey, I've made a right pig's ear of things, haven't I?"

Babs took my hand and squeezed it. "Is nothing that cannot be fixed."

"But how?" I said. "What if I've lost her? What if I've sent her scurrying back to him? What if…" Babs placed a finger on my lip to silence me.

"Nyet!" she said. "No 'what ifs', only 'what will'. What will we *do* to help Sophie? What will we *do* to stop Vegan?" She dropped her hand and stared out of the window where the sky still teemed. "Things look not-so-good right now," she said, "but there is saying, 'After rain, we will walk in green fields.'" She squeezed my hand again. "We will figure this out. Already, the Vegan's plans with Burt and Margot are unravelling. We will find ways to drop more flies in his ointment."

"But what if..." I started. Babs held up her hand.

"Ah!"

I took a deep breath and reframed my question. "What will we do to make sure Sophie and the baby are safe from him?" I asked. Babs placed her elbows on the table and rested her chin on her hands. She stared off into the distance again then shook her head slowly.

"I am sorry, my friend, I do not hev answers... yet. But," she lifted her head and set her jaw, "you are Black Agnes and I am Baba Yaga. Between us, we hev conquered kings and changed the course of history. Together, we *will* bring down this Vegan."

Chapter Twenty-Two

I woke to Babs standing over me, her face close to mine, which is a fate I wouldn't wish on anyone.

"Come, up, up!" she said and whipped the duvet off me. A blast of cold air blew through the cocoon of warmth I'd swaddled myself in and I flailed about trying to grab the sheets.

"Wozgoinon," I mumbled.

"Is time to be up and doing," Babs declared. She marched over to the window and pulled the curtains open, for all the good it did. The sky still spilled across the horizon like pooled ink, with only the faintest smear of cobalt over the rooftops to indicate dawn was near.

"Bugger off," I muttered and buried myself deep into the comforting folds of my bedding. Babs was back at my side in an instant. She snatched the duvet away again and this time kept hold of it.

"I hev been thinking of your problems -"

"—my problem is I need more sleep," I said.

"—and I hev decided you are spending too much time indoors," she said, ignoring my protest, "so come. Up. The day is wasting."

"The day doesn't even know it's begun yet," I grumbled but the cold had got under my nightie now and I knew I wasn't getting back to sleep any time soon, so I slunk out of bed and headed for the bathroom to prepare myself for whatever Babs had in store.

House was taking us on our mystery tour – just as well, as I know I wasn't in a fit state to drive and I didn't know if Babs could. Babs' familiar opened its door for us and lowered the steps. I followed Babs inside. I hadn't been inside House in years and I was always surprised by how roomy it was. Babs' bed, already neatly made with its corners tucked in, nestled in a cosy inglenook, while a pot-bellied stove rested by the opposite wall. Copper pots and cast-iron skillets dangled from low-hung rafters, interspersed with bunches of dried lavender and chamomile. The cold cupboard, where Misty now lay, sat in another section entirely, discreetly hidden by a long, woven curtain I'm sure House had magicked up. It was a sweet but unnecessary gesture. I couldn't bring myself to look at him again. Instead, I sat myself at Babs' little table, with my back to the curtain.

Babs stroked House's walls and whispered softly to it before joining me. A few moments later House lurched first to one side, then the other as it rose up on those great, clawed legs. The pots and pans clanked and clanged on the beams and the herbs swayed wildly but we were off and on our way to Babs' secret destination.

It was a forest. Of course, it was. If you spend any amount of time with Babs, at some point you're going to end up in a forest in the arse-end of nowhere before the sun even has its pants on. At least we weren't dragging anything heavy on this occasion. I should've put my wellies on. You'd think I'd know better by now; this wasn't my first rodeo, after all.

"Why are we in a forest, Babs?" I asked. "… this time?" I added.

"You are not remembering?" she asked. I thought back to the previous night, when we spent a happy couple of hours plotting a myriad of tiny ways we could make the Vegan's life miserable. The weight of the argument with Sophie and all the revelations that followed had hung heavily in the air. I had lit basil and rosemary candles for clarity and Babs had pulled out her usual fallback of slivovica. Shots had been fired now, after all – great cannon balls, in fact – and we couldn't let that stand.

"We're collecting supplies?" I guessed. By supplies, I meant plants we would use to torment vile Vegans.

"Da," she said. "Collecting supplies and getting some fresh air – *your* house is far too stuffy." I scowled in response but said nothing. She had a point; for months, years perhaps, I'd done little more than trudge from my front door to the cafe and back. Oh, I'd shopped when I had to but beyond that, I couldn't remember when I'd last gone somewhere just for the fun of it.

"We'll start with rosehip," Babs stated, clearly still clearly disappointed we weren't hunting for common rue or liquorice, but we'd talked about this last night. I'd explained – again – that this wasn't like the good old days and we couldn't just meddle with someone's manhood willy-nilly, if you'll pardon the expression. The biting air soon cleared her irritation though and before long, Babs was skipping happily into the depths of the woodland – of course, *she* was wearing tough leather boots and of course, *she* had her long, waxed coat on to keep out the damp air. Me, I was in the flimsy anorak I'd grabbed on the way out and I was really regretting binning my nice warm cardy the other day. The morning dew soon seeped through my trainers and reached chilly fingers up my legs until my entire body felt cold and…

"Oh." I clenched and crossed my legs.

"What?" Babs said.

"I feel a bit of an urgency," I whispered. Babs frowned.

"Is no urgency," she said. "We're not in rush."

I wriggled uncomfortably. "No. I mean I need to spend a penny," I said. Babs' frown deepened.

"What? Is forest, not shop." She stopped then. I suppose she noticed my jiggling, since realisation spread across her face. "Ahhh. You need piss. Go behind tree then. I'll wait." She dutifully turned her back and I hobbled off into the undergrowth.

I croodled down with my back against a sturdy tree – what? You don't squat without a means of getting back up again at my time of life – and let nature take its course. As relief trickled out of me, I gazed at my surroundings. For all my grumbling, this really wasn't so bad. Despite the thick, autumnal carpet, snatches of green still pushed through the undergrowth and speared the air with a sharp-scented promise of spring. Birds chirruped around me and above me, the first rays of dawn prised their way through the naked fingers of the praying trees. The ghost of a smile tugged at the corners of my mouth. This wasn't too shabby at all. A blackbird launched itself off a nearby sapling, setting the branches shaking. A few twigs broke loose and I followed their progress as they fell to the ground. The air grew still – even the birds ceased their wittering.

A calming fog rolled across my mind. Images formed in the swirls and eddies, vague at first but growing clearer. Sophie, the baby, Babs, a bloodied fist, dirty orange flames gorging thickly on something black and charred… The acrid stench of death and burning was suffocating. Through it all, a shrill whistle of tinnitus grew to a nauseating crescendo, blocking out all thought until it ended in a dam burst of noise – the hiss and spit of fire, a sickening thud, a baby's cry cut off mid wail… Sophie's face pressed against a window, screaming silently while fronds of smoke wreathed around her.

The glass pane splintered and I could hear again. Her cries morphed into a terrified cat yowl. And then he was there. The Vegan. He strode through the mist in my mind and stood before me. His face morphed – one moment he wore his habitual sneer, the next it shifted into a soft smile, one that haunted my dreams more than twenty years after I'd last seen it. It was the smile of Sophie's mum. I saw him then, for what he was and what he could become. And I knew what he was capable of.

I won't lie, I yelped loud enough for Babs to hear me.

"What? Did you sit on nettle?" she called over.

"Babs, get over here!"

"Seriously? Just find dock leaf!"

"No – you need to see this."

"…" Her silence spoke volumes.

"Not that! Something else."

She sighed heavily and I heaved myself up using the tree as leverage – told you it was useful. I pulled up my drawers and was somewhat presentable by the time she joined me. I nodded at the twigs.

"I don't think rosehip is going to cut it," I said. She stared at them and her face hardened.

"No. I think we will be needing knife… big one… perhaps machete," she replied. I nodded my agreement, peered back at the twigs and pursed my lips.

"A blunt one," I said and turned and abruptly left the glade. For once, Babs was playing catch up with me. I was torn between euphoria that I had accessed my power again and terror as to what the vision could mean, so, ignoring the protests of my lungs and knees, I high-tailed it back to House, leaving Babs to follow on. House obviously sensed Babs approaching because the door creaked open and the steps rolled out like a lolling tongue before I even got there.

The instant we were inside, House heaved itself up onto its legs and waited, poised to spirit us away to wherever we needed to go. I wanted to go straight to the shop. I wanted to bang on the door until he let us in so I could squeeze his throat – or anything else I could get my hands on – until he delivered Sophie and Grace into our care, but Babs insisted we take our time and make a clear plan. I gritted my teeth and snarled that it was a fine time for her to decide she was the responsible one, but in the end, she was the designated driver and I didn't have much choice, so we headed back to my little terrace cottage to regroup.

I'd calmed down somewhat by the time I got out of the shower. Babs was right, better to know what we were up against rather than going in, all guns blazing. Besides, there was time yet – I'd know if something terrible had happened to Sophie, much as I'd known when it happened to Misty. I knew all of this, but my stomach was still tight with fear. Babs had made me breakfast but I could only pick at a piece of dry toast.

"We do not even know that she returned to him," Babs said.

"Where else would she go with the babby in all that rain last night? Even if she still plans to leave him, she'd have wanted Grace out of that weather."

"But he does not know there is problem. I am doubting she left note saying, '*You are stinking, flesh-eating liar and I can do better.*' Even if she has returned, there is no reason she will not be safe. She is smart girl. She will be fine."

I chewed my bottom lip. I knew logically she was right; the Vegan had been horrible to Sophie for ages and she'd managed him well enough but I could still see Sophie's face pressed against the windowpane, her eyes wide and her mouth gaping in a silent howl of terror… it meant something, even if I wasn't sure what, yet.

"If he's touched a hair on either of their heads, all bets are off," I said and Babs nodded her agreement.

"First, we take stock of situation. If she is in shop, we speak to her, find way to convince her to come with us. If she is not, we make… other arrangements."

"Promise?" I said.

"Promise," she replied.

We walked to the cafe in the milky morning light as though we hadn't a care in the world. Babs said it was important we act as though it was just another day so we didn't spook the Vegan, but I still nearly sprained something craning my neck to peer through the darkened windows of Sophie's shop. Burt waved as we passed. Babs nudged me to force a response and I plastered a false smile on my face. We'd decided it would be best to keep Burt and Margot out of it until we knew what kind of situation we were dealing with.

We opened the cafe and waited.

Babs busied herself brewing coffee and pottering in the kitchen but I couldn't rest. A couple of our builders came in for their morning cuppa and I let Babs deal with them. I stood by the window, much as I'd done the day before, but this time real fear gnawed at my insides. I knew what he was capable of now – his own confession about Misty and my vision in the woods had shown me. The Vegan was a man capable of real violence.

Chapter Twenty-Three

I practically fainted with relief when the lights went on across the way. I'd squeezed past the chairs and tables and had my hand on the doorknob before the neon had stopped flickering. Babs whipped off her pinny and thrust it into the hands of a bemused builder.

"Watch shop," she ordered and joined me at the door.

I didn't sprint over, much as I'd have liked to, partly because I didn't want to alert Himself to the fact we were wise to him but mostly because my exertions in the woods had done me no good whatsoever and my knees were officially not speaking to me. I prepared my thoughts while we walked. If she was on her own, I'd start with an apology and an offer of help, even if she didn't want to stay with me – anything to get her away from him. If he was there… well, I'd find a way to get the message through to her. I was just relieved I could speak to her.

My relief was short-lived. She wasn't in the shop. *He* stood there alone and his charming fake-smile dropped into its habitual sneer when he saw us.

"What do you want?" he said. I tried to peer around him to see if she was in the back but there was no sign of her.

"Where's Sophie?" I demanded. He crossed his arms and leaned against the counter, further blocking my view of the rear of the shop.

"What's it to you?" he replied. "Always sticking your nose into other people's business. Perhaps if you had a family that cared for you, you'd leave my family alone."

"*Your* family? Oh, I know a thing or two about your family…" I said. My pulse throbbed in my temples and my fingers itched to knock the sneer off his face.

"Agnes."

Babs' warning stopped my tongue though it may have been too late. The Vegan's skin mottled and the veins stood out in his neck.

"You know nothing," he spat. "You and your so-called sister, swanning around, stirring up trouble. You think you're so clever." He was bearing down on me now, but I wasn't backing down, not now or ever again. I tilted my chin up so I could match his stare. He frowned and stepped closer still, so close my throat burned with the smell of his aftershave.

"Agnes," said Babs again. I could hear the tightness in her voice and wanted to take her hand and tell her it was alright, but I had to keep eye contact. I would not be cowed again. I gritted my teeth. My fingers weren't just itching, they were tingling. It was a sensation I hadn't felt for years, subtle, but growing stronger. A faint buzzing reverberated at the back of my mind and I started to picture all the ways I could harm this man. My own lip curled to match his.

"Where. Is. Sophie?" I repeated. His eyes narrowed and he drew himself up taller still. What he planned to do, I'll never know. What *I* planned to do, I'll never know because at that moment, the doorbell jangled and startled us both apart.

"Everything alright, Hen?" The Foreman poked his head around the door frame. His tone was mild but his eyes were fixed on the Vegan and his face was ice. "One of the lads called. Said there might be trouble."

"No trouble," said Babs, easing herself between the Vegan and me. "We were just asking after Sophie and the baby." The Foreman looked around, suddenly noticing Sophie's absence.

"Aye, where is the wee lassie?"

The Vegan's head snapped round then and he eyed up the Foreman.

"Why do you want to know?"

"I just…"

"Just what? You think I haven't noticed you sniffing around her? Think you've got a chance, do you?" The Foreman's shoulders swelled slightly as he pulled himself up to his full height.

"You wanta watch what yer sayin', pal." He took a step forward and the Vegan matched him until they were standing eye to eye, both of them granite-jawed and unsmiling. I swear, if the testosterone levels in the shop got any higher, Babs and I would have to start wearing Y-fronts. It was then that I noticed something strange about the way the Vegan glowered at the Foreman. He wasn't just squaring off, he was scrutinising the Foreman's eyes, searching for something.

"Or perhaps you've already had your chance," said the Vegan. Finally, the penny dropped for me. He knew Grace wasn't his. My previous words came back to haunt me. *I know a thing or two about your family.* I'd been talking about the Silver Fox, of course, looking to put the wind up him a bit, but out of context, they sounded like confirmation of his suspicions.

"Oh bugger," I whispered. I looked sharply at Babs who gave me a curt nod. Clearly, she'd reached the same conclusion.

"I don't know what yer on, pal, but I'd lay off it, if I was youse. It's makin' youse talk shite." The Foreman muscled closer still and lowered his voice. "I've heard about men like you, playing all tough, bullying women… maybe you should play with people yer own size…" The tone remained civil but the meaning was clear. Nothing good could come out of this confrontation. They seemed evenly matched but whether the Foreman won or lost, until I knew where Sophie was, I couldn't run the risk of the Vegan taking his temper out on her. I cleared my throat but Babs was a step ahead of me.

"Gentlemen, gentlemen, such words!" She edged her way between them and subtly prised them apart. She kept her eyes on the Vegan while I gently pulled the Foreman away.

"We were worried about Sophie because she looked a little unwell yesterday. Once we know how she's feeling, we'll be on our way," Babs was saying to the Vegan. He reluctantly dragged his glare away from the Foreman and shifted it to Babs.

"If you must know, she's in bed with a headache. *Someone*—" and he looked significantly from Babs to me and back again "—upset her yesterday. I told her to take the day off and rest." The words seemed innocent enough but a faint sheen of sweat glistened above his top lip. That's the thing with lying, there's always a tell, even for someone as practised as the Vegan. I decided to push my luck a little.

"And the babby?" I said. "Little Grace alright, is she?" I'd have missed the twitch of his eye if I hadn't been watching for it.

"Of course, why wouldn't she be?" he replied.

"There," said Babs, magnanimously. "That was not so very difficult, now, was it? That is all we wanted to know and now we shall leave. Please pass on our regards." The look on his face made it clear he'd do no such thing. "Come, Agnes, let us go."

"Yeah, piss off," said the Vegan, turning his back on us and giving the Foreman one last vicious look, "and take your Scottie dog with you."

We pissed off and once we were back in the relative safety of the arcade, the Foreman rounded on us.

"What are ye playing at? Did we no agree yesterday that he was a bad sort? Ye want tae steer clear of that one, it would nae surprise me if…" He stopped talking and bit his lip, leaving the rest of his sentence unsaid. He narrowed his eyes and looked at Sophie's shop for a moment then sighed. "Let me see youse back to the caff."

I shook my head. "We just have something to do first," I said, my eyes still lingering on Sophie's shop. I heard the intake of breath as he prepared to argue. "We'll just be a few minutes. You go, get back to work."

Babs gave him a mischievous grin. "Da, we will send your worker back to you when we hev finished." The

Foreman gaped goldfish-like for a moment and Babs patted his cheek. He turned on his heel and stomped away, muttering how we'd be the death of him.

"Poor lad," I said. "It's sweet that he wants to look after us."

"Da," said Babs. "Imagine how foolish he will be feeling when he realises *we* are what others need protecting from." I gave her a sidelong glance but made no comment. I didn't need to; Babs was like the proverbial dog with a bone. "You were quite the terrier in there," she said. "I assume you hed plan for if our friend became violent."

"Of course!" I declared, injecting as much righteous indignation into my tone as I could muster and fooling absolutely no one, least of all myself. I had no idea what would have happened had the Foreman not shown up. The truth was, the memory of my anger scared me. The red-hot rage still tingled in my fingertips, but I couldn't think of that now. I changed the subject. "He'd be rubbish at poker," I said.

"Mmm," agreed Babs. "He was not happy to be speaking of the baby. You think he is aware he is not father?"

"I do. Which means someone told him because if he hadn't noticed by now, he was never going to notice." I tugged her elbow. "Come on."

"Where are we going?"

"To see the person who told him, so we can find out how much trouble Sophie's in."

I opened the door and batted away the dream catchers. Little Miss Magick hadn't bothered with the fake smile when we came in and when she saw it was us, her resting frown pitched into a scowl. Her expression was more like a dog licking a pissy thistle than ever. Speaking of dogs, I heard a faint snuffle behind me and turned to see Babs sniffing the air like a bloodhound.

"Why does it smell like dairy in here?" she asked. I could hazard a guess and if I did, I'd guess there would be a pot of natural yoghurt in the little staffroom at the back of the shop. Very good for neutralising certain burning sensations, is yoghurt – gives instant, if temporary, relief. I could feel Babs smirking without even looking at her. A wicked little thought shimmied across my mind, so I plastered my face with sympathy and spoke to Miss Magick.

"Touch of trouble down there, is it love?" I asked. I could have cooked dinner on her face.

"*That* is none of your business!" she sputtered. "What do want, anyway?"

"Oh, not much," I replied. I picked up a pebble of rose quartz from the display on her counter and turned it over between my fingers. "This is meant to be useful for – ahem – feminine issues, you know," I said, conversationally. "'Course, I never held with that myself. I think you're very wise to go down the practical route…" She was so outraged she couldn't speak. She stood there, flapping her lips like a landed fish. I grinned wickedly. "Assuming your little bit of trouble is of a natural – as opposed to supernatural – nature." I raised my eyebrows in question and a bit of the colour left her face.

"What do you mean?" she asked.

"Hmm? Oh, nothing really. Only I've heard there are

times when a guilty conscience can cause adverse effects—" I smiled sweetly "—not that that should bother you. I'm sure you've nothing to feel guilty about." She swallowed but shook her hair back in defiance.

"Of course, I haven't."

"Just as I thought. Although, I have heard it's possible to curse someone into discomfort," I said and she shifted a little.

"Oh?"

"Yeah," I said. I bounced the quartz in my palm a few times then placed it back with the other stones in the display. "But you'd have to be really good at curses to pull that off. You'd have to really know your stuff. You'd have to know things like..." I pointed to various other stones "... smokey quartz causes nausea and vertigo in an enemy, shark's teeth cause insatiable hunger, usually leading to weight gain, fun one, that, and then there's this one..." I picked up a polished orange stone and held it up to the light. "Carnelian. You'd have to be *really* good at curses to know about carnelian. Used positively, it's said to restore vitality and stimulate creativity, but used in cursing, it can inflict pain." I moved my face closer to her. "Burning, searing pain," I added. She was sweating now. Her top lip was glistening.

"How do you...?"

"Know all this?" I asked. I returned the stone to the display. "You didn't think you were the only 'practitioner' in these parts, did you?" The girl actually blanched.

"You're... witches?" What the hell, I hated the word, but it served its purpose. I nodded. So did Babs.

"Da, darling. But some of us don't need to announce

it with fripperies," she said, waving her hand disdainfully around the shop.

"But anyway," I continued, "don't you trouble yourself with us. I'm sure your affliction can be sorted with a bit of dairy... it is getting better, isn't it? Positive effects of the yoghurt not wearing off?" The girl squirmed uncomfortably. Babs snorted behind me and I stepped back onto her foot to stop her from laughing.

"What do you want?" Miss Magick repeated. Her voice was barely a whisper now.

"What did you tell Sophie's fella, yesterday?" I demanded, my voice granite. The girl took a step backwards.

"N-nothing," she stammered.

"Liar, liar, pants on fire," murmured Babs.

"I've heard that curses, left untreated, only get worse." I addressed Babs now. "Can you imagine how awful it must be, living with constant burning and itching, with no possibility of relief?"

Miss Magick whispered and I leaned close to the girl again. There was a collection of lava lamps on the floor and I managed to catch the switch of one with my foot so my face was suddenly bathed in flickering 'firelight'.

"Try again," I said. She took a breath and then confessed.

"I told him the baby wasn't his. He came round last night... but just kept on and on about her, so I told him," she said.

"I see. And how did he take it?"

"He left. He just went really pale and left. But I saw him this morning. He said he'd spoken with her and she'd gone to spend some time with her mum while they sort things out."

"Ha!" I said. Gone to stay with her mum indeed!

"Look, I've done her a favour in the long run—"

"Finally, something we can agree on."

"He'd have figured it out himself, soon enough. Any fool could see it."

"Any fool could but not every fool did," I said. I spoke quietly so she had to strain to hear me. "You've brought trouble where you had no cause to, girl, and if anything happens to her or the baby as a result, you'll have more than itchy unmentionables to worry about, I promise you that."

She took a step back and looked around anxiously, then in a feeble facsimile of her usual bluster, she threw back her shoulders and tossed her head.

"What are you talking about, 'anything happens'? She's gone to her mum's for a few days, that's all!"

"Her mum's dead," I said. "Has been for years, so that's at least one lie he's told you. I wonder what others he's told?" I let that statement hang and by her dumbstruck look, I knew it had hit home. "Come on, Babs, we're done here." I gave her one last look of contempt and turned on my heel. I'd almost reached the door when she spoke.

"She doesn't deserve him, you know," Pissy Dog Face's voice rang out. I barely graced her with a glance.

"You can say that again," I said. And then, because I'm basically a good person, I faced her full-on and sighed.

"Bicarbonate of soda," I said. "Otherwise known as baking soda. Mix it with water to form a paste and apply to the… ahem…" I dipped my eyes briefly to crotch level "…afflicted area. Leave it to dry and then rinse it off. That should stop the burning… And next time someone gives you fancy knickers, run them through the wash before you put them on."

Pissy Dog Face flushed crimson again.

"How did you…?" she began, but I'd already battled my way through the dream catchers and out of the door.

I stormed across the Arcade, stomping so hard I nearly cracked the pavement. Babs caught up with me at the door of the cafe. She blew air through her teeth.

"Well, that was… interesting."

"Stupid girl," I stormed. "Now she *does* deserve him."

"You do not mean that," said Babs and I sighed.

"Maybe not, but we're no closer to finding Sophie and now we *know* there's something amiss," I said, but Babs was looking elsewhere. She spun around to stand in front of me, blocking my view of Sophie's shop.

"Agnes," she said, "I think we hev found Sophie." She jerked her head backwards and rolled her eyes up. I took the hint and looked towards the second storey of the shop. There, with her hand pressed against the window, was Sophie.

Chapter Twenty-Four

Sophie looked so much like she did in my vision that I yelped. She was even shouting silently behind the glass, just as I'd seen her. I took a step forward, ready to wave my hands and acknowledge her, for whatever comfort that would bring, but Babs touched my arm and shook her head. She nodded briefly at the shop below the flat where the Vegan watched us from the counter. I stayed my hands and bustled into the cafe.

I craned my neck behind the curtains to see if I could spot Sophie but the flat wasn't visible from here and I let out a *Gah!* of frustration which alarmed the tea drinkers at the window seat. Babs glided behind the counter and relieved the poor workman we'd left there, who was struggling with the coffee machine. She sent him off with a smile and a flapjack whilst I seethed.

"Now what?" I demanded.

"We continue as normal," said Babs, smiling at a customer.

"How can you say that?" I hissed. "You saw her."

"I can say that because he is watching and we do not know how he will react if he knows we saw Sophie. Right now, he is coiled cobra. We do not want to provoke him – it may not be us he bites." Her smile never wavered but her eyes were deathly serious. I nodded and forced my own face into a more amenable expression.

"What can we do? I'll bet the cafe he's taken her phone. We can't make a move outside without him seeing us."

"Then go to somewhere he can't see you," she said, nodding graciously at another customer as she gave him his change. I looked blankly at her and she sighed. "You are also heving flat, no?"

The flat. I'd almost forgotten about that. I only used it for storage but it was directly opposite Sophie's window and if I couldn't see her from down here, then *he* wouldn't be able to see me when I was up there. I rushed towards the back of the cafe.

"*Walk*, don't run," said Babs through her fixed grin. I slowed my pace and walked with deliberation until I reached the kitchen, out of sight of the street, and then I pounded up the stairs, two at a time.

By the time I got to the top, I remembered the other reason why taking things slowly was a good idea and stopped to catch my breath before opening the door to the living room.

There wasn't much to the flat – lounge, bedroom, kitchen, bathroom, all sporting a faint patina of dust. I didn't get up here that often, as shown by the furniture that was the same rag-tag collection of mismatched chairs and patterns that would make the 1960s blush as was in the place when I bought it. I'd added a few boxes over time – tins and cartons that would be underfoot in the cafe kitchen but that was of no concern now. I wasn't here to admire the decor; I was here for Sophie. I went to the window and plugged in the old standard lamp that stood next to it. I flicked the lamp on and off several times to get her attention. Sure enough, I caught her eye and her face sagged with relief. She breathed on the glass and wrote in the condensation

DEPPART

ENOHP ON

I sighed. Good job she was dealing with someone who had read enough things she wasn't supposed to over the years to be able to read back-to-front, upside-down and even inside-out if need be. I nodded to show I'd understood, then hoofed up my own window.

GRACE WITH YOU? I took care to write from right to left so she didn't have to translate. She nodded.

GOT FOOD?

She glanced away and hesitated before nodding.

DRINK?

Another pause before she nodded. That didn't bode well. I bit my lip then wrote again.

LEAVE IT WITH ME.

Another nod. I gave her what I hoped was a reassuring smile and returned to Babs.

"He's got her trapped with no phone to call for help," I reported. "She's alright, for now anyway, but we've got to get her out of there."

"Agreed," said Babs. "And without informing anyone else." I understood what she meant. Involving anyone else would probably also involve the police, but truth be told, if keeping Sophie safe meant an uncomfortable conversation with the authorities, I'd suffer the latter to secure the former any day. I told Babs as much and she nodded along.

"Agreed, but I believe we can solve it without such intervention – Ah!" She held up her hand to stop my interruption. "If we fail, we call police, da?"

I bit my lip, then nodded.

"But we will not fail," she continued, "because I am heving plan."

"Oh?" I said.

"Da, and it is, how you say, humdinger."

Normally, I would have left it there. I could tell she wanted to milk it a bit and there's nothing more enjoyable than leaving someone hanging when they're fishing like that, but I didn't have time for that right now. "Well, let's have it then," I said. "Ideally before I grow another grey hair."

Babs' eyes twinkled with mischief. "We are just needing Vegan out of way, da?"

"Da – yes, but how can we make sure…"

"We send him on feral duck hunt."

"Feral duck…?"

"Da." She pulled out her phone and waved it at me. "I just need to practise."

She explained her plan and I took over at the counter while she sat on the stairs and played the recording from the day before over and over. Every so often, I heard her repeat a word or phrase. Finally, she joined me and gave me a single nod to indicate she was ready. We waited until there was a lull in the cafe before Babs picked up the phone. There was a clear line of vision from Sophie's shop to our cafe, so Babs went out of sight of the window. I stayed put, where I could keep one eye on Babs and the other on the Vegan. She dialled the number of Sophie's shop and I watched him answer the call. I knew she'd been rehearsing but it still made me jump to hear the Silver Fox in my kitchen.

"We need to meet." His deep voice resonated from Babs' mouth. She switched on the speaker so I could hear the Vegan's response.

"Tough, I'm working on something here." His tone was as arrogant as ever and even from this distance, my fingers itched to slap some manners into him.

"That can wait," the Fox's voice came. "I've had some alarming reports we need to discuss."

"What kind of reports? No one knows anything… unless… I bet it's that old bitch from the cafe, isn't it? Her and that deranged sister of hers." The Vegan's head shot up and I felt the malice in his look even from this distance. I promptly busied myself with cleaning so he wouldn't think I was looking. "They've been sticking their beaks into everyone's business lately. Had the greengrocer and the other woman round all the time. Well, I know how to deal with—"

"ENOUGH!" Babs' shout made even me jump. "I'm not going to discuss it now. I want to meet, tonight, at…" She looked at me and I quickly wrote down the name of a motorway service station. She repeated it to the Vegan and I heard him baulk.

"That's over an hour away!"

"Of course it is," snapped Babs. "Do you think I want to be seen with you? This is my business reputation on the line, Boy. I'm beginning to wonder if this venture is worth the trouble."

The Vegan shifted uncomfortably. "But your plans... The investors..."

"All I know is I've paid you a lot of money to shack up with some shopgirl. I'm haemorrhaging cash here while you're playing happy families."

"It's not happy families we're playing," he muttered. "Sh—"

"I'm not interested in your personal life." Babs cut him off and across the way, the Vegan squared his shoulders and sniffed.

"Yeah," he sneered, "so I remember." At that moment, I caught a little glimmer of the past – a small boy holding a drawing up to an indifferent man. The years flashed forward like a flip book animation; the child grew and the object changed but the man's indifference remained the same. The glimmer faded. That explained a lot. I might almost have felt sorry for him if he wasn't such a prick. I might have given this more thought but my musings were interrupted by a gaggle of customers heading towards our door. I shot Babs a panicked look. If the Vegan heard them, it would give the game away. I made a wild 'wrap-it-up' gesture and Babs nodded.

"Look, just be there. Nine pm," she said. The customers were getting closer. "And don't call me back. I'm in meetings the rest of the day," Babs added, picking up speed.

"Fine," huffed the Vegan. One of the customers had their hand on the doorknob and Babs was gabbling now.

"Fine, see you then. Ok. Love you. Bye," she said

and ended the call exhaling with relief. The door jangled open, the customers poured in and across the Arcade, the Vegan stared at the phone, looking perplexed. Finally, he shrugged, put the phone down and headed into the stock room. I smiled at the customers to let them know I'd seen them then rounded on Babs.

"'Ok. Love you. Bye'?"

She held out her hands in helplessness. "I was panicking."

I rolled my eyes at her. "You handle the customers. I'll let Sophie know," I said and climbed the stairs – at a regular pace this time – to the flat. She was already at her window and I hoofed my own up.

"8 PM. BE READY," I wrote. She nodded, then turned sharply, as though hearing something. I quickly rubbed out my words and flicked the light off so there was no trace I was there. I peered at her window from behind the dusty curtains. *He* had entered the room. He stood, jaw jutting, skin mottled, his face mere millimetres from hers. Sophie was crying, Baby Grace clutched close to her chest while he screamed at her. I saw her mouth move and he raised his hand. I grasped the windowsill to steady myself. I felt clammy. Fire stirred in my belly and tingled down my arms. Sophie flinched, covering the baby with her body. The Vegan dropped his hand. I saw his lip curl and he left the room. Sophie dropped to her knees and I did the same. I rested my head against the windowpane. The condensation cooled my raging forehead and I listened to the thudding of my pulse. The sooner we got Sophie out of there, the better.

Chapter Twenty-Five

We waited in the gloaming, Babs and I. We'd closed at the usual time and made a great show of leaving for home, then waited in the alley behind the Arcade. We sat on a couple of Burt's upturned crates in the ley of the wheelie bins. Babs delved into her trusty bag and pulled out her usual bottle. I scowled at her.

"Is that really appropriate?" I snapped. She raised her eyebrows slightly.

"But of course," she said mildly. "We hev long wait and little but the cold for company. I think it most appropriate." She took a swig, smacked her lips appreciatively then offered me the bottle. I hesitated for a moment – she wasn't wrong about the cold. Babs rattled the bottle at me and I gave in. I took it off her, wiped the rim on my sleeve and took a shot. She had finished the slivovica and moved on to becherovka. The warm liquid glided down my throat and nestled in an amber pool in my stomach. I sighed, relishing the slight aniseed aftertaste that lingered, and passed the bottle back to Babs. We sat in silence for a moment before Babs rifled through the bag again. This time, she pulled out a foil carton.

"Belish?" she said, offering me a slice of filled flatbread.

"Do you just take a picnic with you everywhere you go?" Babs bit into her belish and chewed thoughtfully.

"Da," she said, finally. "I find it is for the best. That way, you face whatever comes to pass with full belly." She rattled the box in front of me as she had done the bottle. The potato and cheese filling wafted over and my mouth watered. They were still warm. My resolve crumbled before the box had finished shaking. Besides, there was logic in her words and I didn't want to risk feeling faint with hunger when I rescued Sophie. The bread outer was buttery and had an almost pastry-like crispness that gave way to the soft, comforting filling and I tried not to moan as I chewed.

Neither of us spoke for a while. The seconds played at being hours. I finished my belish and dabbed at the crumbs with a moist finger. Babs offered the bottle again and I took another drink. Finally, she broke the silence.

"You think he has hit her before?" she asked. We hadn't discussed what I'd seen earlier yet. I think Babs knew I'd been too shaken to give a coherent response. I shrugged.

"No idea," I replied, "but that's neither here nor there, really, is it? You and I both know that the emotional batterings can be every bit as dangerous as anything physical."

Babs blew air through her teeth. "Oh, you can say that again. I was asking only to get a feel for damage control."

I gave another shrug. "I think we'd know if he'd been violent but…" I trailed off and Babs delicately let the sentence drop, no doubt guessing I was berating myself for not spotting his other controlling habits earlier. Perhaps if she'd known she had a friendly ear, a safe place to turn, we wouldn't be in this predicament now. If I'd paid more attention, if I'd not been so caught up in my own issues... who knows, maybe he'd have been ousted before he did any damage, maybe Misty would still be alive. But if wishes were horses, beggars could ride. I rubbed a stiff spot on the back of my neck and rolled my shoulders.

"I don't know if he's raised his hand to her before," I said. Sophie's petrified expression filled my mind and I gritted my teeth. "But I promise he'll not do it again," I added. Babs nodded approvingly.

"I will drink to that," she said and took a swig of becherovka and I elbowed her gently in the ribs.

"You'll drink to anything," I said.

"Da, I'll drink to that," she said and took yet another drink before passing the bottle to me and we huddled together to keep out the cold.

I'd almost dozed off when the Vegan finally put in an appearance. He looked around shiftily before getting into his shiny German car. I'd wondered who owned that one, now I knew – no doubt funded by Daddy. I nudged Babs and she snorted awake.

"Look," I said, pointing at His Nibs.

"Nice car," commented Babs. "It would be shame if someone put wrong fuel in it." She narrowed her eyes and made a little gesture with her hand. She grinned wickedly and I realised she'd just planted mischief in the Vegan's mind and bought us some more time. It wouldn't even occur to him he was using the wrong pump until it was too late. I could have hugged her, but instead I yanked her further behind the bins so she didn't get caught in his headlights as he peeled out of the car park.

"Ready?" she asked.

"Ready," I said and we let ourselves into the Arcade. Mindful that Little Miss Magick might be watching, we skulked in the shadows to the door of Sophie's shop. We stared at the lock for a moment.

"Well?" I asked. "Do you want to do the honours or shall I?"

"Be my guest, darling." Babs motioned me toward the door and I reached into my bag for the lockpicking kit... What? Listen, you live as long as I do and you come to realise certain skills, though dubious in nature, are useful to have in your arsenal. Yes, theoretically you can pick a lock with a bent screwdriver and a paperclip, but why make life difficult? I knelt by the locks and twiddled with my instruments. It took me a few goes to find the sweet spot, thanks to the after-effects of the becherovka, but it wasn't long until I felt the tell-tale give in the lock and the door swung open.

Babs helped me up with a theatrical grunt that was entirely uncalled for and we crept into the building, behind the counter to the back of the shop and up the stairs. There was another locked door between us and Sophie's home but that was soon dispatched. It swung open with a creak and I stepped quietly into the hallway.

"Sophie?" My voice was a hoarse whisper. "Soph, love, where are you?" Then Babs slammed the door behind me and I nearly jumped out of my skin. She grazed her hand over the wall until she found the light switch and we blinked in the sudden glare.

"For heaven's sake," she said. "Vegan is out, there is no need for cloaks and daggers. SOPHIE!" Her voice bounced down the corridor.

"Oh, yeah," I said, sheepishly. I probably shouldn't drink before rescue missions, I get carried away with myself. I didn't have time to feel too embarrassed though as Sophie's voice rang out.

"Hello? Babs, is that you? Is Aggie there?"

I almost staggered with relief. "Yes, Love, it's us. We've come to get you."

"Oh, thank God." I heard the tears seeping through her voice. "I'm in the baby's room." She didn't need to tell us. We'd already followed the sound of her voice through the open-plan kitchen and lounge to a door with a dining chair lodged under the handle. At least we didn't have to deal with any high-tech security. We moved the 'lock', opened the door and Sophie tumbled into my arms.

The reek of stale urine hit me and with a jolt, I realised it came from Sophie. I held her at arm's length to get a proper look at the scene. The baby was fine – that was a blessing, at least. She lay swaddled in a little nest of blankets on a pull-out bed. Clearly, Sophie didn't feel comfortable leaving her in the Moses basket. Sophie herself was not faring as well. Her eyes were rimmed with red and her complexion, never glowing with health, looked even more sunken. I traced the stench to the dark, damp patches on her jeans. She caught me looking at them and buried her face back into my chest.

"He didn't even let you use the toilet?" I asked, my voice low. Sophie shook her head. I could feel the heat from her cheeks through my top. Her whole body trembled like the wings of a hummingbird. "I see," I replied carefully. "And what about food and drink – you're nursing, after all." She waved over at the window ledge. The water bottle she normally carried with her was there – empty, by the look of it – and some sweet wrappers and then there was the food he'd left – the curled-up edges of the sandwich revealed a meat filling and next to it, a pint of cow's milk, which was sure to be on the turn by now even if she did drink the stuff. It was a calculated insult and a fresh layer of malice on an already unforgivable situation. I drew air sharply between my teeth and swore. Babs placed a soothing hand on my shoulder but her eyes were glittering as dark and dangerous as my soul. I took the hint though and calmed myself before responding. *He* wasn't the priority here. I placed my hand under Sophie's chin and gently tilted her head upwards.

"Don't you worry, my love, Babs here will go and get you a glass of water while I get you a change of clothes and you gather little Grace's belongings. You'll be staying with us for a spell until we sort things out." I kept my voice soft and low. I had thought she might protest at the thought of leaving her home and shop, but by now she was so worn down, I think she'd have come had I said we were taking her to a shack in a swamp. She simply nodded, her head bowed. Babs had already wandered off to the kitchen for the water. She returned moments later with the glass and a pair of jogging bottoms.

"I found these on radiator," she said quietly. Sophie was still staring at the floor. She hadn't moved since she'd pointed at the sandwich. I tried to get her to speak to me but she wouldn't lift her head.

"Soph? Sophie, Love?" I pressed the glass into her hand but still, she didn't move. She stood, knock-kneed and trembling, like a whipped foal. Babs raised one eyebrow at me and I shook my head. I took the water again and lifted the glass to her lips.

"Come on, Love, you've got to drink. You need to keep your strength up for feeding Grace." At her daughter's name, she opened her mouth and sipped, gently at first but then she took the glass and drank deeply. The instant she had finished, Babs was ready with one of her apple-filled toffees.

"Don't worry, is vegan," she said and we watched it work its magic on Sophie. The sugar brought colour to her cheeks and when the liquid apple centre burst to life in her mouth, she looked up and blinked. Babs nipped back to the kitchen to refill the glass and Sophie swiftly downed that too and wiped her mouth on her sleeve.

"You've got to go," she said. "Thank you, but I don't want you to get into trouble with him. I don't even know where he is. He could be back any moment."

"I think not," said Babs. "I think he will hev missed appointment and then he will be heving car trouble." She grinned at me and I remembered her comment about the wrong fuel. She was good. It would take a good few hours and a fair wad of cash to put it right. He'd be lucky to be back before dawn. Sophie looked puzzled and I patted her arm.

"Don't fret about it, Love. Just trust us. We've time so let's pack and get you two out of here, yes?" She glanced at Grace, then at the milk and the ham sandwich he'd left and nodded. "Good girl. You get the baby sorted and I'll pack you some clothes. Babs will get your toothbrush and whatnot. Now, which way to the bedroom?" Sophie pointed me in the right direction. I grabbed a pillowcase to put her stuff in and Babs and I peeled off to take care of our tasks.

Finding her clothes in the bedroom wasn't hard. I just had to look for the tatty stuff: threadbare t shirts and jeans with holes that had nothing to do with fashion. There was nothing new, in stark contrast to *his* clothes, some of which still bore designer tags. In fact, there was hardly a trace of her in the bedroom at all – a small, wooden box with a mandala carved on it, a framed picture of her dad… I took these and placed them carefully into the pillowcase before I looked around the rest of the room. Everything else in there reeked of him. It had a shiny, superficial look as though tainted by association. Cheap and nasty, just like him. It was as though he was slowly eroding her very existence, replacing her life with his, treating himself to anything and everything plastic could buy while she muddled through with what she already had.

I'd have asked her about it but I already suspected the answer. He'd taken her card to 'take the load off her', no doubt telling her if she needed something, he'd get it for her. The reality would be she'd have to ask for her own money and justify every expense whilst he bought knickers for his mistress with his girlfriend's cash. I perished to think what her bank account looked like. I shivered, then shook my head. One more thing to sort out. I stuffed her clothes in the sack and padded out of the bedroom.

The kitchen and lounge weren't much better. I couldn't believe the TV that took up half the wall was Sophie's choice, or that she got much use from the golf clubs in the corner and I knew she didn't drink coffee, so the shiny coffee machine wouldn't be hers either. There wasn't so much as a pacifier or baby's bootie to show she and Grace lived there – everything of the baby's was confined to her room.

A dark thought unfurled like smoke from the recesses of my mind; how easy it would be to make someone disappear by inches, chipping away at them, day by day, until they may as well not exist at all... I clenched my jaw and the thought dug deeper. We were getting her out in the nick of time, that was for certain, but it didn't feel *enough*. Part of me wanted him to suffer, wanted to dole out punishment while I was here.

I scanned the kitchen for something, anything to make his life that bit more unpleasant. I didn't have time for anything serious but my sense of justice demanded something, no matter how small. My eyes landed on a used teaspoon in the sink and before I had time to properly think about it, I was at the cutlery drawer. I pulled it open, took out a spoon and licked it. There. He might never know, but I would and I felt a warm glimmer of happiness about that. I'd lick each and every piece so he couldn't avoid me. I was about to return it and pick another piece when Babs' voice made me jump.

"Agnes, I am surprised at you!" My cheeks flamed and I stared at my feet as the full pettiness of the situation hit me. How could I defend myself? I was meant to be a grown woman.

"I just wanted to... I don't know, I just wanted to feel like I'd made him pay..." I mumbled. Babs tutted.

"Not that! I mean I am surprised you are merely licking. Surely *this* would be better..." She took the spoon from my hand, reached behind her and pulled at the elasticated waist of her trousers. I could only watch, jaw dangling open as she rubbed the spoon between the cheeks of her backside before returning it to the drawer. She looked at me then, an open challenge glittering in her eyes. I bit my lip in a futile effort to stem my smile but I could feel the mischief bubbling inside me. I snatched another spoon and tugged at my own waistband. Babs nodded her encouragement and in one swift motion, I felt cold steel between my cheeks.

Laughter sneezed through my nose in bullet blasts and Babs' shoulders shook. We each raided the drawer again and again – I confess, I went carefully with the knives and forks but by the time we'd reached the last knife, we were both red-faced and gasping with mirth. It was at that moment Sophie came out of Grace's room, her arms full and the baby strapped to her chest. She took one look at us and dropped the bags.

"What on Earth...?" But I missed the rest of her sentence. I was laughing too hard. My ribs and jaw ached and I could hardly draw breath. Sophie put her hands on her hips. She looked better for a change of clothes and a drink.

"Are you two drunk?" she demanded.

"Of course we are," I gasped between laughs, "you don't think we'd do this sober, do you?" Sophie stared from each of us to the other then held out her hand.

"Give me the knife," she said, hoarsely. I looked at the knife in my hand, shrugged and handed it to her. She stared at it for a moment, then reached behind her, pulled the waistband of her joggers and deftly swiped it. "There," she said, nodding with satisfaction. She passed it back to me, handle first, and I dropped it into the drawer with a clatter. Babs crowed with laughter behind me and I grinned at Sophie.

"Good girl. You ready to go?"

She lifted her chin and looked at me. "Yes," she said. "Yes, I am."

Chapter Twenty-Six

House was pacing the garden when we arrived home. I swear it lifted one leg to stare at an imaginary watch. Babs headed straight over and stroked its shingles.

"There, there, Mielasis, were you worried?" It shuffled around and turned its back on us, but Babs followed its circuit and rubbed her face against the rough walls. "I am sorry, my darling one, I did not mean to scare you. We hed important business but I am home now and look, Mielasis, we hev visitors."

She threw her arm wide to show Sophie and Grace and House's whole demeanour changed in an instant. It rushed over to Sophie, who cringed against the garden fence, cradling the baby, her eyes squeezed shut. House eased back a bit and precariously plucked the last, forlorn rose from my mangled bush. Ah, well, easy come, easy go.

As though sensing House had stepped back, Sophie opened first one eye, then the other and slowly, carefully and oh-so-gently, House offered her the rose.

"Erm… thank you?" she said, looking from me to Babs for reassurance before taking it. House bobbed a strange kind of curtsey and stepped back.

"Oh, House likes you," said Babs, clapping her hands. She patted House again. "My darling one, you are so thoughtful," she gushed.

"Yeah, with other people's flowers," I muttered. Sophie just stared.

"So, I didn't imagine it," she said to Babs. "Your house really has legs?"

"Da," said Babs. "House is very special." She peered closely at Sophie, who was rubbing her arms. "But that is tale for another evening. We are needing to get you indoors and heving hot meal." I nodded my agreement and shepherded her inside my front door.

Babs was in the kitchen before we could blink, mixing chickpeas and tomatoes with goodness knows what. For my part, I brewed a pot of chamomile tea and added a hearty dollop of agave nectar. While she sipped it, I ran her a bath, adding a muslin pouch of dried plantain and lavender to the water to soothe her mind. The hardest part was convincing her to let go of the baby for long enough to enjoy the water. Finally, she agreed to me sitting outside the open bathroom door with the baby in my arms, so she could get to Grace if she needed her. She needn't have troubled herself; the little mite had barely stirred since we left the flat, but I knew her caution had nothing to do with me. So, I sat. I rocked her gently and breathed in the soft, sweet cheese scent of her head.

By the time Sophie was clean, Babs had finished cooking. I led her downstairs to the kitchen table. It's remarkable what good food and a hot bath can do for the soul. Sophie looked better than she had in ages. Her lips had colour and the dark rings beneath her eyes seemed to have faded. She looked almost well enough to hear what I had to say next.

It wasn't fair, I know it wasn't, but there was still so much Sophie didn't know about the past, about my part in her parents' story. I wondered if I should wait for a better time, but I doubted there would ever be a good time to discuss it and if she was going to be staying with me, she should know it all. I did wait until she started nursing Grace, so I knew she'd have to hear me out. She settled the baby to feed and Babs nodded at me and discreetly went upstairs to get the spare room ready for them. I cleared my throat and began. I told her everything and she sat very still and listened.

"So, there you have it," I said, finally. I stared at my hands, clasped together in a penitent's grip. Sophie said nothing for a minute. She finished feeding Grace and rested the baby against her shoulder, patting her back gently. Finally, she spoke.

"You weren't responsible," she said. "You didn't stop him from protecting himself."

I smiled softly but shook my head. "I don't think you understand, Love, and why would you? This is the first you've heard of it, but a binding – a good binding – would have stopped him from so much as shoving her hand away. And I was *very* good at binding. I'm sorry, Love, but I may as well have struck the fatal blow for your mum."

Sophie shook her head now. "Did you never ask anyone what happened? A neighbour? My gran? Did you never read about it in the paper?"

"No. I hadn't the heart."

"Perhaps you should have. It might have spared you

years of guilt." I frowned at her and she bit her lip. "She's dead now, you know?" I nodded. I'd felt the twinge in my breast when she went, as I had with all of them. Sophie took a breath. "She contacted me a few years ago. She knew she was dying. She said she wanted to make amends while she still could." Sophie spoke as though the words left a bad taste in her mouth. "Gran would never talk about what happened so I decided to visit her in the prison." She closed her eyes and buried her face into Grace's warm body.

"Sophie, Love, you don't have to… if it's too hard, you don't have to say any more."

Sophie opened her eyes and sat up straighter.

"No. Enough people have been hurt by this. I want you to know. I visited her in prison and she told me what happened. She wasn't attacking dad that night, she was attacking me." My stomach lurched at her words and a trickle of ice threaded through my veins. "She lunged at me and dad stopped her the only way he knew how. He covered me with his body. She couldn't get the blade back out of his back and she couldn't move him off me."

I closed my eyes. Maybe it was the witch blood in her but, as she spoke, I saw them in the room. I felt the flecks of spit from her mother's crease-faced screams, heard the raw-throated wails of the baby, trapped beneath her father, smelt the iron in the air, so thick it coated my tongue… I took a shaky breath and opened my eyes. Sophie shifted Grace to the crook of her arm and continued with her story.

"Apparently, a neighbour heard the commotion – some busybody who'd always had it in for her, *she* said.

They called the police. She tried to claim self-defence, but one look at the scene told them she was lying. And then, when they -" she stopped and swallowed. I passed her the tissue box and she carried on. "When they did the post-mortem, they discovered so many defensive wounds... *She* laughed when she told me that part." Sophie shook her head. "She wasn't interested in making amends. I think she just wanted one last victory... to let me know I'd never been loved."

I clenched my teeth at that and reached over to cover her hand with mine. "You know that's not true, Love. Your dad loved you, and your gran... and I've always been there, lurking... granted, that doesn't sound as wholesome as I intended, but you know what I mean."

She smiled softly. "Thank you."

The silence that fell then was a comfortable one. For my part, I was thinking of Sophie's mum and her final act of spite. She must have gone to her grave happy, knowing the poison she'd poured in her daughter's ear would fester and spread long after she was gone. No wonder the girl had been so quick to fall for the Vegan's lies – the promise of love would have been as hard for her to resist as a hot meal to a starving man.

"He'll come for me, won't he?" Sophie's voice made me jump but I recovered enough to answer her.

"Yes," I said, "and you'll have to speak to him. But not tonight. Tonight, you rest and let Babs and me handle things, yes?"

The tentative smile flickered on her lips again and she nodded. Moments later, warm, dry and full of food, her head started to nod, so I gently led her up to the spare room where Babs had constructed a nest of sorts for baby Grace to sleep safely next to her mother. She didn't so much as stir when Sophie placed her in it. I left them to it, closing the door softly behind me and went to join Babs on House's roof.

"So, you are off hook?" She cut another slice off her rope of tobacco and tamped it into her pipe. The wind had dropped now and the night was fine and clear. I pulled the blanket on my knees further up and cupped my hands around the mug of warming brew Babs had given me. I considered her question.

"I'm not responsible for his death," I said, slowly grappling with my thoughts, "but I'm not blameless. It could easily have been my fault and I have to keep that in mind."

Babs looked at me severely.

"Am I heving to strike you again? You were misled by bad person. Is Sophie to blame for Vegan's behaviour? Nyet. Are you to blame for her mother's behaviour? Nyet. You are not responsible for the suffering of Sophie's father." She finished filling the pipe bowl and took out a box of matches. "You are responsible for *your* behaviour afterwards. By letting this wound fester, you hev allowed infection to spread around you. *That* is what you need to forgive yourself for." She rasped the match against the box and it hissed into life. I watched her suck and puff on the pipe until she had a decent draw and I let her words sit in my mind. There was no rebuke in her voice, no reproach of any kind, just a simple statement of fact. I thought about the events of all those years ago, the dark secret I kept to myself which, now I'd dragged it out into the light, was more of a grubby, off-white secret. Sophie's revelation had robbed it of its weight. The burden felt lighter. What bothered me now was the arrogance with which I had taken the mantle of martyr, assuming blame that was not mine. And how many had suffered as a result? Would the Vegan have got his feet under the table if I'd had my eye on him instead of moping? I bit my lip. Babs patted my arm.

"Enough now," she said, seemingly reading my mind. "No more hair shirts." I took a breath and nodded my agreement. It was time to let that go. Babs smiled and offered me her pipe.

"Good," she said, "because I think we are about to hev company." She pointed at a figure reeling down the road. I squinted at it. It certainly looked like the Vegan.

"SOPHIE!" the figure bellowed and removed all doubt. Babs took back the pipe and stowed it safely, then House lifted us to the ground and we stood together, blocking the door to my house while the Vegan's shouting lit windows up and down the street.

He didn't bother to unlock the gate; he simply booted it open and it swung back and forth a few times on the quivering gatepost.

"SOPHIE!" he yelled again on his march up the path. Thankfully, she had the sense not to respond or turn on the bedroom light, though I know she must have heard him. Ah, well, time to make *my* voice heard.

"Do you mind? This a respectable street." He turned the full force of his gaze on me. The malice in his eyes glittered in the porchlight. It had been a long time since I'd seen hate like that.

"Where is she?" he said.

I shrugged. I didn't see any point in lying. "Upstairs, sleeping. She's had a trying day." He made as if to barge past us but we moved closer together, barring his way. He clenched his jaw and glowered at us in a way that was no doubt intended to be menacing.

"Move," he ordered, through gritted teeth.

"Don't think so," I replied calmly. He balled his hand into a fist, his arm twitching as though struggling to keep it down – a sideways glance at Babs showed her face full of concentration and her lips moving subtly as though in silent prayer, so maybe he was really struggling to lift it up. Either way, his jaw jutted and his eyes bulged. He thrust his face close to mine.

"I said, SHIFT," he roared.

"NO!" I shouted, louder than I expected because I was actually speaking to House, who had crept up behind the Vegan and was now poised on one leg with a stone from my rockery grasped in the raised claw of the other. House dropped the stone with a clatter and the Vegan swung round. House shifted, tilting upwards as though trying to look innocent – I swear it would have whistled nonchalantly if it could. Not that any of it mattered; all the Vegan saw was a gypsy caravan. He turned his attention back to us.

"And what's to stop me shoving you interfering cows out of the way and going up there to get her?" he said. I blew air out of my mouth slowly and squinted as though considering the question.

"Well," I said finally, "there's Mrs Leadberry, for a start." I gestured over the road to where the light in a lounge window flickered as the curtains twitched. "Frightful old busybody, she is," I explained. "Nasty, too. She'd call the police on kiddies for sniffing her flowers, if she could, and I don't doubt she's on the phone to them now. Then there's Mr Jones." I pointed at another house. "He's got to be up at the crack of dawn to get to the dairy. He'll be none too pleased about having his sleep disturbed. And, of course, you know Burt." As though on cue, Burt came out of his home and sauntered across the street, tying his dressing gown.

"Everything alright, Aggie, Love?" he called. I waved and nodded to indicate we were fine, then looked back at the Vegan.

"I should leave if I was you," I said. The Vegan looked around. All over the street, windows glowed like the eyes of Serengeti predators in the darkness. He took a breath and relaxed his jaw.

"I just want to talk to her." His tone was wheedling, almost seductive. "It was just a stupid fight. We belong together. She needs to come home. She needs me." Honestly, where's the sick bucket when you need it? Babs had been muttering away under her breath to make sure his arms stayed firmly by his sides, but now she tutted.

"Needs!" she huffed. "Da, people hev many needs – access to toilet and food they can actually eat," she said. I raised my eyebrows at him and folded my arms.

"She's got a point. Didn't exactly cover yourself in glory earlier, did you?" He opened his mouth to object but I held up my hand. "And before you try and deny it, we saw the state of the room." His lip curled, all pretence at sweetness gone.

"I knew it," he sneered. "Well, while your neighbour is calling the police, she can tell them to arrest you two for breaking into my house and keeping me from my girlfriend."

I tilted my head to one side. "It's not actually your house though, is it? And I'd think long and hard about involving the police in what went on behind those walls today." His gaze dropped to his shoes, though I suspect it was embarrassment at being caught out rather than shame for his actions. "As for the other part, I'll not stop you from speaking to her, but it will be when she's good and ready, and not before. Now go – and don't let the gate hit you on the arse on the way out." He looked up at me again and the fire was banked in his eyes again.

"Aggie?" Burt was on the pavement outside the garden now. The Vegan shot one last venomous look at me and Babs.

"You'll regret this," he said quietly and backed away, still glaring at us… of course, had he actually been walking the right way, he might have noticed House's outstretched leg lying across the path. I suppose I could have warned him but I'd already foiled House's fun once; it seemed churlish to do it a second time. And for the record, it's hard to maintain a menacing glower when you're flailing your arms and stumbling backwards onto the pavement.

The Vegan staggered back to his feet and whirled around looking for what tripped him but by now, he was over the garden boundary and with a discreet nudge of the foot, House closed the gate behind him… And yes, it did hit him on the arse. I bit my lips to stop myself from laughing. Babs had no such qualms and held onto the doorpost while her laughter followed the Vegan onto the street. He dusted himself off and stomped away, kicking a random pebble, sending it skittering down the road ahead of him. One by one, the windows in the street winked into darkness.

I sagged against the other doorpost and let myself smile. Burt joined us under the porchlight.

"What was all that about?" We quickly filled him in and he frowned. "This won't be the end of it," he said, his face creased with worry. "I've met his sort before." He rubbed his chin as though reaching a decision. "I'll be driving you all in and home again from now on," he said and held up his hand. "It's no good arguing. I've made up my mind."

Babs reached up and patted his cheek. "Dear Burt," she purred, "we would not dream of arguing. Of course, you will escort us."

Chapter Twenty-Seven

Burt beeped his horn for us at an ungodly hour in the morning. Well, half seven, but it felt ungodly when I'd been up half the night. The three of us traipsed down the garden path – four if you counted Grace, snuggled in her sling. Burt stood proudly by the rear door of his car and pointed to the back seat.

"What do you make of that, then?" he said. I looked blankly for a moment, my brain still thinking of the warm duvet upstairs. It was Sophie who cottoned on first.

"Burt! You've got a car seat!" she said. Burt blushed happily.

"Yes, well, I didn't think you had one for the little mite – don't think I've ever seen her out of that sling." He reached over and stroked Grace's head. "She's a grand little thing, isn't she?"

Sophie didn't answer. She was squinting at him, bemused. "But how…?" she asked, looking at the seat and Burt shifted uncomfortably.

"Well, after that set-to last night, I couldn't sleep, so I popped over to the all-night megastore on the outskirts…" Sophie stared at him, open-mouthed. To be fair, it was all I could do to keep my own jaw from dropping.

"But Burt, you *hate* the megastore," I said. "In fact, I believe you referred to it as 'the scourge of small businesses everywhere,' and said it would be a cold day in hell before we caught you stepping foot in there."

Burt reddened further.

"Well, needs must. I knew the little one would need a seat and I didn't think you'd want to be asking your fella for the seat back, assuming he's got one in that monstrosity he drives… I picked her up some nappies and onesies and whatnot – they're environmentally friendly, or so it says on the label. I know that's important to you…" He trailed off seeing the tears that now spilled down Sophie's cheeks. "Hey, what's this about?"

Sophie shook her head. "Nothing," she sniffed. "It's just so kind of you. You must let me pay you back." Burt waved her comment away.

"Nonsense, I've been meaning to get a little something for her since she arrived. I'm ashamed it's taken me so long… I should have been looking out for you better." My head shot up at that. Surely Burt didn't think he bore any responsibility for Sophie's situation. Babs elbowed me in the ribs.

"It seems you do not hev monopoly on being martyr." She stepped over and linked her arm through Burt's. "So, tell me of this megastore," she said to him. "Are their plums as big and juicy as yours?"

I thought Burt might burst into flames, he was so red now, but instead, he threw his head back and laughed.

"Do you know what, Babs? They were rubbish – not a patch on mine."

Babs patted his cheek. "This is what I thought," she said, then turned to Sophie and me. "Well? Shall we go?"

Burt parked a good distance from the Vegan's car and scouted around before opening the doors for us. He needn't have bothered. A flock of hi-vis vests descended upon us and escorted us to the cafe. I raised an eyebrow at Burt who had the grace to look sheepish.

"I may have called in reinforcements," he said.

"Alright, Hen?" The Foreman was at the centre of things, helping Sophie to extract Grace from the car seat. "Dinnae worry aboot a thing, you'll no have tae speak to Himself if ye dinnae want tae," he told her. Babs nodded her approval and it was sweet, I grant you, but they clamoured and fussed around Sophie and the baby and I had to shoulder my way through them to get to the shutters. Finally, I raised my voice.

"ENOUGH! Anyone *not* coming in for breakfast can kindly bugger off." No one moved so Babs stepped forward.

"Gentlemen, it is lovely to hev you here but we cannot get to building. You must form orderly queue, that is right, just like that – you can still protect us in organised line." She clucked and cooed them into a semblance of order and I finished opening up. Sophie, Babs and the builders filed in and Burt wandered off to his own shop. A movement across the Arcade caught my eye and I saw him, leaning against the darkened door of Sophie's shop, watching.

We kept Sophie safe behind the counter for most of the day. It was no accident that there was at least one hi-vis jacket on display all morning. The Foreman seemed to have set up camp. I wondered if Sophie realised how many people she had looking out for her. There's only so long you can delay the inevitable for though, and like death and taxes, sure enough, he came.

He startled the doorbell and the door itself quivered in the frame. He must have been biding his time until there were no builders apparent. He strutted over to the counter like he'd been watching too many cowboy films. He treated Babs and me to a dark look. Stubble grazed his chin and his eyes were red-rimmed. I sniffed the air. The tang of stale sweat and alcohol swirled around him.

Babs responded with a concerned tilt of her head. "Oh, you do not look happy. What is matter? Shitty breakfast?" I thought back to the cutlery drawer the night before and sniggered in spite of myself. There was no trace of a smile from Sophie, though. The colour had drained from her face the instant he barged in and now she gripped the countertop as though it was all that kept her upright. The Vegan ignored Babs and me and positioned himself in front of her.

"Soph? Sophie." The Vegan's voice was soft, as intimate as when he'd tried that tone with me the night before. "I just want to talk." Sophie looked at him. She was gripping the counter so hard her knuckles were white, but I could still see her trembling. I shifted my weight, preparing to stand next to her but Babs placed a hand on my elbow and gently shook her head. He was leaning across the counter now. He'd taken one of her hands between his and was caressing it tenderly.

"Babe. I'm sorry that you were scared…" Typical, even his apology wasn't an apology, placing the blame on her, as though he had nothing to do with her fear and debasement. I tutted loudly and his eye twitched. Babs stepped on my toe to shut me up. I knew why; Sophie had to make her own choices... but what if she made the wrong one again? The Vegan carried on stroking her hand.

"I was angry. It's the effect you have on me. I simply couldn't bear the thought of anyone else touching you..." He lifted her hand to his mouth and kissed her knuckles. Sophie stared at him, transfixed. Then he made his mistake. "I'd forgotten how gorgeous you are," he said, nuzzling her hand. "It's been so long since I saw you without that baby strapped to you..." In an instant, the spell was broken. Sophie snatched her hand away. She shot an anxious look at Grace, who was enjoying a post-feed nap in her car seat, then turned back to the Vegan.

"You need to leave," she said.

"Sure, as soon as you tell me when you're coming home."

"No. You need to leave home. *My* home," she said. He stepped back and looked at her incredulously.

"You don't mean that, Babe, I know you don't." He reached for her hand again but Sophie pulled it out of the way and stood with both hands behind her back. Her eyes flicked toward Grace again and as though drawing strength from her, she stood up taller and lifted her chin.

"I *do* mean it. I'll give you until the weekend to move out but I want you gone."

His face hardened and the real him grubbed its way to the surface.

"Oh, that's what you want, is it? You're the one slagging around but you expect *me* to move out – planning to move your other man in, are you? Think you're going to play Happy Families? Think again." His lip curled and he looked her up and down. "He'll toss you to the curb like the piece of used-up trash you are. You and the brat."

"Hey, that's enough!" We'd been so focused on the Vegan, none of us had noticed the Foreman coming out of the toilets. The Vegan flashed him a worried look then rallied himself. He squared up to the Foreman, pigeon-chested and full of swagger.

"I might have known you'd be sniffing around. Can't wait to get your feet under the table, can you?"

The Foreman smiled mildly. "Naw, Pal, I just dinnae like hearing women spoken to like that, ye ken?"

Babs' fingers twitched on my elbow and I knew why. I wouldn't call my worst enemy Pal, the way he said it. *Pal.* That was only three steps away from someone leaving with their teeth in an envelope. The Vegan clearly picked up on the tone as he deflated a little. His eyes flicked around the cafe at the other diners who had stopped eating to watch the show. As for Sophie, I didn't think it was possible for her to look any paler but she did now. I'm surprised the counter didn't have indents where her fingers gripped it.

Time stood like a collective held breath while we waited for the Vegan to respond. You could almost hear the cogs in his brain ticking and then a nasty smile slimed across his face – physical violence was out, but he wasn't done yet.

"Well, you and your boys are quite the heroes, but I wonder what your boss would think of you spending all your time in this dump? Must be hitting his pocket pretty hard. Maybe I'll give him a call."

The Foreman's smile didn't falter.

"Aye, you make a fair point, right enough. Maybe you should give him a call." He reached into his pocket and pulled out a business card. The Vegan stared at it for a moment before taking it.

"If you think I'm bluffing…" he started, pulling out his phone but the Foreman maintained his placid composure.

"I don't think someone like you bluffs aboot anything," he said. "Phone him. I insist." There were creases round the Vegan's eyes now and a wary, uncertain frown. He pressed the keys on his phone and moments later, the Foreman's back pocket trilled. The Vegan's chest lost some of its puff. The Foreman's smile broadened into a beatific grin and he pulled his own phone out with a pantomime tut of frustration.

"So sorry, I just have to take this call," he said apologetically before answering the phone. "Hallo… Is that Twatty McTwatface? I hear you've a complaint tae make aboot me and mah boys…?" The Foreman ended the call and looked the Vegan directly in his scowling face. "It's mah own company, ye patronising wee jobby," he said. "Now, the lady said you'se got till the weekend to get oot the house so I suggest ye concentrate on packing instead of bothering these fine people, ye ken? And I'm sure me and the lads can find plenty tae do around here if your focus starts tae drift, ye get mah meaning?" His tone was conversational, friendly almost, but his meaning was clear. The Vegan held his ground for a few moments and glowered at the Foreman's impassive face, then he snorted, spat on the floor and swaggered out.

The whole cafe let out an explosive breath – a few people clapped their hands tentatively but that soon fizzled out into an embarrassed silence until Babs clapped *her* hands together with a ringing slap.

"Come now, we will not let bad manners spoil our lunch. Not when we hev freshly baked honey cake to enjoy." She bustled through to the kitchen and returned moments later with the promised cake. The warm aromas of honey, ginger and lemon wafted through the cafe and people gradually settled. The sound of clinking cutlery and chatter again filled the air. I took a cloth and the anti-bacterial spray and cleaned up his spit. Sophie leaned against the counter, taking long, deep breaths. She smiled gratefully at the Foreman.

"Thank you," she sighed. The Foreman shrugged.

"Nae bother." He hesitated, then said, "I know his sort. He'll sink a ship just 'cause he cannae be the captain." Sophie said nothing but the Foreman passed her his business card. "If he gives ye any more bother, ye tae call me, right?" Sophie bit her lip and then nodded.

"Thank you…" she peered at the card. "Cameron." There was something about the way she said his name that made me look twice. A warm glow infused her face and I saw them in glorious technicolour in a world of black and white. There was potential there. I shook my head. Best to untangle her from one relationship before entangling her in another.

Chapter Twenty-Eight

Our honour guard appeared again at closing time. They clucked and fretted around us like so many day-glo geese until we were safely ensconced in Burt's car. Not that they needed to worry; Himself was in the flat, silhouetted in the window. The glass glowed in the gloaming, and his form slit the pane like the pupil in the eye of some ancient, malevolent beast… or maybe it was just some nasty git in a window and I'd been reading too many novels. Either way, I shuddered and hustled Sophie into the car in case my imagination was catching.

House was waiting, as usual. It waited until Burt was safely out of sight then opened the gate for us and stood there, shifting from one leg to the other.

"You are excited, Mielasis?" House dipped in response to Babs' question, which I took to mean *yes*. House moved slowly, carefully towards Sophie. Its shingles and boards cracked inwards and I realised House was trying to appear smaller, less intimidating. It balanced on one leg and handed her something wrapped in an old leaf. Sophie looked surprised.

"For me?" she said. House shook and pointed at the car

seat. "For Grace?" *Yes*. She opened the leaf to reveal a small wooden butterfly carved from wood so old it shone. Only someone familiar with House would have recognised the shade and texture of the wood perfectly matched House's own. Only someone used to noticing small details would have seen the missing shingle brick from beneath the fringe of House's roof. Sophie didn't notice but that didn't stop her from being delighted with the gift. She was still cooing about it when she entered my house. I held back for a moment and laid a gentle hand on House.

"Thank you," I said, simply. I nodded at Babs, whose eyes shone with pride and I left her with her second soul whilst I started dinner.

It was a quiet night in the end. We ate and we played with the baby a bit. She had recently discovered her hands and was very seriously trying to stuff both of them into her mouth while the three of us looked on indulgently.

"Does she look like her father?" Babs' question came out of nowhere.

"Babs!" I admonished. "You can't ask that!" I let the silence sit for a moment before turning to Sophie. "But now that she *has* asked… does she?" Sophie flushed a little but recovered quickly enough and shrugged.

"I don't really remember what he looked like." She flushed crimson now. "That's awful, isn't it?" Babs shrugged and I held up my hands to reassure her.

"No judgement here, love. One-night thing, was it?" Sophie looked down, her face now beetroot.

"Yes," she said, then, "No, not really. It was… *He'd* gone out." No need to ask who *he* was. "I knew he was seeing someone else. I'd tried to raise it with him but he told me

I was paranoid and that *I* must have something to hide if I was questioning him. He made me…" She trailed off and I rubbed her shoulder.

"It's alright, Love. You're safe." Sophie took a breath and tried again.

"I felt like I was going mad and then, one night when I was home on my own again and I knew he was with his bit on the side, something flipped and I just thought, *blow that for a game of soldiers, two can play at that.*"

"Da," said Babs. "What is good for duck is sauce for gander." I was about to translate that for Sophie but her smile showed she already understood.

"Something like that," she replied. "Anyway, I put on a skirt and some lipstick and headed across town to the club." She shook her head ruefully. "I knew the second I got there it was a mistake. I mean, how ridiculous must I have looked? All those leggy teens in their sequins and six-inch heels and there's me in my tartan mini-skirt and lippy I'd had since high school."

"'Leggy teens,'" I scoffed. "You talk like you're ancient."

"I felt it," she said. "I stood there, sipping a glass of red wine I didn't want because I thought it would make me look sophisticated when it just made me look even more out of place – everyone else was drinking neon drinks out of bottles with straws. I was about to leave and then I saw him…"

"Eyes met across crowded dance floor, time stood still?" proffered Babs. Sophie chuckled.

"No, nothing like that. I just thought he looked nice. He had a kind smile – I remember thinking he'd look a bit ordinary if it wasn't for that smile. He came over and introduced himself, which I couldn't hear because the music was so loud it made my shoes buzz. We danced for a bit and he kept his hands to himself, unlike the other lads on the dancefloor, and at chucking out time he bought me a bag of chips at the takeaway and I thought… why not?" She tweaked the toes of Grace's romper suit. "It sounds so sordid when I say it like that," said Sophie, "but it really wasn't. He was… nice. Kind."

I raised my eyebrows at that and Babs bit her lip. I suppose we were both thinking the same thing – how starved of affection you have to be to drop your drawers for a bag of chips. Babs broke the silence in typical Babs fashion.

"Well, he is very lucky boy. He must have thought all his Christmases had arrived at once."

Sophie lifted her chin. "I don't regret it," she said, a touch of steel in her voice, "whatever you think of me."

I touched her arm to soothe her. "And nor should you," I told her, and nodded at the baby, "especially when you consider the outcome." Grace gurgled and cooed. Sophie cleared her throat.

"Afterwards, he asked if he could see me again," she said. "He told me I had sad eyes and he'd like to make them happy…" She stared off into the past for a moment, then shrugged. "I said no. I didn't need any more complications. I was all set to go home, turf *him* out and start again." She sighed. "Well, that didn't happen. I found out I was pregnant and everything changed. *He* changed, for a while at least. He said he'd take care of us, started managing the business and the household finances and I was so scared he'd find out I just let him, I let him take over everything."

Her shoulders were heaving now. I moved closer and wrapped my arms around her until her breathing slowed and she stopped shaking. Babs had disappeared into the kitchen while this was happening and now she returned with another of her bottles and three glasses. Sophie had calmed herself now.

"Sorry," she said, her voice scarcely a whisper. "I've made a right mess of things. Sometimes, I wish…"

"Nyet, no wishes." Babs' sharp tone had the desired effect; Sophie swallowed her maudlin train of thought and sat up straighter. Babs nodded her approval. "This is better." She started to fill the glasses. "We hev saying, 'If wishes were horses, beggars could ride.' You think you are Cinderella and wishes will make for Happy Ever After?"

"No…" began Sophie.

"That's right," Babs said. "Wishes are worth spit. So here, we do not wish. Here we plan and we do and we make the most of everything life throws at us, da? Here we make our own future."

Sophie said nothing at first, she simply stared at Babs, her eyes shining, though whether it was through fear, awe or excitement, I couldn't tell you. Finally, she nodded.

"Yes," she whispered. Babs cupped her hands around her ear.

"I am not hearing you."

"*Yes!*" Sophie said louder, laughing.

"Good girl! It is like I am always saying, it does not do to worry the bones of the past. Bury them and let them be. The future is what counts."

"I've never heard you say that," I said. Babs shot me an irritated look.

"I say it when you are not here." She passed a glass to Sophie and I promptly took it off her.

"She's nursing, remember." Babs rolled her eyes.

"I am aware of this, which is why I am serving non-alcoholic drink." She took the glass off me and passed it back to Sophie and another to me. "And now we will toast." She raised her glass. "To the future."

"The future," I said. Babs and I downed our drinks. Sophie sniffed hers warily, then shrugged, threw caution to the wind and drank. She finished spluttering much sooner than I expected. She stayed downstairs a while longer, clearly trying to distract herself from the events of the past few days. Every so often, I saw her hand dip into the pocket she'd put the Foreman's card in as if she was clutching some protective talisman. Ah well, that was a worry for another day. Finally, though, she could stifle her yawns no longer and I packed her and the baby off to bed.

Once I heard the creak of her bedroom door closing, I let out an explosive breath.

"Well, what do you make of that?" I asked Babs.

"They must hev been very good chips," she replied and I snorted with laughter and reached for my knitting. Babs sighed wistfully and flopped down in the armchair.

"It has been long time since I had… chips."

"What's that?" I said, untangling a piece of yarn.

"I said it's long time since I had chips."

"Well, I've got some potatoes and a pan… or there's a chippy down the road," I said, picking up my needles and coiling the yarn around my finger. Babs tutted and gave me an incredulous look. "I'll pay," I said. I could quite fancy some myself. Babs shook her head. She stood up, paced across to the living room window, twitched the curtains and peered out. Then she stomped back and flopped back down with a sigh in the overstuffed armchair. We sat in silence; the only sound was the click-clack of my needles. Babs repeated her circuit to the window and back twice more before I cracked.

"What's the matter with you?" I said. "You've had a face like a split clog since Sophie went to bed."

Babs glared at me for a moment, then sighed again. "I just… I hev itch to scratch, you know?"

I set my needles aside and got up.

"I think I've got some ointment for that."

"No!" she said and rolled her shoulders irritably. "I want… hmmm, something to make me feel good."

I frowned. "I've a bar of chocolate in the fridge. I'm happy to share." Babs fixed me with a pitying stare.

"Chocolate will not be cutting it." She walked to the window and twitched the curtains again, opening them a crack. She pursed her lips. Across the road and three doors down, a light still shone in Burt's front room. Babs clapped her hands together.

"I think I will see if Burt is wanting Borscht," she said.

"What? Now? It's gone eleven!"

Babs grinned wickedly. "Da, darling, the perfect time for… Borscht." She sashayed towards the door.

"I thought you wanted chips!" I called after her. The penny dropped as the door closed behind her and I realised she hadn't taken any Borscht with her. I chuckled to myself. *Lucky old Burt won't know what's hit him* I thought. Then, *I hope he's been eating his greens.* I paused and hoped Babs remembered her promise not to hurt him. And then

I sighed and thought sadly how long it had been since I'd last had Borscht and how nice it might be to taste some again… what? Just because you haven't made the dish for a while, doesn't mean you want to throw away the recipe entirely, does it? So, I took a moment to feel sad. Just a moment, mind and then I smiled. At least I wouldn't have to share my chocolate now.

Chapter Twenty-Nine

I woke to screaming. I sat up and clutched the duvet, willing my heart to stop hammering long enough for me to catch my breath and figure out where the noise was coming from. My brain threw pieces of last night at me. Babs went out, I went to bed, Sophie… My heart froze. Had the Vegan got in somehow? Was it her I could hear? The baby?

I stumbled out of bed and had flung open the door before common sense took hold. The blackness beyond my bedroom door was still and serene. Unlike me. I dropped to my knees. My skin was clammy. My head pitched and tossed like a doomed ship and I had to swallow quickly to stop myself from gagging. I took a few deep breaths and forced myself to focus. This was no natural reaction.

Wherever the noise was coming from, it wasn't inside the house; the shrill, piercing shrieks rolled and boiled through the corridors inside my mind. I fought down another wave of nausea and let my eyes adjust to the gloom. Slivers of colour flickered at the edges of the blackout curtains – fingers of dirty red and greasy orange curling past the fabric, beckoning me to the window. My stomach dropped, and I realised the last time I'd felt this way was when Misty died. Cold dread spread through my veins. My other senses caught up. Beyond the screaming, the hiss and crackle of flames reached my ears and the stench of smoke seared the back of my throat.

I staggered upright and was at the window in a heartbeat. I yanked open the curtains and winced at the sudden glare. Bright flames filled my vision. They leapt and licked the sky with insatiable hunger and at their core, writhing and quivering, was House.

I thundered down the stairs. Sophie poked her head out of her bedroom but one look from me silenced whatever question was forming. I opened the front door and raised my arms against the sudden gust of hot air that blasted my skin and singed my eyelashes.

By now, the distant wail of sirens startled the sky, growing louder with each passing second. The fire engines would be here soon – I've no idea who called them, but they would be too late. House had stopped twitching and the screaming in my mind had ceased. The core of the blaze seared white hot and began to collapse in on itself.

House was gone.

A new scream wrenched through the air, torn, bloody and raw from an anguished throat.

"HOUSE!"

Babs. My own heart plummeted. I edged past the pyre in the garden, shielding my face with my arms, then sprinted out of the garden gate to meet her. She stumbled through the street, barefoot and naked. Her face was streaked with tears and soot, though there was no way the grime could have settled on her yet. Tendrils of steam snaked off her body in the cool night air. In the flickering firelight, it looked almost as though Babs herself was ablaze. Burt hurried after her. He held a towelling dressing gown before him, but every time he got close, Babs shook him off.

"Babs, love…" Burt spotted me then and looked at me helplessly. "Aggie, thank God. She just sat bolt upright in bed and started screaming," he said. "Then she ran out of the house to here – wouldn't even stop to put some clothes on…" He stopped short and stared at the fire. "That's her caravan, isn't it?" But I didn't answer him. I tugged the robe from his hands and made to intercept Babs before she reached House.

The fire engines were here now. Their sirens blared and blue and red lights bounced off the houses. I'd nearly reached Babs when I saw him, lurking behind next door's wheelie bins. The grin he gave me crawled straight out of Hell and his eyes glowed orange in the firelight. My fury was a lead weight in my chest, crushing against the inside of my ribs, clawing up my throat, desperate to get out. My hands didn't just tingle, they burned, from wrist to tip. The burning didn't stop there either. I could feel it seething through my body. Darkness coiled through my mind, seeping and spreading like ink in water.

I'll kill him.

I might have, too, but at that instant, he spoke.

"You gonna let your pal burn, are you?" He smirked the words at me and I frowned, too far gone in anger to understand, but then Sophie's shout smashed through my rage.

"Aggie! Help!" She and Burt were clinging desperately to Babs, dragging and wrestling her away from the bonfire she was desperately trying to reach.

I shot the Vegan one last, venom-filled look and ran to help Babs.

Chapter Thirty

I sent Burt away. He looked for a moment as though he might argue with me but I'm guessing the look on my face made him think twice. Between us, we corralled Babs indoors and covered her with Burt's dressing gown.

I dealt with the authorities, too. A faulty heater was the suggested cause. I let them believe I agreed and all the while, Babs stood in the doorway like a marionette whose strings had been cut. Now I led her gently to the sofa and sat her down. She didn't resist. In all the years I'd known her, I'd never seen her like this. Her face was slack and her eyes stared off into nothing. She'd stopped screaming – on the outside, at least – but that wasn't necessarily a good thing. Her silence was unnerving, as was her stillness. I realised that I'd never really seen Babs still. She was always on the go, always busy. I took her hand; it felt like marble. I chaffed it between my own to get the blood moving a bit.

"Come on, Pet, let's get you warmed up," I said. Sophie jumped up.

"I'll switch on the fire…" she stopped and quailed under the heat of my glare.

"A blanket will suffice," I replied. I took the old candlewick from the back of the sofa and wrapped it around Babs' shoulders. "She needs to rest," I said. "I'll get her something that will help. You stay with her." Sophie looked panicked.

"What should I do?" she asked. I bit back a sigh of exasperation.

"Just *be* there," I said. "Sit with her. Let her know she's not on her own." I threw Babs another anxious look then marched into the kitchen and rolled up my sleeves. In the last few days, Babs had turned it into the culinary equivalent of Da Vinci's studio but she wasn't the only one who knew her way around a kitchen, albeit for different purposes. In all the years I'd lived here, it had been little more than a place to reheat food while I licked my wounds and felt sorry for myself. It was time to change that. I opened the broom cupboard and took out my wooden apothecary box. Babs had ordered new supplies for me from her phone and they'd arrived promptly, so everything was fresh.

I cracked my knuckles and set to work. I filled a small copper pot with water and set it to heat on the stove. I blended chamomile and lavender, then added valerian root to soothe her spirit. Sophie was speaking in low tones in the living room, but there was no response from Babs. I stood for a moment, tapping my teeth, then added magnolia bark to the other herbs and tied them in a muslin bundle. I took the pot off the stove and set the bundle to steep in the boiling water.

The warming scents soon filled the kitchen and steamed the windows. I watched the second hand chase around the clock five times before I lifted the sodden sack from the pot. I decanted the tisane into a cup and added a teaspoon of honey. Then, because it was Babs and she had the constitution of an ox, I added a heady dose of rum.

I sniffed the concoction. The floral of the lavender and chamomile overruled the day-old-sock stink of the valerian and the magnolia lent a sweet citrus fragrance. The honey and rum added richness and depth. I nodded in satisfaction. Not bad considering how out of practice I was. I added a drop of cold water to cool it and took it through to the other room.

Babs was still catatonic. I crouched before her and stroked her face.

"Here you are, love, I've made something to help you rest." I held the cup up to her face but Babs didn't even blink.

"Come on now, Babs, it will do you good." There was still no reaction. *Damn.* I had to get the drink into her. There was only one thing left. It had been over a century since I'd last had cause and I didn't know if I could still do it but one look at Babs' grief-bleached face told me I had to at least try. I took a deep breath and squared my shoulders. My fingers tingled and the heat prickled up my arms and down into my stomach. The corner lamp flickered and the rest of the room grew dark. I drew myself up and pulled my voice from the depths of my boots.

"BABAYAGA. DRINK!" My words rang with the iron of an anvil and brooked no argument. Sophie yelped behind me and baby Grace began to wail. Babs blinked as my words struck her hindbrain and she reached out her hand, obeying the instruction automatically. She downed the brew and I gently took the cup away from her and put it on the floor. The room had returned to normal now and my hands had cooled.

Grace's cries had subsided to a gentle whimper. I could feel Sophie hovering at my shoulder, no doubt brimming with questions I was in no mood to answer. I ignored her and kept my attention on Babs. The potion was a good one and I knew it would work. I waited and watched until her eyes began to droop and her head began to loll, then I eased her round and lay her gently down on the sofa. I spread the blanket she'd been wearing across her and tucked her in, then gently stroked her forehead until her eyes closed and she sank into unconsciousness. Only then did I allow myself to unleash an explosive breath.

"That bloody man, I could swing for him!" Sophie jumped at my words and quickly started rocking to soothe Grace before she could cry again. I looked around the room, briefly searching for something to hit or kick before common sense tapped me on the shoulder and reminded me we didn't need any further injuries. I swallowed down the bile that burned my throat. "Wait until I get my hands on him. He's only lucky I didn't put him down then and there." I didn't add that if it hadn't been for her and Burt, I might have done. I've never killed before, not directly, but at that moment, I was tempted. I didn't know if my abilities were sufficiently restored to let me do it but I was angry enough that if magic failed, I'd have throttled him with my bare hands. Sophie looked hunted.

"No," she said. It was almost a whimper. "Can't this be an end to it?"

I shot her a filthy look. "Oh, so Babs rescues you from him and ends up paying the price?"

"It might not have been him," she said. I spun around so fast I nearly got tangled in my clothes.

"Might not have… who else could it have been?" I spat at her. Sophie stared at the floor, her face red.

"The firemen said it was probably a faulty heater…" she said.

"Ha! As if House ever had a faulty anything."

"Well, even if it was him, I'm sure he didn't mean any real harm…" She sounded desperate but I didn't care. My legs trembled with rage.

"You're still making excuses for him? After all he's done?" I whispered my shout and Sophie took a step back from me, holding Grace close to her body. I pointed to Babs drowsing fitfully on the sofa. There was a deep crease between her eyes and every now and then she whimpered. "How can you defend that?" I hissed.

"I'm not, I'm just saying it could have been worse. At least no one was hurt."

I took a deep breath and counted to ten. Then I counted again. Sophie jigged in that way of hers that set my teeth on edge.

"Aggie? I'm not defending him, really, I'm just… he *can't* have meant to cause her real harm – he simply can't. Babs isn't physically injured; she just lost her home." The way she said it sounded like a mantra or a prayer – a verbal life jacket to keep her afloat.

"You think that's not bad enough? Losing your home? Losing a beloved pet?"

"No, it *is* bad." Sophie was backpedalling. "But it could

have been much worse. I mean, it must be a terrible shock and obviously, it's sad House is gone, but Babs wasn't actually hurt, was she?" she repeated.

"Only because of sheer, dumb luck," I said. "If it hadn't been for Babs deciding to visit Burt, we'd have more than House's charred remains on our hands. That man intended murder tonight… and he succeeded, even if he doesn't know it." Her eyes widened but she shook her head.

"No, I can't believe *that* of him. And he didn't know what House was… I mean, you can't call it murder if it…" She stopped and tried again. "I know House moved and all, but it wasn't exactly alive, was it? It was just a house."

I didn't know whether she was trying to convince me or herself. I shook my head. Of course, she didn't understand, there was no reason why she should, but a little barb of disappointment stung inside me at her words and I looked at her sternly.

"You don't know what you're talking about," I said. "Let's say you're right and House was little more than a collection of timber and soft furnishings, but what about Misty? How do you marry *his* death with your vegan principles?"

Sophie frowned. "He might be bad, but he didn't have anything to do with your cat," she said.

"He bloody did!" I said. "I've got it straight from the horse's mouth, recorded on Babs' phone. Ask Burt or Margot if you won't take my word for it; they've heard it too."

Sophie's forehead wrinkled but I was in no mood for pulling my punches. Seeing Babs so pale and pathetic made my chest hurt. My blood was seething and *someone* was going to know about it. "So, what now? Will you tell me *that* doesn't matter because Misty was 'just' a cat? And stop that infernal jigging, will you? You'll give that poor mite hiccups."

Sophie froze. Her eyes filled. "I didn't know," she whispered.

"Didn't know or didn't want to know? Because while you've been hiding away from his uncomfortable truths, the rest of us have been paying for it." The words rattled off my lips and ricocheted around the room. Sophie looked like she'd been slapped and the expression on her face pulled me up short. It had to be hard for her, too. She'd lived with him, cheek-by-jowl, built a life of sorts with him, perhaps even loved him. Even knowing he'd lied and cheated, it must be difficult to realise you'd been so very mistaken about someone. That little worm of guilt squirmed inside me again and I pinched the bridge of my nose. I took yet another breath and forced myself to speak calmly.

"I'm sorry, that was unfair. I know you've had a rough time of it. What you've got to understand is that House was so much more than Babs' home, in the same way that Misty was more than a pet."

Sophie swallowed and nodded. "I understand," she said.

"No, you don't," I replied, not unkindly, "but I'll try to explain." I sat on the edge of the sofa, being careful not to disturb Babs, and motioned for Sophie to take a seat in the armchair. "When you live as long as Babs and I, things are different." I bit my lip and thought about how best to explain it. "We spoke about your mum a while back."

Sophie nodded. "Well, *my* mum died over a thousand years ago." Sophie baulked a bit at that but I shrugged. "I've no idea anymore what she looked like. I remember my daughter's face though… well, bits of it… her smile, the shape of her eyes. Sometimes, I catch a glimpse of her in the mirror or a stranger's face and I think, 'Yes, there you are, that's what you looked like.' She's been gone so long, there's not even dust left of her now."

Sophie glanced at her own baby and cradled her a little more closely. I dragged my mind away from the brink of distant memories and sat up brusquely. "The point is," I continued, "when you live as long as we do, you lose everyone you ever cared about eventually and you have to make a choice. You can either keep yourself aloof and alone, living out the centuries in solitude… but that way leads to madness. We were none of us built to be alone." I trailed off.

"Or?" prompted Sophie. I smiled warmly at her.

"Or we can love anyway…" I smiled wryly, "which is another form of madness, I suppose, especially when you know that all love stories end with goodbye. But once you accept that, you can take a part of yourself – a bit of your soul, a bit of your heart, the best bits of yourself – and you can place them in another being. A vessel for your love, you might say. Someone to stand with us when all is dust and ashes. Someone to love us when love has died." I sighed. "Someone to help us carry on. That's what House was to Babs. That's what Misty was to me, so when I use the word 'murder', I mean it."

I looked at her seriously. She could barely meet my eye. Instead, she busied her hands, tugging at the baby's sling. I ran a weary hand across my face.

"Look, love, I'm not telling you this to make you feel bad or because I want your pity. I'm telling you because I want you to remember what he's capable of. He locked you and your baby up, for heaven's sake! And you do know, deep down. Do you think we haven't noticed that you never put the baby down? That you never leave her alone with him? You've excused him for so much for so long, but there's enough of me in you that you can see the truth of what he is."

The tears welled in her eyes and I gave her a moment. I reached over and stroked a lock of hair away from Babs' forehead. "These coming days will be hard," I said, almost to myself, then echoed Babs' words from a few days ago, "because let me tell you, nothing is ever 'just' anything. Your fella knows that even if he doesn't respect it. He watched and waited and looked for the thing that would hurt most and he destroyed it. Maybe he thought Babs was inside House, maybe he didn't…" I thought of those first few hours after Misty died and shuddered. "It would almost be a kindness if she had been."

There was no malice in my voice but I heard Sophie's gasp.

"She… she will be alright, won't she? I mean, you are, so…" My answering laugh was mirthless and I couldn't keep some of the bitterness I'd suppressed in the last few months from leeching into it.

"You think so?" I looked at her and held her gaze. "Because *I* think the only thing that keeps me from waking up every morning screaming is the fear that I won't be able to stop." I took no pleasure from the stricken look on Sophie's face. Rather, I wondered if I'd said too much. I'd learned, over the centuries, that people tend to be uncomfortable with the emotions of others. Perhaps I'd been too harsh, but if it helped her understand why the Vegan needed to be stopped, I hoped it was a pain worth sharing. I might have said more, but at that point, Babs groaned and I turned my attention to her. The Vegan could wait. He wasn't going anywhere and even if he was, I was determined to hunt him down.

Chapter Thirty-One

I woke to the sound of Babs sobbing – not the guttural keening of the previous night, but the plaintive cry of one who has woken from their worst nightmare to discover it was real. She stood at the window with her palm pressed against the glass, staring at House's remains. I dragged my crumpled form out of the armchair and eased her into it. She winced slightly as she moved and I realised her feet were muddy and grazed from her barefoot walk from Burt's. I fetched a bowl of warm water and some ointment and she sat, expressionless while I treated them.

Sophie came downstairs while I was applying the bandages and I sent her straight back upstairs to fetch some of my clothes. I pulled the woollen dress over Babs' unresisting form – it looked even dowdier on her than it ever had on me, and that's saying something, but it would do for now. I helped her on with some underwear and socks. My feet were a little bigger than hers but between her bandaged feet and a pair of thick socks, she was able to fit into my boots. That done, I brushed the hair from her forehead.

"Come on, love. Let's get you out of here." Sophie's

silence was deafening. "Yes?" I asked her, not bothering to turn around.

"Nothing!" Another brief silence, then, "It's just, do you really think it's a good idea to take her out?"

"It's a damn sight better than keeping her here with *that* staring at her all day." I nodded towards House's blackened ashes. "Besides, she needs some grub in her and I'm in no mood to cook. So yes, we're going out. You coming?" I guided Babs to the front door and threaded her arms into her coat while Sophie made up her mind and moments later, I heard her footsteps behind us as she joined us.

The day was dirty yellow. The meagre sunlight was smoke-drenched and heavy, but it was enough to make me grimace and blink and that's when I lost my grip on Babs. She slipped from my hand and bolted for the greasy black circle of House's remains. Charred wood bleached ash-white rose like the blanched bones of an ancient beast and Babs knelt in the very centre, at the heart of the fire, scrabbling through the dead cinders. My heart wrenched.

"Babs, love, don't do this." Still, she clawed at the ground. The ash billowed up in great clouds. It got everywhere. I tasted it on my tongue. It mingled with the bile in my throat until I had to spit but I knelt with her and placed my arm gently around her shoulders. As I prised her gently away from the grave, she made one last dart for the ash with her hand. This time, she pulled out something small and round from the embers. She clenched it within her fist and looked around wildly, as though daring anyone to try and take it from her. I held up both my hands in supplication and her shoulders relaxed.

She put the object in her coat pocket and let me lead her away.

I needed to get Babs to Margot's place in the Arcade and the walk was slow going. I kept my arm linked through Babs', talking softly to her about who-knows-what and Sophie walked a step or two behind, with the baby in her sling. I hadn't given any thought to the Vegan since my explosion last night – I'd been too caught up with caring for Babs to pay him any mind but I saw him now, leaning against the door of Sophie's shop, and I cursed myself for not thinking ahead. Of course, he'd be here; there was no fun in gloating from a distance. He sauntered over to us and I tightened my grip on Babs' arm.

"Ladies," he said, cheerily, then tilted his head in mock concern. "You don't look happy. What's the matter? Shitty breakfast?" He laughed then. I sucked air through my teeth. He had some nerve. My arm was trembling though I couldn't tell if it was through my rage or Babs'. She stared at him intently now, as though he was a particularly vile insect under a microscope. The Vegan pulled a package out of his coat pocket and unwrapped it to reveal a bacon sandwich. "*My* breakfast is lovely," he said, taking a big bite.

Sophie grunted and he grinned at her. "What?" He spoke with his mouth full, spraying bits of masticated bread and chewed bacon over us. "Oh, the meat? Well, I don't have to pretend anymore, do I?" He swallowed his mouthful. "No more crappy lentil stew or bean bake for me. Nah, I'm back to proper man food… might treat myself to some veal for dinner, you know, the proper, crate-reared stuff you have to import." Sophie said nothing. She had her hand cupped over Grace's head and had backed herself up against Margot's window. I was torn between placing myself between them and needing to keep hold of Babs. The Vegan took a step closer.

"Makes you sad, does it? Thinking of those poor baby cows? Well, perhaps if you'd spent less time worrying about baby cows and more time thinking about me, you'd have been a better girlfriend." His eyes flicked down at Grace and his lip curled into a vicious sneer. Sophie instinctively wrapped her arms tighter around her daughter. "Perhaps if you'd had more meat in you, you wouldn't have gone whoring around, eh?" said the Vegan, peeling the top layer of his sandwich back to reveal the pink filling. "What do you reckon? Shall we find out?"

He lunged at Sophie before I could move, rubbing the meat of his sandwich against her face, smearing her skin with bacon fat. Sophie cowered, too busy covering Grace to be able to fend him off. Grace's shrill shriek rent the air and Babs wrenched her arm from my grasp, presumably driven by some ancient, protective instinct. She thrust herself between the two of them and shoved the Vegan away. He stumbled backwards then regained his balance and came up panting. He looked at Babs.

"Think you can take me on?" He looked her up and down and a smirk oiled across his face. "Look at you." His smirk hardened with concrete malice and his eyes glittered with caustic glee as the next words tripped off his tongue. "How's your house?"

She didn't think before she reacted – she didn't have time. She simply whipped her head back, snake-like, and spat. Old she might be but she was also accurate and a glob of ash-filled phlegm splattered on the Vegan's cheek. He lunged again, this time with his hand raised to strike Babs. This time, I had my hands free and placed myself in front of Babs. The Vegan looked at me, his face twisted with hate.

"Your turn now, is it?" he said. I said nothing but met his stare. I remembered last night and the burning fury that had seared through me, the seething desire to break him and raze his bones to dust. Something of it must have shown in my eyes because the Vegan hesitated. Uncertainty clouded his features and he backed down. He spat on the ground at Babs' feet.

"Like I'd waste time on you," he said to her. "You're nothing but a pathetic old woman." And with that, he stalked away. I dropped my shoulders and bustled the others into Margot's shop.

Margot hurried through when she heard us, her face tinged the pale green of the pistachio ice cream in her chiller, and she practically hurled herself on us.

"Oh, Aggie, Babs, I've just heard." She tried to engulf us all in her embrace at once. "Burt just got off the phone; he told me everything. It was that slimy bastard, wasn't it? He's been going frantic – Burt, that is, not the Vegan Git. He's been knocking on your door for ages. I must let him know you're here…" she yammered on while I attempted to disentangle us from her hug. We finally broke free and Sophie hurried to the toilet to wash the worst of the bacon off her face. I walked Babs over to a chair and sat her down.

"Oh…" That was Margot again. She had finally caught

sight of Babs and turned several shades of vanilla paler, as well she might. After her burst of activity outside, Babs had returned to her semi-catatonic state. The fire had taken its toll physically, too. It hadn't been as noticeable last night when everything was in turmoil, or outside in the fresh air, but in the enclosed space of Margot's shop, the stench of smoke lay so thickly on Babs, you could almost see her smoulder. Soot still clung to her hair and skin and etched into the lines and creases of her face. I'd never seen her look so old; even the feathers on the collar of her coat drooped. She stared blankly at the melamine table.

Sophie returned and started nursing her grizzling baby. I ordered three sundaes and she said she wasn't hungry but I waved away her protest. We waited for the food in silence, broken only by the occasional whimper from Grace. The sundaes arrived and I lined all three in front of Babs. Sophie frowned at me.

"I don't think she'll fancy all that…" But I shushed her again and passed Babs a long-necked spoon.

"Eat," I said. She took the spoon and started – just a smidgen of cream at first, then another and another until she met resistance from the first scoop of ice cream. Her backside squeaked in the plastic seat as she wriggled into a better position and then set back to work, gripping the stem of the ice cream glass to get a better purchase on the food within.

I'd seen this before, many times. When Misty first went missing, the very sight of food made me feel sick. Once I knew he was dead, though, a great hunger opened up inside me. I was ravenous. I gorged myself. No food was too fine or too common – creme brulee with rich, gloopy custard, steak so rare it practically mooed, fish finger sandwiches on white bread with tomato ketchup that dribbled down my chin. It was unseemly, really, but in the midst of death, the body searches for life. Had I been younger, I might have looked to other appetites to reaffirm life, and maybe Babs would prefer that, but Burt wasn't around and all she was getting from me was the ice cream. Her spoon tinkled and scraped on the bottom of the glass now as she chased the last bit of sauce. She looked up at me then, her eyes full.

"He called me '*old woman*'," she said. Hurt and bewilderment swagged every word. I reached over and patted her hand.

"I know, love." I pushed the second sundae in front of her and she began eating again in a workmanlike manner – first the edges, then raking the sides of the ice cream turret in the centre. Sophie opened her mouth to speak but I shook my head at her. The second sundae was finished more quickly than the first. Babs looked at me again, her eyebrows raised.

"He called *me* 'old woman'." Incredulity dripped from every word. I pushed the final sundae towards her. There was no grace with this one, no finesse. Her spoon dipped again and again, moving in a blur from glass to mouth and back until it was empty and pushed away with such force only Sophie's quick hands stopped it from smashing to the floor. Babs thumped the table. The spoons rattled in the glasses. She leaned forward, her eyes glittering like the fires of Hades.

"*He* called *me* 'old woman'!"

I grinned back at her. "That's right," I said. "So, what are we going to do about it?"

Chapter Thirty-Two

The Vegan had lit another fire – unintentionally this time. His words burned through Babs' shell of grief and galvanised her into action. She stormed out of Margot's and into the Arcade like a woman possessed. For a moment, I worried she was going to confront the Vegan there and then, but instead, she strode over to the cafe and waited for me to unlock the door. She shifted impatiently from one foot to the other, clearly eager to be inside and start plotting. The Foreman trotted over while I fumbled with the keys to the shutter. His face was creased with concern.

"I heard aboot the fire, are youse alright?" he said. He caught sight of Babs who, though somewhat recovered, did not look great. "Surely, yer no opening? Ye need tae rest."

"Nyet, no rest," Babs replied with uncharacteristic sharpness. She hesitated when she saw the expression on his face and patted his hand reassuringly. "But today, da, we are closed." He pursed his lips but said nothing more to her and instead turned to Sophie.

"And you and the wee bairn? Yer okay?" Sophie blushed

but nodded. "I'll be on mah way then. Remember, you've got mah number, should ye need it." He left as I finally got the shutters up and the door open and we trooped inside, leaving the lights off and the door sign turned to 'closed'.

We hadn't discussed the decision to decamp to the flat instead of my house; it just happened naturally. I think we were all keen not to see House's burnt carcass or smell the acrid stench of the familiar's death. We moved boxes around to form a makeshift living room. I called Burt and sent him over to mine to collect some clothes and other essentials. He dropped them off while Babs was in the shower and I sent him on his way before she got out. Sophie stared after his retreating form and frowned.

"I don't understand," she said and I shook my head.

"Burt's a complication she doesn't need right now."

"No, I don't understand why she is so hung up about him calling her old. Don't get me wrong, I'm glad she's speaking and moving again, but I don't understand... I mean, it's not nice but compared with losing House..." I sat on one of the boxes and wondered how to explain it. Finally, I sighed.

"Compared with losing House, it's a bearable pain, alright?" I said, "It's the one she can handle and so that's what we'll do. We'll help her deal with the small hurt..."

Sophie nodded, as though understanding. "Ah, and in time, she'll be able to deal with the bigger hurt," she said.

I rubbed my ankles where they still prickled for Misty's soothing presence.

"I doubt there's world enough or time to deal with the bigger hurt," I said grimly, "but I'll help her learn to cope." I straightened up. "But that's later. Right now, there's work to be done, and you'd be surprised how therapeutic a hearty dose of fury can be." I paused and looked her up and down. "Are you up for this… whatever we plan? You were with him for a while, so if you feel you can't be part of it, we'll understand."

Sophie rubbed her cheek where the faint sheen of pork fat still lingered.

"He's never going to stop, is he?" she asked.

"No," I replied, "not someone like him." She knelt beside Grace, who was cooing happily in the nest of blankets we'd made on the floor.

"Then we have to stop him," she said simply.

"I am happy to hear that," Babs' voice came from the doorway, "because I am heving idea."

She was dressed in a pair of jeans and an oversized jumper that Margot had sent over. Her eyes were red-rimmed and her face so pale it was practically blue, but she was upright and acting more like her usual self and she held her phone in her hand – she'd left it at Burt's last night but now she held it aloft like it carried the secrets of the universe. I smiled warmly at her and patted the box next to me.

"Come on, then. Let's hear it."

She walked over, still a little unsteady on her feet and sat next to me. "We get coven together," she said. I blinked.

"A coven? We've not had one of those for years."

"What's a coven?" asked Sophie.

"It's a group of, well, our kind," I explained. "When you get a large number of us, it kind of…" I hesitated, searching for the right words.

"Magnifies power," finished Babs. "Neither Agnes nor

I hev strength to risk taking on Vegan alone. We must ask for help."

I took a deep breath and nodded.

"You're right," I agreed. "I'll pop downstairs to get a pen and paper. Do you have their addresses?"

Babs looked at me like I'd grown two heads. "No, I do not hev addresses. I hev instant messaging group." She showed me her phone and I peered at the screen, which showed numerous ancient and familiar names in a group communication. I frowned.

"Why am I not part of this group?"

"Because *your* phone is older than Sophie. Now let's decide who to contact." She had a point. I'd got a phone for emergencies years ago. I mostly used it as a paperweight. I shuffled closer to Babs and stared at the names on her list.

"Marie Laveau?" said Babs.

I bit my lip. "Hmm, bit of a trek over from New Orleans. We could do with striking quickly."

"Da," said Babs, nodding. "They must get here fast, which also rules out Moll Dyer, Merga Bien and anyone east of Germany or south of Sicily." She tapped her teeth.

"Who does that leave us with?" I asked.

"La Befana," she said and I felt a spark of hope.

"Befana? That's great. Who else?"

"Malin Matsdotter could probably make it from Sweden. I'd ask Muma Padurii, but she is currently in Africa."

"Is she? Since when?"

"About ten years ago – part of cultural exchange, I believe. You are really out of loop!" I shrugged and indicated for her to keep looking. "Let's see, there's… Ah."

"What?"

"Walpurga…"

"Ah… maybe not."

"Da, perhaps we keep looking."

"Why?" asked Sophie. "What's wrong with Wal… Wall…"

"Walpurga," I finished. Sophie nodded. "She's not exactly," I said, delicately.

"Not exactly what?" said Sophie.

"Just… not exactly," I said. Sophie looked at Babs for clarification and Babs tapped the side of her head.

"Wheel is turning but hamster is dead," she said. "Is very sad but this is what happens when you do not hev…" she trailed off and stared into the distance. My ankles prickled again and I finished Babs' sentence in my head. *This is what happens when you don't have a familiar.* I shook myself and gave Babs' back a brief rub.

"Never mind that, who else have we got?"

Babs scanned the list.

"Well, with those that hev died or are otherwise unavailable or unsuitable, that only leaves Biddy Early."

I winced. Sophie noticed. "What's wrong with Biddy Early?"

"Nothing," said Babs decisively. "She is kind, thoughtful person, she is just a tad… talkative."

"She never shuts up!" I said.

"She is young, remember, scarcely three hundred," Babs pointed out, "and she has many good qualities; she is honest and open…"

I snorted.

"Very open," I said. "There's not a thought enters that girl's head that doesn't immediately roll off her tongue."

"You were young too, once," Babs reminded me and I sighed, conceding her point.

"You're right, ask her."

"I already hev," Babs replied. Moments later, her phone pinged and she read the response. "They will be here before dawn."

"So quickly?" I gasped and Babs rolled her eyes at Sophie then looked at me.

"Da, so quickly. There are many ways to travel at speed. We hev cars and aeroplanes now, Agnes… not that they will travel that way."

I blushed in response. "I know that," I said. "It's just been a while since I travelled." Babs smiled at me.

"Well, perhaps when all this is over, I shall take you travelling. House…" She caught the sentence in her throat and nearly choked on the black ice ball of loss that hit her. I blinked away tears on her behalf and fished around for something, anything else to talk about.

"Shame there will only be three of them. It would have been good to have nine of us."

"Why?" asked Sophie.

"It concentrates the power further," I said. "Don't ask me why, because I don't know, but three is a good number, and three times three is better yet."

"Well," said Babs, clutching onto the new topic like a castaway to a life jacket, "there will be the three of us as well, and we can bring Burt and Margot in – they may not hev magical blood but they hev strong connection to this place which may work in its stead."

"That's eight," I said, then Babs and I both slowly turned to look at the baby.

Sophie followed our gaze and her expression hardened. "No, absolutely not."

I shrugged and Babs smiled softly at Sophie.

"Quite right, too," she said. "No magic until at least sixteen, is what I always say. Eight will be enough to handle Vegan."

We sat quietly for a moment, then Sophie cleared her throat.

"What will we do to him?" she asked. I looked at Babs, sitting so straight she could snap. I looked at the faint smear still on Sophie's face. I looked at the empty space around my ankles.

"Whatever is necessary," I replied.

Chapter Thirty-Three

It was a day of waiting, that prolonged feeling of anticipation that stops you from settling to any one activity. I found some old knitting needles and yarn in one of the boxes and I worked a row of stitches before setting it down, then picking it up again, setting it down, picking it up, setting it down, before Babs informed me if I picked it up again, she'd shove the needles where the sun didn't shine. Sophie paced the floor, jigging the baby in that irritating way of hers. What we all needed was to get out but every time we glanced out of the window, we saw him lurking in the doorway of Sophie's shop or lounging in the Arcade, like a shark circling its prey.

Burt and Margot showed up at lunchtime with food and an ultimatum. They stood, side by side, wearing matching expressions of determination.

"It's time to put a stop to this, Aggie," Burt declared. "It's time to call the police in—" he held up his hand to interrupt any argument "—I know you're not keen on the idea, but we *know* that bastard was responsible for burning Babs' caravan and we've got that recording to say he did for your cat and…"

"Yes," Margot spoke now, "and we've got him saying he's been bullying me."

I stared at their earnest faces. A bloom of warmth and affection battled with a red itch of annoyance. They meant well. I stared longer than they were comfortable with, just long enough for those determined expressions to falter, then I replied.

"I see," I said, "and when we've been to the police, what then?" They looked at one another and frowned. "You see, we've no proof at all he was involved in the fire and as for the recording, it could be anyone, he'll say, or he'll tell them he was just bragging – a stupid bit of bravado aimed at the people who have made his life hell."

Margot gasped.

"*We've* made *his* life hell?"

"That's how he'll tell it." I shifted my posture to look broader, more masculine and then slumped my shoulders in a facsimile of humility. "'*It's relentless, Officer. They're always on at me for something.*'" I matched the tone and cadence of the Vegan at his smarmiest almost too well and Sophie blanched. "'*Ever since I cancelled that order of flapjacks, anything that goes wrong, they blame me for. I've had the local builders coming into my shop and threatening me because of them; they attack anyone they think is on my side – just ask the girl in the shop next door, and now…*'" At this point, I pretended to wipe a tear from my eye. "'*…they've turned my girlfriend against me. She's left me, Officer. She's taken our baby and gone. They've destroyed my life.*'"

I finished talking and looked back at Burt and Margot. They gaped back, open-mouthed. "Don't you get it?" I said. "He's good at this. In his mind, he truly is the wronged party and when he speaks to the police, he'll be so charming, so credible... He will make it hard for us, all of us. And in the meantime, he'll be out and about and free to cause chaos." Burt opened his mouth to argue but I slammed my hand down on the nearest box. "*No!* Burt, now you just listen to me. I've seen enough people I care about hurt because of him. I'm not about to let that happen anymore. If it were simply a case of getting Sophie and the babby away from him, then yes, we'd go to the police or take her to a safe house or refuge but it's about more than that."

I took a breath then continued in a calmer voice. "I've got some friends coming this evening. They're going to help us put a stop to his nastiness."

Burt's brow creased.

"What type of friends?" he asked, suspiciously.

"The type who know how to deal with people like our so-called vegan."

Burt paled and took a step backwards.

"Oh no, Aggie, no. If you're talking about what I think you're talking about, I can't condone that, I won't -"

I stopped him in his tracks.

"I guarantee I'm not talking about what you think I'm talking about, Burt, but in any case, we want you and Margot to join us."

Margot jumped. "Us? Why?"

"Well, for starters, you've both had run-ins with him but also, Burt, you can see first-hand that none of us will lay a finger on him."

Burt looked visibly relieved. I didn't add that we wouldn't need to touch him.

"So, you're doing an intervention type of thing, then? Talking to him, showing him the error of his ways, that manner of thing?" I didn't dare meet Babs' eye when I nodded in response.

"Something like that," I replied, vaguely.

"And do you think that will work?" asked Margot. This time, I did meet Babs' eye and we shared a long look.

"It will the way we do it," I muttered, darkly.

It took a little while longer before Burt was reassured enough to go along with our plan. Even with our assurance that no one would be physically harmed, doubt lingered on his face. It was Babs who finally turned the tide.

"Burt, we are asking you to trust us. If things are no better in twenty-four hours, we will *all* accompany you to the police station but, please, give us this time." She spoke so quietly. Her voice breathed out of her body as though trying to spare her energy. The discussion had wearied her and she looked so frail and vulnerable, it would have taken a much harder heart than Burt's to deny her. He swallowed down the last of his argument and agreed.

They closed up their respective shops early and returned to our flat. Burt brought camping beds and sleeping bags, and Margot brought food, which we were grateful for. Babs had ventured down to the cafe kitchen earlier and spent twenty minutes staring blankly at the ingredients for Borscht before I took her by the shoulders and gently guided her back upstairs, where she sat, periodically checking her phone for updates. Margot and Sophie took turns pacing the living room. Burt found an old carriage clock and busied himself tinkering. The air in the flat was thick with the words we didn't speak.

Finally, I sent everyone off to bed. It would be a long night, I told them, and a little rest now would help. Sophie and Margot took the bedroom – there was a serviceable bed in there and Margot had brought enough supplies to keep Grace comfortable. Burt decided to set himself up in a chair in the cafe itself in case the Vegan had any ideas.

That left Babs and me in the living room. She took something out of her coat pocket before she settled down – at first, I thought it was the carved shingle House had given Sophie. I'd noticed Sophie quietly trying to press it into Babs' hand earlier, but Babs had simply smiled sadly, shook her head and told Sophie that House had meant it for Grace so she should keep it. The item she had now was whatever she'd dug out of House's ashes. It looked to be a small pebble. She wrapped her hand around it gently and shot me a wary look as though expecting me to berate her, but I wasn't going to judge; I kept Misty in the freezer, for heaven's sake. I sighed then. Poor Misty, burned up with House. I hadn't even been able to say goodbye.

We both lay down in the dark. The evening drew on. I listened to her breathing and the erratic tick of the carriage clock that marked the night's progress. Finally, I heard the sound I'd been waiting for. A stifled sob reached out to me – the sound of grief snared. I was at Babs' side in an instant and pulled her into my arms. She resisted for a moment, then curled herself around me and wept. I held her while her body shook and her chest heaved. I held her while her tears soaked my neck and shoulder and when the tears and the sobbing stopped, I held her while she trembled and shuddered. And when those stopped, I simply held her and we sat in companionable silence until her phone lit up the room. Babs sniffed, wiped her face and read her message.

"They are here," she said.

Chapter Thirty-Four

Befana, Malin and Biddy arrived together. Burt let them in and escorted them upstairs. I heard them before I saw them: well, I heard Biddy, at least. She was busy telling Burt how we hadn't seen each other since the old queen was on the throne. I wonder how he'd have reacted if he'd known she was talking about Victoria rather than Elizabeth. As it was, he simply wore the bemused expression of most people when confronted with Biddy's verbal diarrhoea. Finally, she drew breath and he managed to get a word in edgeways.

"It was good your planes all got in at the same time," he said.

"Planes?" said Biddy. "What are you... ow." Malin stepped on her foot.

"That will do, child," she said. "We are not here to bore the nice man with our travel plans." Biddy scowled and I could understand why. It set my teeth on edge when I was her age. It's not easy being referred to as 'child' when you've seen the turn of three centuries but I was over five hundred before the older ones acknowledged me as experienced enough to drop the term, so she had a way to go yet. Befana rubbed her arm and soothed her ruffled feathers a bit before they turned to greet Babs and me.

Academics and experts in mythology would have wet themselves at the sight of them and waxed lyrical about the Triple Goddess and the maid, the mother and the crone. I wouldn't, and not just because Befana, sweet-natured as she was, had a left hook so hard you'd see next week if she used it, but because it's rude. Besides, while it's true that Malin had a somewhat maternal air about her, with a good few centuries under her belt, I doubt Biddy could call herself a maid with a straight face. She was the first to step forward, her copper curls bouncing obscenely.

"Geez, are youse alright? I couldn't believe it when we felt House go, and so soon after Misty, Aggie! I can't imagine how youse are both even standing; if anything happened to my Donal, well I just don't know what I'd do. I mean, youse must both just feel like -"

"Ahem." Malin cleared her throat significantly and Biddy blushed. She took a step back and cast a guilty glance at the holdall she'd placed on the floor. It shifted slightly, which told me her cockerel, Donal, was probably secreted inside, out of sight to spare our feelings. The other two had similar bags and my heart swelled at their thoughtfulness, though Burt's eyes were bulging at the moving bag.

Malin stepped forward then, all high cheekbones and Scandinavian chic. She pulled Babs, then me into a warm embrace that filled my eyes and tightened my throat.

"I am so, so sorry for your loss," she said. "Whatever I can do to help you through this time, it shall be done."

Babs and I nodded our thanks and she stepped back to make way for Befana.

No words were offered. None were needed. She simply took each of our hands in turn and pressed them first against her lips, then against her forehead. The network of lines across her tanned leather face creased into an expression of sorrow and concern that nearly broke me. I fished in my pocket for a tissue and handed another to Babs. She took the tissue and held it close to her face to hide the tremor of her bottom lip.

The trio gave us a moment to recover ourselves while Burt went to get Margot and Sophie, and then we filled them in on the story over tea and thick slices of apple cake. The double hit of cinnamon and sugar helped calm my frazzled nerves and even Babs had some colour in her cheeks.

"So, when are we giving this 'Vegan' a hiding, then?" said Biddy when we'd finished talking. She was lying on her belly, fussing over the baby, with whom she'd been instantly smitten. "No time like the present, I say. He sounds like a right hole, sure enough, doesn't he darlin', yes he does." This last bit was to Grace.

Burt looked at her sharply. "What do you mean? Surely, you've got to wait for the others?" he said.

Biddy raised her eyebrows and looked at me. "Others? Are there more than us coming then?"

I shook my head. "Not as far as I know. What 'others' do you mean, Burt?"

Burt's cheeks pinked and he tugged on his earlobe.

"I just thought there might be some... that is to say, I'm sure you ladies are all formidable in your own way, but this man means business and I think you could do with a couple of, you know, people of the male persuasion."

Only years of friendship and affection stopped me from laughing in Burt's face. The others had no such compunction. Biddy's snort was as unladylike as they come, Malin tutted and rolled her eyes, and Befana just looked at him curiously as if the thought that she might need a man's help had never crossed her mind, which to be fair, it probably never had. I looked at Babs who graciously stepped forward to explain things.

"Dear Burt, you are all the man we will be needing."

His pink cheeks flushed red now. "That's kind of you to say, but I can't protect all of you…"

Another snort from Biddy drew a harsh look from Malin and I had a go at explaining.

"We don't need protecting, Burt. We have means to protect ourselves."

"What do you mean?" he asked.

"We're witches, you daft apeth," Biddy exclaimed. "We're what other people need protecting from." Malin glared at her again and Biddy shrugged. "Well, we are," she said.

Burt gaped at her and then stared at Babs and me. Margot's eyebrows had disappeared into her hairline.

I sighed. "It's true, Burt. Babs, Biddy, Malin, Befana and I, we're all witches."

"Though we do not care for the term," added Babs.

Burt started to back away. "Babs, Aggie, I know you've been through a lot lately, but you can't go around saying things like that. People will think you're mad."

"You don't have to believe us, Burt, but it's true. And between us, we're taking down the Vegan tonight."

Burt planted his feet and squared his shoulders. "Oh no, Aggie. I can't allow that. You're clearly not in your right minds."

I gritted my teeth. I know he meant well but I could have fetched him one about the ear at that point. Then Befana shuffled forward and I caught the look in her eye. I turned back to Burt.

"What if I could prove we're not delusional?" I said.

Burt cocked his head. "And how do you propose doing that?"

At that moment, Befana threw out her arm and pointed at a jug of water resting with the tea things. In an instant, the water fizzed, boiled and then exploded into flame with a crack that made Margot yelp and set Grace crying. Biddy helped Sophie soothe her and glowered at Burt.

"Wheesht. Now look what you've done!"

Burt was pale and shaking and I took the opportunity to capitalise on it.

"Like I said, we're not delusional, we are protected and we are going to stop the Vegan now. You coming?"

Burt nodded and stepped aside.

It would have been so wonderfully dramatic if I'd been able to lead them in battle formation from the flat and into the fray, but that sort of thing only happens in fiction. In reality, it took us a while to get out of the flat – first Sophie had to wrap the baby up and then Biddy couldn't find her shoes. Burt and Margot watched the casual chaos with haunted expressions. I was a little disappointed at how easily they were convinced of Befana's power, if I'm honest. I mean, yes, she made water burn but any fool with a basic grasp of chemistry knows you just need a bit of sodium for that, or is it potassium? One of the -iums, anyway. That's not how she actually did it, but that's not the point. If they had just used their brains a bit, perhaps they wouldn't have flinched any time Befana moved.

Eventually, though, everyone was as ready as they were going to be and we made our way downstairs and out of the cafe. We filed across the Arcade. I felt like a primary school teacher, counting and recounting the number of people to make sure we didn't lose anyone, with Babs as my trusty TA, bringing up the rear. Burt and Margot's faces were dough grey in the gloaming. Only Biddy seemed to be enjoying herself.

"When witches go riding and black dogs appear, the night shall be filled with terror," she crowed, then glanced at Sophie. The girl's teeth were chattering. Biddy gave her a one-armed hug.

"Don't you fret, love. Just think of it as a grand day out with yer pals," she said, and started whistling, 'Oh, I do like to be beside the seaside'.

Sophie gave a high-pitched giggle which she quickly stifled under Malin's disapproving glare.

"Don't mind her," Biddy whispered to her. "She's had a face like a slapped arse ever since ABBA split up," and Sophie stifled another giggle. By then, we had reached the shop and Sophie started rooting in her bag for her keys. She didn't need them. One hand, placed gently on the doorknob was all it took for the door to swing open.

"*Oh.*"

I'd eased in front of Sophie, determined she shouldn't be the first into the lion's den,. Products had been pulled off the shelves and strewn across the floor. A bent nine iron, no doubt from his collection of golf clubs upstairs, lay bent and twisted next to the display cabinets it had vandalised. Obviously, the Vegan had not taken his girlfriend's departure well. There was another "*Oh*" behind me, this time from Sophie. I couldn't shield her from the mess and destruction of her beloved shop. Her eyes shone in the darkness.

Burt and Margot followed her.

"Oh, Sophie, love." Margot was aghast.

Burt clenched and unclenched his jaw in anger. For all his talk of non-violence, I began to wonder if we'd have to hold him back from the Vegan. "What sort of person does this sort of thing?" he asked.

"The type that would sink a ship just because they can't be captain," Sophie replied. She looked so pale but still, she lifted her chin. "But that's why we're here, isn't it? To throw him overboard."

I smiled warmly at her, a glow of affection filling me.

"That's the spirit," said Biddy. "Nothing a sweeping brush and a lick of paint won't solve but let's get that steaming turd of an ex flushed away first." She had her arm around Sophie again and I could almost see the warm energy flow from her into Sophie. She winked at me and I smiled back. It was a simple trick, but Biddy's little boost would be a sustaining nip of brandy on a cold night. Sophie stood a little straighter and nodded us onwards and upwards.

The stairway up to the flat had also suffered, with holes punctuating the plasterboard. Sophie braced her shoulders to see the state of her home. She fumbled with her keys in the dim light and snicked open the lock. I tried to slide in front of her again but she shook her head, took a deep breath and opened the door. *His* voice carried down the corridor.

"You're back, then."

Chapter Thirty-Five

Sophie stepped forward to allow us all to shuffle in behind her and I caught sight of him, sprawled across an armchair with one hand tucked in the waistband of his joggers and the other clutching a can of lager. The detritus scattered across the floor indicated it was not his first. Another golf club rested against the armchair and the shattered remains of ornaments told us he'd been practising his stroke. He followed our collective gaze around the room, then he looked at us and let out a belch.

"Oh, and you brought some friends," he said. He looked us all up and down and his lip curled in derision. "You really think this pathetic bunch can get me to leave? One has-been soldier and a clutch of fossils? I'm a bit offended, to be honest. Although…" his eyes lingered on Biddy's chest, "I wouldn't mind the redhead having a go." He smirked salaciously at Biddy who smiled back impassively.

"Ah, no, darlin', yer not my type. I've sworn off snakes."

He shrugged and popped open another can.

"Might've known, fucking dyke," he said and I heard Befana grunt behind me. Biddy merely grinned.

"Yes, that's a much easier explanation to take than 'I wouldn't touch you with a bargepole.'" Sophie stepped forward and we followed her further into the flat. She swallowed and faced him, her hands trembled but her voice was clear.

"I'm going to ask you once more nicely. I want you to leave."

He didn't even bother to look at her. "No," he said. "Your name might be on the deeds but all payments have been coming out of my account. If you want this place, you're going to have to fight me for it." Now he looked at her. His eyes narrowed and he snorted, "And you don't have the balls."

Burt pushed to the front.

"That's enough!" he said. "There's no need for any of this. She's asked you to leave, so just pack up your stuff and go before there's any more unpleasantness."

The Vegan stared, startled for a moment, then he fired off a mock salute.

"Sah, yes, Sah!" he said. He dissolved into laughter, sloshing the contents of his can everywhere.

Burt puffed out his chest. "I mean it," he said.

The Vegan stopped laughing and jumped out of the chair. He loomed over Burt and the first curl of panic fluttered in my stomach. He was at least a foot taller and twenty years younger than Burt. He prodded Burt in the chest.

"You mean it, do you?" he said. "Yeah, I bet you do. Very quick to defend her honour, aren't you – not that she's got any. I'd bet you were sniffing around the little whore as much that Scottish prick was if I didn't know you were more into grave robbing than cradle snatching." He fired a smirk at Babs to make sure his shot hit home. Burt drew a breath to answer back but the Vegan cut across him. "In fact, for all I know, you might've fathered her filthy bastard; the brat's got the same useless look about her."

He looked Burt up and down and laughed again, "Nah, I doubt you've got it in your pathetic little shrivelled dick…"

The Vegan stumbled backwards but not because of Burt. Befana now stood between them. She raised her hand and waved one finger in warning in front of the Vegan's face. She whispered something in her soft, Italian voice and the Vegan frowned.

"What's her problem?" he snarled.

"La Befana does not care for bad language," Babs explained.

"Yeah?" He curled his lip at her. "Well, she can kiss my ar—"

It happened so quickly he didn't have time to finish his sentence. Befana made her soft utterance and I felt the tingle of power burst from her, trailing the scents of citrus and sea salt in its wake. The Vegan flapped his lips like a landed fish. He tried to speak but was unable to make a sound. He clutched his throat and stared at us, wide-eyed.

Biddy wheeshed air between her lips.

"Sure, there's two village eejits round here and yer man there is both of them," she said.

"What just happened?" asked Burt. His voice was a little higher than usual and there was a nervous trill to it.

"Befana is one of the most powerful of our number," I explained. "If she tells you she doesn't like bad language, you'd do well to take notice." I looked at the Vegan, now shouting, red-faced and silent. "She's also one of the sweetest of our number, which is why she merely snagged his voice and did not rip his throat out."

The Vegan froze and gaped at the little old lady who smiled serenely back at him. Babs' snort let me know which option *she* would have preferred. The Vegan, still bug-eyed, was puce. His face twisted into a silent snarl and he lunged for Befana. He was fast, but Biddy was faster. She blurred past me and wrenched his arm up behind him, pulling him up short.

"Ah, no. There'll be none of that," she whispered in his ear. His cry of pain would have rattled the windows had it been audible. He flailed for a moment but Biddy's grip grew stronger until he finally stood still, sullen and panting. "Look on the bright side, darlin'," she said, "you got me to touch you after all."

Malin spoke then.

"Now that dreadful racket has stopped, what shall we do with…" she wrinkled her nose at the Vegan "… this?"

I frowned and rubbed the back of my neck idly. "Well, his power comes from his charm," I said. Biddy pulled a face and whirled him round by the arm to take a better look. His face scrunched up in pain. Biddy raised one doubting eyebrow and looked at Sophie.

"Really?" she said. Sophie blushed.

"He can be charming," she said. "He convinced me, anyway."

"Yes," I said, "that's the trouble. He hides his true self

and spins a good story to convince people he's decent. As long as it is worth his while, he can put on a show to fool the world. And he's good at it."

"So let us remove those talents," said Babs. The other witches nodded their agreement.

"But how?" Margot started to speak, but Malin shushed her sternly and she instantly fell quiet. Biddy winked at her sympathetically.

At Malin's suggestion, I positioned everyone in a circle around the Vegan. I gave Burt's hand a reassuring squeeze. The poor man looked ready to run if any of us so much as blinked at him.

The Vegan had stopped panting now. He was pale and sweating and his eyes were fixed on Befana who had stepped into the centre of the circle with him and Biddy. Befana smiled in a way that was not at all comforting and raised her arms. She muttered some words in that quiet voice of hers and her hands began to glow. I felt a tug in my midsection, a persistent pull, like thread drawn through a hole. It had been a long time since I'd felt this draw of energy. I relaxed into it and let Befana take what she needed.

Sophie was next to me. She looked wild around the eyes. It was easy to forget how alien this must be to people who weren't of our kind. I grasped her hand to let her know it was alright and her shoulders softened a little. Around the circle, the others had done likewise. Babs had Burt's hand in her own and Malin was speaking softly to Margot.

The room hummed with energy. I half closed my eyes and faintly saw it – thick, golden ropes of light connecting us to Befana. It lasted no more than a few seconds and then the feeling was gone. Befana's hands stopped glowing and she lowered her arms. The room was quiet now. Even the Vegan was still.

Margot was the first to speak. "Is… that it?"

"You were expecting maybe fireworks?" replied Babs.

"No! I just… what was that?"

"Is tricky curse," explained Babs. "One person could do it but would be like lifting big boulder. Much easier with more people."

"Yes," I said, "Befana took a little bit of energy from each of you – except the baby, of course," I said before Sophie could protest, "and except for himself there as well." I nodded at the Vegan.

"That's why you needed me and Burt? To make up the numbers?" Margot sounded disappointed.

"Don't sell yourself short," I told her. "You and Burt helped a lot more than you realise." Burt looked sick.

"We cursed him?" he said. "Do you mean he's going to die?"

The Vegan's head shot up, panic scored into his face. Babs' laugh was like the tinkling of a chandelier.

"Burt, you are too good for this world. He will not die," she said and walked forward to look the Vegan in the eye, "at least, not because of this curse. We hev made it so his true self will no longer be hidden. It will shine like oil slick on ocean. Nor will he be able to lie. Every word he speaks will be absolute truth."

The Vegan shrank from her and looked imploringly at Sophie. Sophie turned away.

"How will we know it's worked?" she asked. I looked

at Befana, who shrugged. No use saying we just knew it had worked. Sometimes, people had to see to believe.

"Oh!" exclaimed Biddy. "You said he was doing the nasty with the ride from the Magick shop. Why not get her in?" It was a decent idea, to be fair. Babs grabbed his phone from the side and held it up to his face to unlock it, too quickly for him to turn away. She started thumbing through his contacts.

"Look under 'Dave'," Sophie told her and the Vegan glared at her. Sophie looked straight back at him and raised her eyebrows. "You really think I didn't know?"

Babs was still scrolling.

"Hmm, Dave, okay, I hev him and is definitely her… oh my." She glanced at the Vegan. "You are very naughty boy. Okay, what shall I write?"

Biddy piped up again. "Oh, I know, send her one of those aubergine-eggplant emoji things and say, 'Come to the flat.'"

Babs and I looked at each other blankly.

"Aubergine emoji?" said Babs. "He is inviting her to dinner?"

"What are you like?" Biddy hooted.

"Confused," I replied, honestly.

Sophie glanced discreetly at Befana, then leaned in and whispered in my ear. I nodded with understanding then whispered into Babs' ear.

"He has penis shaped like aubergine?!" shouted Babs incredulously and Biddy hooted even louder. Sophie and I groaned. So much for discretion. Babs clicked send and we waited.

Malin leaned against a wall like a retired supermodel,

Befana lifted herself up onto one of the barstools by the kitchen counter and sat there, kicking her legs. Burt and Margot stood close together, not making eye contact with anyone else. Biddy maintained her grip on the Vegan, and whistled tunelessly through her teeth.

"Will we put the kettle on?" she asked after a while. No one answered and she resumed her whistling. Another minute went by, then, "Fancy you not knowing what the aubergine emoji means," she said to Babs. "Aggie, I get, but I thought you kept up with the times."

"Hey!" I objected, a little spark of indignation flaring.

Babs shrugged. "It will be very sad day when I hev no new things to learn."

Biddy started whistling again. There have been more awkward waits throughout history, but not many. Finally, we heard the scrabble of a key in the lock.

"You gave her a key?" Sophie hissed. The Vegan swallowed and looked down, perhaps realising today was not the day to be on the receiving end of a woman's ire. Malin positioned herself behind the door and we waited for Little Miss Magick to enter.

"Babe? Are you here? Why's the shop all broken up? I've been so worried." She walked into the flat and the door clicked shut as Malin closed it.

"Come in, dear. We've been expecting you."

Miss Magick jumped. "Who are you? Where's—"

"Your friend is through here. We require your assistance." Malin had the young woman's arm in her own vice-like grip when she guided her where we waited. Miss Magick's eyes widened when she saw us all and when they finally landed on her lover, she gasped.

"What's going on?" she asked. The Vegan immediately opened his mouth, violently and silently protesting at his handling. Miss Magick blanched.

"What's happened to his voice? Why can't I hear him?"

We all looked over at Befana, who shrugged and clicked her fingers to restore his voice.

"—king bitches have done to me. Babe, you've got to help me." But Miss Magick's expression had changed. Gone was the look of concern and revulsion crept across her face. Her stomach twitched visibly as she looked at him, as though she was trying not to gag. The Vegan saw the change.

"Why are you looking at me like that? Babe, don't look like that. *I love you.*" That's what he intended to say, at least, but the curse strangled his last three words as they formed and they left his mouth like a sigh in a hurricane. His mouth twisted over them and spat out, "I think you're pathetic," instead. Miss Magick's hands flew to her face and the Vegan desperately tried to backpedal.

"Babe. No, listen, babe, *I didn't mean it* I meant every word." He clamped his mouth shut, trying to stop the new words escaping, but they spilled out regardless.

"What the hell is going on here?" Miss Magick demanded.

"We hev been making improvements," Babs replied. "From now on, you will see your friend here for exactly what he is and he can only speak the truth. Observe." She looked at the Vegan and said, "Tell me, did you ever love your aubergine friend here?"

"*Yes* Of course I didn't, you stupid bitch, She's just tits and an arse to me."

I half expected Miss Magick to cry at that point, but she straightened her shoulders and observed him with haughtiness an empress would envy.

"And your promise that you'd leave Sophie and live with me? What of that?"

Sophie stood next to Miss Magick. "Yes, dear, do tell the nice lady."

The Vegan had at last learned to keep his mouth shut; his lips were pressed so tightly together they were white. His skin glistened with the effort of keeping quiet but he needn't have bothered. His silence spoke volumes. The rest of us grinned smugly at a job well done. But it seemed the Vegan wasn't licked yet.

Chapter Thirty-Six

It happened so fast, I almost missed it. Lulled into a sense of security by his humiliation, Biddy must have relaxed her grip because the Vegan shook free of her grasp and pushed her away. He lunged for the golf club. Anger and hatred radiated from him until it hurt to look at him and in that instant, he found a focus for it – Baby Grace, sleeping soundly against her mother's chest. In two steps, he was before them, the thick metal rod raised high in the air. Blood coursed through my veins, beating a tattoo in my ears and throbbing in my chest and at that moment, time slowed. The club had already begun its descent when my legs kicked into gear and I ran between them, my arms flung wide to shield them from the blow.

The ponderous inhale of a collective breath froze to glacial speed. The drops of lager, still beaded on the Vegan's face, inched their way down cheeks contorted with rage. My own breath hung in the air before me. I looked at the metal club, still moving inexorably downwards and I reached my hand up to meet it.

Time returned. The frozen gasp was released and Sophie curled up with a yelp to protect her child from the blow that didn't land. A moment of confusion reigned in which everyone stared at the striking end of the club resting lightly in my hand. The Vegan held the other end. He tightened his grip and tried to yank it out of my grasp but it didn't shift. He pulled again, tugging harder and harder until sweat trickled down his ruddy face and into his eyes.

I kept my grip gentle and faced him down, the enormity of what he'd attempted slowly creeping along my nerves and spreading, spider-like across my brain. He would have killed them. He would have killed them and never thought twice about it. My blood crystalised in my veins. It wasn't enough – the curses we'd placed on him wouldn't stop him.

The thought worried at my brain while he tugged away at the club. It burrowed deeper and deeper until I could almost see Sophie and baby Grace, battered and bloody on the carpet beside me. Other images filled my mind: Misty's sodden corpse, House writhing in flames, Babs screaming, soot-streaked and naked. I still heard the hiss and crack of the fire, smelled the scorched air.

Suddenly, the chill in my body had gone, replaced by a searing bloom of heat. The air fizzed and hummed again. There was no tingle in my hands, this time they burned. I drew myself upright and as I did so, I felt the curious pull in my belly I'd felt before, but instead of exhaling energy, I was the one drawing it, syphoning it from the others. It poured into me in a glorious spectrum of colour. My arms burned, my chest, and surely my hair must be aflame. I felt reborn, rising from the ashes of the lives he'd torched. The rage I felt when he destroyed House burned anew.

I looked at him and the fire must have shown in my eyes because he stopped pulling and tried to back away. I muttered a word and sent a bolt of heat along the shaft of the golf club, welding his hand to it. He yelped, twisting and thrashing, desperate to pull away but I had him held fast. I could kill him.

The thought rang with such clarity through my mind and a dozen or more deaths proffered themselves for my consideration. It would be so easy. It would solve a problem. He would never hurt anybody ever again. He knew it, too. I could see the fear in his eyes, the jump and quiver of the pulse in his neck. It would be mercy, really, like putting an animal out of its misery.

"Agnes." Babs' voice reached me as though from a great distance. "This is not who you are." The words were spoken softly, but they were enough. I looked at her, then at Burt and Margot, Sophie and even Pissy Dog Face. Their faces were rigid with terror and they were looking at *me*. Time froze again while a number of futures unravelled before me; I saw my loved ones scatter, fearful and sick at the Vegan's demise. I saw them struggle and separate, living out their lives alone. I saw myself, bitter and unloved, sinking beneath black seas. I had never killed before – I had helped people find the door when pain or old age blurred their vision but I'd never crossed that line.

I looked at the Vegan, cowering before me. I straightened my shoulders and made my choice. I would not cross that line for him. I smiled at my friends reassuringly. Their faces relaxed and the burning in my hands soothed to a golden pulse. The Vegan shifted. He'd seen the change in my demeanour. The dread mask of his face faltered and the ghost of his habitual cockiness fleeted across his features. But the rage that seared through me was now a vibrant warmth of a fire tempered, not doused. I cocked my head to one side and smiled at him. Uncertainty chased across his face once more and I raised my hand. It was time to end this.

"Manum tuam mulieri iterum, ego te asinum pabo."

The words came unbidden and rang through the flat with the weight of a funeral bell. The fire in my hands shot across the room and wrapped around the Vegan in a golden chain, pulled tight around his body. It lingered there for one heartbeat, two, three, then flickered and vanished beneath his skin.

The humming stopped. The heat in my body faded and awed silence blanketed the room. Naturally, Babs broke it. She punched the air.

"*Yes!*" she crowed with delight. "The witch is back!" And with that, the spell was broken. Everyone who wasn't a sleeping baby or a fake vegan let out a long breath and sagged with relief. Befana grinned at me and nodded her approval and even Malin cracked a small smile. Biddy pulled the Vegan back into an arm lock but she needn't have worried. He wouldn't be hurting anyone ever again, and he knew it. He knelt, trembling, a damp patch spreading across the front of his joggers.

"Behold the thrice-cursed man!" Biddy cried and she cackled like a two-bit crone in a Shakespeare play. Malin tutted, Babs and I shook our heads and Befana rolled her eyes.

"There's always one who lets the side down," I sighed.

Biddy morphed her cackle into a cough and looked at us shame-faced.

"Sorry," she muttered, "I got carried away."

Burt was frowning, sounding out the words I'd used.

"I did Latin at school. Manum tuam… *if your hand upwards then shall… asinum…?*"

"Your donkey stand in a pasture?" Margot finished. "No, that can't be right… your ass stand…?"

"If you raise your hand in anger again, your arse will be wheelbarrow stand," Babs translated, laughing.

"Or words to that effect," I muttered, my cheeks flaming. "My Latin is a little rusty."

"Words do not matter. Your meaning was clear."

"What just happened?" asked Miss Magick. Her eyes filled her head and she looked from me to the Vegan and back again.

"Ah, Aggie just cast a wee binding on yer man here," replied Biddy casually.

"There was nothing wee about it," corrected Malin. "That was some impressive work, Agnes."

I inclined my head in acknowledgement.

"You… you can do that?" Miss Magick stammered.

"You mean you can't?" I asked innocently. "I'd have thought as a fellow practitioner, you'd know how to do a simple binding." A flash of devilment flowed through me. She'd been the Vegan's victim too, but she hadn't been blameless. I leaned closer to her. "You're in amongst the big girls now, are you sure you want to play?" I held her gaze for a moment and watched her breathing become shallow. I lowered my voice further so only she could hear me. "Itching stopped, has it? If it comes back, you let me know, and I'll put a stop to it like that." I snapped my fingers and the residual energy I held sparked at their tips. Miss Magick yelped and bolted for the door.

"Will you not stay for a cuppa?" Biddy called after her, then tutted. "She didn't even say goodbye. Rude is what I call it." Then she laughed, long and hard.

I looked at Babs and she smiled back at me. She was right. I was back.

Chapter Thirty-Seven

Befana, Malin and Biddy left soon after. I said before that we're not the most sociable of creatures and Malin's pursed lips told me she was already tiring of Biddy. Babs saw them off. They took the Vegan with them, or at least I assume they did, because he wasn't littering the apartment anymore. Not that it mattered; he was well and truly neutered.

I stayed behind to make sure Burt, Margot and Sophie were alright. Burt and Margot were still wrapping their heads around my dodgy Latin and seemed strangely pragmatic about everything. I asked them about it and Margot shrugged.

"He needed to be stopped," she said simply. I looked at Burt who nodded then looked shamefaced.

"I'm sorry about the fuss earlier." He glanced over at Sophie and Grace. "He'd have killed them, wouldn't he?"

"Yes," I replied. "Maybe not today, but he'd have done it eventually." Burt nodded again, taking in my words.

"I wouldn't have believed it if I hadn't seen it." His voice was heavy and my heart ached for him. "I mean, you hear about people like that on the news, but you don't really think they exist."

"You're a good man, Burt," I told him. "And good men find it hard to conceive of bad men, but maybe it's time to remove the blinkers."

I patted his arm and left him to his thoughts. Sophie stood by the window and I put my arm around her shoulder. She gave me a wan smile.

"You okay, love?" I asked. She bit her lip.

"I just keep thinking… that last curse, it was really strong, wasn't it? I mean, I felt it… and there were nine of us, including, you know…" she looked out of the window at the Magick shop.

"It was strong," I replied. "It won't break, if that's what you're worried about."

"And the other curses?"

"Befana knows what she's doing. They won't break either," I said and Sophie sighed.

"Then that's it. We've ruined his life," she said. I raised my eyebrows and she hurriedly continued. "I don't still care for him or anything, I just… it seems like he'll have a hard and lonely life and I feel sad for anyone in that situation."

I squeezed her close.

"You've a kind heart, Sophie. As for himself, well, the rest of his life is up to him. We took away his ability to lie, but he can choose to be honest. We took away his ability to hide his true nature, but he can choose to cultivate one he doesn't need to hide. And the not hitting people is just common decency." I looked at her seriously. "There's always a choice, Sophie. You say we've ruined his life, I say we've given him the opportunity to make better choices. The rest is up to him."

I let my words sit with her and we both continued our vigil at the window.

"It's so quiet now," Sophie said after a while and I chuckled softly.

"Yes, Biddy tends to have that effect when she leaves a room. And as for Malin, well…"

"She walks in the front door and the cat runs out the back? That's what gran would say," and I laughed again.

"It's a fair description. She's been cultivating that disapproving look for centuries – I think Medusa learned from her."

Sophie shook her head. "I don't get it. You wind each other up but they still came."

I rubbed her shoulders. "That's what family does," I said.

Sophie went back to the cafe a little while later. Her flat and the shop were in too much of a state for her to deal with then and there so it was decided she should stay in my flat until it was sorted. She salvaged a few of her belongings and left. Margot went with her to help her get settled while Burt lingered, his hands in his pockets, whistling tunelessly. The man had no guile.

I pottered around and pretended not to notice the way he perked up when Babs returned. She entered the room and I gave her a look and announced I was going to get a few more things for the baby. I took myself off to the nursery and left them to it. I left the door open, mind; privacy's one thing but I'm still a nosy so-and-so at heart.

For a while, neither of them spoke, then Burt broke the ice.

"So, you're a witch, then?"

"Da."

"Not Aggie's sister."

"Nyet, not in the way you think."

"But you've known her a long time."

"Many, many centuries."

There was silence and I could imagine Burt mulling over her words, chewing the inside of his cheek.

"Well, I've always had a thing for older women," he said finally and Babs' answering laugh lifted the air.

"Dear Burt, what we had the other night was wonderful and I shall never forget your kindness."

"Well, that sounds like the brush off," he said.

"You are good man," Babs said, unconsciously echoing my words.

"But not good enough," Burt replied and I winced at the unfamiliar note of bitterness in his voice.

"On the contrary, Burt, you are *too good*. It would kill me to lose you."

"Who says you'll lose me?" I sighed inwardly at his response and imagined Babs doing the same.

"I lived for many years before you were born, darling," she said, "and I shall live for many more when you hev gone. There would be a parting and it would break me. Do not think of this as 'brush off', think of it as self-preservation."

More silence, followed by the crunch and shuffle of Babs' footsteps kicking through the detritus on the floor. "Oh look," she said, too brightly. "There is Margot, leaving cafe." Still more silence, then Babs cleared her throat. "It is still quite dark, perhaps you should see her home." I don't know if Burt caught her real meaning but he took the hint anyway and I heard him walk to the door. He was near the nursery when Babs called out to him.

"Burt?"

I peered through the crack in the door and saw him turn.

"Thank you," said Babs. A soft smile eased across his lips and he doffed his imaginary cap.

"My pleasure," he said, and left.

I waited long enough to hear his footsteps disappear before I joined Babs. She watched from the window as he caught up with Margot at the entrance to the Arcade.

"You heard."

It wasn't a question so I didn't answer. I linked my arm through hers and stood with her.

"I'm sorry," I said. "You've lost so much because of me."

She looked sharply at me. "What is this nonsense?"

I swallowed and that nasty little worm squirmed in my mind again. The dark thought I'd kept at bay since House burned made itself heard at last.

"I mean, if I'd let you deal with the Vegan as soon as you arrived, I'd have spared you a lot of heartache. House would still…"

"You cannot hold yourself accountable for that man. There is no way you could hev known what he would do. Even I could not see."

"But still."

She squeezed my hand and shook her head. "I hev my friend back," she said. "I would not change that for the world." My heart swelled at her words and I coughed to clear the lump in my throat.

"I am sorry you lost Misty again," Babs said. "I am sorry I insisted we put him in House for safekeeping." I sighed.

"I'd already resigned myself to his loss. I don't need a grave to remind me of him."

Babs grunted and we stood a while longer.

"What now?" I asked and she shrugged.

"Now, we open the cafe."

Chapter Thirty-Eight

They were queueing down the street before we even turned the sign to open. I stared in wonderment, unable to account for it until Sophie showed me the article in the paper – a national paper, too, not just the local rag. The journalist had written about us again but this time, his words had been glowing. His descriptions leapt off the page and made even my mouth water when Sophie read them to me during a rare lull. He even spared some words for my flapjacks.

Babs sniffed modestly. "This just proves he has taste buds," she replied and sashayed off to the kitchen where moments later, we heard her chuckle. Sophie looked at me questioningly and I rolled my eyes.

"She's been doing that every time she spots an aubergine," I explained. I looked out across the Arcade. It teemed with life. Burt had people waiting three deep to be served. Those who weren't shopping were enjoying one of Margot's ice creams. Even Miss Magick's doorbell was chiming more than it had done for quite some time and when Sophie re-opened, she'd find herself busier than ever too. Thankfully, she'd finally relaxed and placed Grace in a pram rather than having her permanently strapped to her front, so at least she'd have both hands free.

Babs had forwarded the incriminating recording she'd taken at the other cafe to the Silver Fox, so I suspected he'd back off. The deli owner she'd spoken to that day had accepted her offer to move into Margot's place when she joined me in the cafe and I knew they'd make a brilliant addition. Sun shone through the glass ceiling and bathed the place with light. Yes, I looked across the vibrant Arcade now with a smile. At least I did until our own personal dark cloud swarmed into view.

"Uh-oh, incoming," I muttered to Sophie as Pissy Dog Face strode purposefully across to the cafe.

"What is this?" Babs asked, wiping her hands on a tea towel as she joined us from the kitchen. I nodded at the woman who now hesitated in our doorway. She straightened her back and pushed the door open.

"Can we help you?" I smiled brightly at her and she flinched. She backed away from me and turned to face Sophie.

"I came to tell you… That is, I thought you should know." She took a deep breath. "It was me who told him about your baby – about it not being his, I mean." I heard Sophie's intake of breath, and Pissy Dog Face spoke very quickly. "In my defence, I didn't know he would react the way he did. I just wanted him to leave you, I didn't think for one second that he'd try and hurt you both. I'm not a total bitch."

"Ha! We'll be the judge of that!" I said, rolling up my sleeves. I know this wasn't news to us but it still galled me. Pissy Dog Face blanched but Babs placed a hand on my arm and motioned me to take a step back. I suppose she was right; this was Sophie's fight. I sized the pair of them up. Pissy Dog Face was taller and broader, but Sophie had a dangerous glint in her eye that would make a good bookmaker stop and think before writing her off. *This should be good*, I thought, then leaned back and waited for the fur to fly.

A slap would have been good at that moment and I'm not ashamed to say I was willing Sophie to do it. I clenched my fist, pre-empting the moment of vicarious satisfaction. As it was, Sophie stood for a moment, nodding slowly, taking in her words. Finally, she raised her chin and fixed Miss Magick with a superciliousness that would have looked at home on the face of a queen.

"Her," she said.

Miss Magick looked wary. "Her?"

"Yes, my baby is 'her', not 'it.'"

"Oh, right, of course."

"And you put her in harm's way. You put my baby at risk because you were jealous."

Miss Magick bit her lip and looked at the floor, unable to meet Sophie's gaze any longer.

"Yes," she said, "I'm sorry."

Sophie took a deep breath. Babs and I held ours. This was it, any second now we'd hear the ringing sound of a slap well delivered.

"I forgive you," said Sophie.

"What?" said Pissy Dog Face.

"Yes, what?" I demanded.

"I forgive you," Sophie repeated. For crying out loud! Babs' tut of disappointment said it all; being the bigger person sucked sometimes. Sophie looked at us. "Look, he was very good at playing the role, making people believe he was something special. He's had us all duped at one point or another."

Babs snorted with derision.

"Well, most of us," Sophie conceded. "I can't blame anyone for being fooled by him when I was fooled myself for so long." She looked back at the other girl. "So, I forgive you." She reached forward to wrap her arms around her.

"Woah! What do you think you're doing," said Little Miss Magick, pulling away. Sophie froze, her arms still outstretched.

"Oh, I thought this might be a hug-it-out moment. You know, a fresh start for our relationship," she said.

Miss Magick's top lip curled with distaste.

"God, no!" she said, backing away. "I still can't stand you." She picked up her coat, ready to leave, then sighed – a tad more dramatically than the situation warranted, if you ask me – and turned back to Sophie. "But… I know how hard it is for women in business. I assume it'll be harder still as a single mum so if you need help…" she gritted her teeth and forced the rest of the sentence out "… you can call on me."

Babs gave me a sidelong glance. Both her eyebrows were raised in surprise – I know mine had damn near shot into my hairline. Well, I never, perhaps Pissy Dog Face was not so pissy after all. Sophie went beetroot.

"Th-thank you?" she stammered.

Miss Magick sniffed. "Only as a last resort, mind," she bristled. "Don't expect to be borrowing a cup of sugar every day or whatever." Ah, there she was. Still a bit of urine in her soul, after all. I grinned at Babs and she smirked back.

"Of course," replied Sophie.

Miss Magick sniffed again, she nodded curtly at Babs and me and turned to leave. That was it then? One piss-poor excuse for an apology and she breezed back into her life without a care in the world? Well, Sophie wasn't the only one with a dangerous glint in her eye and I decided it was time to throw a few wrinkles into the red carpet of Miss Magick's charmed life.

"Something's just occurred to me," I called. She stopped in her tracks and eyed me warily, the events of the previous night evidently still in her mind.

"Yes?"

"All this time and I still don't know your actual name," I said. She pursed her lips as though scanning the sentence for barbs or hidden meanings. She must have deemed it safe though as she shook back her hair and replied.

"It's Magenta," she said, not even reddening at the lie.

I smiled at her, letting my teeth show.

"That's pretty," I said, "and very in keeping with your business." She nodded and I continued speaking. "Not what I expected though. Can't say you look like a Magenta to me. I'd say you look more like a Lisa or Tracey or…" I looked her square in the eye. "Maud."

I swear I saw the breath catch in her throat. Her cheeks blazed and her mouth opened in a moue of surprise.

"How did you—?" she began, but then stopped herself. "Someone must have told you."

"Tell many people your real name, do you, Maud?" She frowned at that and I let my smile calcify. "Why don't we just see this as a friendly reminder that I know who you are and after last night, you know who I am… just in case you ever thought of being unfriendly again, yes?"

I've never seen someone go from puce to paper-white so quickly. She gripped the lapels of her coat but I still saw the trembling in her hands. She held my gaze for a moment then dropped her head and nodded.

"I'm glad we understand each other. It's so nice when people get along," I said. She made no reply but straightened her coat and glanced longingly at the door. I actually felt sorry for her when Babs spoke up.

"Wait," cried Babs. "You hev not had Borscht. Let me give you some to take away."

The young woman started to protest but Babs was already in the kitchen, ladle in her hand. I swear that woman can move faster than the devil where food is concerned. She returned moments later and pressed the takeaway bowl into Miss Magick's hands.

"No, really…"

"Nyet, I insist," she said. "You will love it, I promise. Just smell." She reached forward and prised off the lid of the bowl to let the aroma out. Pissy Dog Face sniffed obligingly and Babs winked at her. "Don't worry, *is vegan*."

There was something about the wicked glint in her eyes – it came from the depths of Hades and dragged the evil grin that slid across her face in its wake. The three of us froze and stared at the takeaway bowl. Right on cue, a lump of… something… blobbed to the surface. Pissy Dog Face swallowed and turned green. She thrust the takeaway package back into Babs' hands and bolted from the cafe, her hand clamped over her mouth. The doorbell jangled for a good five seconds after she'd gone.

Babs hooted with laughter. "I do like her," she said. "She is still cowbag, but I *do* like her!"

Sophie and I still had our eyes glued on the takeaway carton.

"Er, Babs?" I said, slowly. "What *did* happen to the Vegan?"

Babs shrugged. "How should I know? Befana was going to drop him somewhere. Remote island in middle of ocean, I think she said… or perhaps just middle of ocean." She waved her hand airily. "Somewhere in middle of ocean, anyway. There may be land."

"So," I said carefully, "you definitely didn't cut him up and cook him in your soup?"

Babs looked aghast. "Nyet! How could you think such a thing? I would *never* cook Vegan into Borscht."

Sophie and I both sighed with relief,

"Sorry, Babs," Sophie said, "I should have known you'd never do something so awful."

"Nyet," said Babs, still looking affronted. "He would quite spoil the flavour." She managed to hold on to her wounded expression for two more seconds before her lips quivered and she snorted with laughter again. This time, we all joined in.

Chapter Thirty-Nine

The sky was dark by the time we closed up. The smoky tang of autumn would wither beneath the bitter snap of winter soon. I turned the sign on the door to closed, turned out the light and stepped outside. I heard Babs' quiet step behind me. The arcade was all but deserted. The dim lights in the Magic Tat shop showed she too had shut for the day. Over in the greengrocers, Burt was helping Margot select fruit for her next batch of ice cream. They stood close, not quite touching but I guessed that would only be a matter of time.

"Da," said Babs, as though reading my mind. "Time that will quickly pass if I am not here, I think."

My throat seized at her words.

"You're going, then?"

"Da, darling. It is time." A strange expression crossed her face briefly but she shook it off and turned back to me. "And what of you? Will you stay here?"

I shrugged. "Dunno. I only took the place to be close to Sophie."

"Da, and before that you took shop to be near her mother and another to be near her mother before that.

Tell me, Agnes, when was last time you did something because *you* wanted to?"

That flummoxed me.

I cast my mind back twenty, a hundred, a thousand years and still, no answer bobbed to the surface. It hadn't been a bad life and there had been plenty of joy, but I'd always felt bound. I worried the pavement with my toe.

"I suppose you're right," I said. "I've been playing 'mum' for so long, I've forgotten how to be anything else." I stared at my shoes for a moment, waiting for Babs to say something but there was nothing, not even a snarky comment. I lifted my head to face her and she wasn't even looking at me. She was staring off into the distance, a wild look in her eyes, clearly thinking of something else altogether. I tutted.

"Oh, don't mind me," I huffed. "I'm only baring my soul here." Babs blinked and looked at me as though only just noticing I was there.

"What?" she said, then, before I could answer, she held up her hand to silence me. "Shh!"

"Well, that's rich!" I said, but Babs was waving her hand, urgently.

"Listen!" she said. I did as I was told and listened, *really* listened, because whatever had caught Babs' attention was clearly not a mundane sound. And then I heard it... or rather, I didn't hear it – the complete absence of sound that comes before an act of magic, like the startled hush that shrouds the earth when snow falls.

Then came the hum, soft at first but becoming louder, swarming around us until I had to clamp my hands over my ears. It lifted the hair on the back of my neck and sent tingles down my arms. Whatever was happening was *big*, bigger even than what I'd done to the Vegan. I winced at Babs but she looked frozen in the moment, her mouth caught in an O of wonder. It looked like she was holding her breath. The humming reached a crescendo then petered away to a sigh, like moths on the breeze. I dropped my hands from my ears.

"What the f-" A woman walked past with a toddler in a pushchair. "-lipping heck was that?" I said. Babs shook her head, still unwilling or unable to answer, but her face was alight with fierce hope. Suddenly, she gasped.

"Oh," she breathed. Her hands dipped into the pocket of her pinny, then jerked away, as though she'd touched a hot coal. "Oh," she said again. Tears sprang in her eyes and she delved into the pocket once more. This time, she grasped something firmly and pulled it out. She opened her hand a little and revealed the white stone she'd taken from the ashes of House. I hadn't noticed before how smooth and round it was. I peered at it, wondering what I was supposed to be looking at, when it twitched. I jumped back and frowned at Babs.

"Did that just -" but I didn't finish my sentence because the pebble twitched again, and again. Its stark white outer seemed to glow and it began to throb and pulse in Babs' hands.

"Oh, my Mielasis, can it be?" she said. She looked at me then, her heart in her eyes. "Quick, we must get to your—"

"—house, yes, of course," I said, catching her train of thought. I had no idea what was happening, but Babs needed me and I'd follow her to Hades if necessary. I jogged over to Burt's and dropped my keys on the counter in front of Margot.

"Lock up for me, will you?" I said.

They both looked bewildered. "Everything alright?"

I waved away their questions. "Yes, just… I'll explain later," I said, and sprinted after Babs.

She was already at the entrance to the arcade. The air thrummed like the wings of a hummingbird. The stone was now the size of a ping-pong ball and practically iridescent. By the time we left the arcade, it was the size of a golf ball. We did that weird, hip-jiggling fast walk – not quite jogging but as near to it as you can get – all the way home, so as not to risk dropping the… whatever it was. By halfway home, it had swollen to the size of a tennis ball and by the time I creaked the gate open, Babs was clutching something the size of a skull between her hands. She knelt on the grass and tipped the stone onto the scorched earth that marked House's pyre.

The sky had bruised to black. She sat back on her heels and waited. The stone was more of a small boulder now. It pulsated on the lawn, growing larger with each heartbeat. Babs clasped her hands tightly in front of her as though in prayer. She was holding her breath again. I held mine along with her.

The thing was massive now. It almost filled the lawn and blocked the view of my front window. Babs and I had been forced back to the gate. I was beginning to wonder how much more it would grow when a sharp crack exploded from the depths of the object and a line chased down its side, rupturing the surface and spreading out until it resembled the crazy paving on my pathway.

The object gave a final, almighty shudder and the white outer dropped away. I followed the trajectory of one of the pieces as it fell and only then did I realise what I was looking at. Eggshell. My jaw hung open. I raised my eyes slowly to see what had erupted from the egg and there, before me, stood House. It ruffled out its damp shingles and lifted first one side, then the other until it stood on two wobbly legs.

"Oh, my darling one!" Babs' voice cracked between a laugh and a sob and she hurled herself forward, her arms outstretched. "You came back to me."

She hugged as much of House's bulk as she could reach and rubbed her face against the walls. Her cheeks were wet with tears and newly-hatched membrane. I felt a drip on my hand and realised I was crying too. My jaw ached from the size of my smile and a golden droplet of warmth beaded in my chest and spread throughout my entire body. I watched my friend reunited with her beloved familiar, with part of her very soul, and I felt younger than I had in years. My heart swelled for her. I wiped my face.

"It's really House?" I asked.

"Da, darling," said Babs, still pressing her cheeks against the wooden shingles. "Is really House."

"But how?" She looked at me and her face practically glowed. Her mouth stretched into a wide grin.

"You know, I always wondered why people said House had chicken legs," she said and I looked at the wobbly limbs – the narrow, ringed shanks, leading to the clawed feet – that inexplicably managed to lift the wooden bulk of House's body. They certainly looked like chicken legs and I opened my mouth to say so but Babs cut me off.

"Nyet, darling. Any fool can see they are *phoenix* legs."

"Phoenix legs!" I laughed out loud. Only Babs would think of such a thing. "House has been reborn!"

"Da, everything within and without is brand new."

I nodded, walking around House to admire its new body. It twisted slightly, this way and that, as though giving me a better look. The moss between the roof tiles was gone; wooden walls that had previously darkened with age now shone with the light copper of youth. I rejoined Babs.

"Looking good on it," I said.

Babs looked at me expectantly and I had the distinct feeling I was missing something important.

"What?" I said and Babs shook her head, grinning at my slow wits.

"Everything *within* House is restored," she said. I frowned, still not catching her meaning. Babs rolled her eyes. "Listen," she said and beckoned me close. I placed the side of my face against House and pressed my ear against the wood.

"I don't hear…" I started, but Babs put a finger against my lips. I listened again and heard it. My heart seized at the sound before my brain even had time to register what it was. My eyes widened and grew hot with new tears. I hardly dared to breathe.

"Was that…?" but Babs didn't have to answer because the sound came again; the faint, but distinct mew of a kitten. House shuddered and swelled again then flung its door wide open. A sudden blast of warm air coughed into the night and steps unfurled from the opening. A pair of bright green eyes blinked in the dim light and a small, black kitten tripped down the steps on unsteady legs. I was on my knees before it in an instant. I scooped it up and held it up to get a better look. House obligingly grew an outdoor lamp so I could see better.

Once again, the centuries peeled back and in the flickering lamplight, I saw him as he'd been in the light of the bonfire, when I'd first forged him so long ago. His fur punked out in erratic tufts and he was still wet behind the ears but when his face met mine, his ribcage vibrated and a deep purr resonated from the very depths of his soul. My world contracted to the size of the tiny bundle of damp fluff which had now scaled my arms and was nuzzling at my body. Each tiny pin-prick of his claws wrenched another joyous sob heaving from my chest. He was back. Misty was back.

Chapter Forty

It was later, much later and Babs and I sat on deck chairs in the garden watching House decorate itself. It had already been through three sets of curtains. Babs had wrinkled her nose at the red polka dot pair, wobbled her hand uncertainly about the pair with the diamond motif and gave an immediate thumbs down to the ones that were made of actual peacock feathers.

"I'd have thought they'd be right up your street," I said, while House shivered another pair into being. Babs shook her head and burrowed deeper into the blanket we shared.

"Nyet, darling, they moult. I would be forever fishing tiny bits of feather from my Borscht."

"Ah," I said.

House shone the lamp on the next set – a simple pair in pale yellow, decorated with tiny blue butterflies. Babs' breath caught in her throat and she clasped her hands under her chin.

"Perfect, Darling One," she breathed. House bobbed with satisfaction and moved on to the flooring. "What will you do now?" she asked me, while House experimented with parquet. "Carry on with cafe?"

I chewed my lip thoughtfully and tickled Misty under the chin. I'd only put him down long enough to feed him and promptly swept him up again once he'd finished. From the gentle spread of his paws against my shoulder, I could tell he was quite content with the arrangement.

"Actually," I said, "I've been thinking about that." And I had been. The train of thought that had been derailed by House's rebirth was back on track. I thought of Sophie and the Foreman – or Cameron, as I now had to remember to call him. I pictured them as I'd seen them earlier, standing together in the ruins of Sophie's shop, discussing the repairs. Like Burt and Margot, their heads were close together, not quite touching. I'd stuck *my* head round to say I was making bacon butties for his team if he wanted one. He'd smiled at me.

"Naw, yer alright, Hen. I dinnae eat meat." The appraising look Sophie gave him then was brimming with possibility and I couldn't help myself; I let my mind unfurl and tried to grasp a few threads of the future for a glimpse of what they could weave. It was all there. They could be together. He would be good for her – steady, capable and kind, just what she needed – and I could make it happen, it would only take a gentle nudge… my fingers began to itch and I'd thrust them deep into my pockets, away from temptation. Whatever happened between them had to be of their doing. They didn't need me; Sophie didn't need me, not anymore. Surprisingly, the thought didn't hurt as much as I expected. I'd spent over a thousand years caring for my family, pushing my desires to one side to see to their needs. And there were so many desires.

I looked up at the stars, pinpricks in the night's shroud,

as someone once described them. I felt the familiar tug in the pit of my stomach, the same tug I felt each year in the call of the geese as they disappeared over the horizon. It was a perverse, gentle sorrow that I was not taking flight with them. I wanted to travel – barring a few exceptions, I'd barely left the shores of Britain. I wanted to explore, discover new plants and learn of the good that could be done with them, perhaps even take a lover – well, why not? If Babs could, why shouldn't I? Most of all, I wanted to live… and I knew just the person to do that with. I glanced at Babs who was waiting patiently for my reply. I cleared my throat.

"I was just wondering…"

"Da?" The garden had fallen silent. House had paused its renovations and was also poised, waiting for my answer.

"Is there room in House for two more?" I held up Misty and crossed my fingers under his body in hope.

Babs' face was impassive. "What of the cafe?"

I waved my hand dismissively. "Margot can have it. She'll make a good show of it… or maybe she won't. Either way, it's up to her now."

"And Sophie?"

I took a deep breath. "Likewise," was all I said.

Babs nodded slowly. "You are certain?" she asked.

"I am."

She looked at me solemnly for a moment and I stroked Misty to hide the apprehensive tremor in my hands. Suddenly, her face split into a wide grin. She flung her arm around my shoulder and pulled me into a hug.

"I was thinking you would never ask!" she cried and burst out laughing. She released me from her hug, delved into the bag by the side of her chair and pulled out her bottle of slivovica and two copper cups while I laughed along with her. She poured two shots and we toasted our plans.

"Together we shall fill the world with wonder..." she said.

"Wonder?" I laughed.

"Or terror," Babs conceded. "Either is working. What was Biddy saying again? Da! 'When witches go riding and black dogs appear, the night shall be filled with terror.' Let us go riding, my friend!"

We clinked cups again and I looked at her seriously.

"You're sure it's okay? You've got room enough?" I said. Babs stood and shook off the blanket. She strolled over to House and patted its side.

"Well, Darling One," she said, "what do you say? Are we heving enough room?"

House remained stock still for a minute then jerked and shuddered, as though sneezing, and in the midst of the motion, an entire second floor shivered into existence. I gasped. Babs clapped her hands together with glee.

"Oh, my clever Mielasis!" she said and then turned to face me. "Is this answering your question?" I could only hug Misty and nod. My chest felt too full for words. Babs rejoined me at the chairs. "Where shall we go to first?" she asked.

I looked up again. The moon still hung from the inky clouds but beneath it, the sky silvered. Soon pink and gold would smear across the heavens like a thumbprint dragged through paint and a new day would dawn, crisp and clear. For the first time in an age, I felt the cool air in my lungs and my skin tingled with the promise of adventure. A formation of geese honked past. They shaved the sky with their arrowhead and I pointed at them.

"That way," I said. "To wherever their horizon leads us."

Acknowledgements

The words 'it takes a village' are often bandied about and I am lucky to have some amazing people in my village.

First, I'd like to give group thanks to the Storytellers' Academy Elite squad for your support and feedback, Miss Trunchbull's Bootcamp for helping me get my word count up and the Cardiff Critters for gritting their teeth through various 'elevator pitch' iterations. You are all amazing.

Now for my special thanks:

To Karen, for my Autor Glow Up.

To the inestimable Abigail. Your courage, enthusiasm and heart are truly inspiring and helped drive me forward.

To my magnificent friend, Claire. Your constant kindness and gentle humour has been the steady hand on the tiller so often. Thank you.

To my wonderful aunt, Christine. You've been my biggest cheerleader for so long and I am so grateful for it.

And last but never least, Deanne – Babs to my Aggie or Aggie to my Babs? We never will solve that riddle but it's no exaggeration to say this book would not have happened without you. You make everything better.

This book is printed on paper from sustainable sources managed under the Forest Stewardship Council (FSC) scheme.

It has been printed in the UK to reduce transportation miles and their impact upon the environment.

For every new title that Troubador publishes, we plant a tree to offset CO_2, partnering with the More Trees scheme.

For more about how Troubador offsets its environmental impact, see www.troubador.co.uk/sustainability-and-community